ABOUT THE AUTHOR

Former naval intelligence officer and U.S. Naval Academy graduate Geri Krotow draws inspiration from the global situations she's experienced. Geri loves to hear from her readers. You can email her via her website and blog at www.gerikrotow.com.

Books by Geri Krotow

HARLEQUIN SUPERROMANCE

1547—WHAT FAMILY MEANS
1642—SASHA'S DAD
1786—NAVY RULES*

HARLEQUIN EVERLASTING LOVE

20—A RENDEZVOUS TO REMEMBER

*Whidbey Island series

Other titles by this author available in ebook format.

Just like wounded warriors, stepmoms and moms-in-law are not recognized or thanked enough. For this reason I dedicate this book with all my love and gratitude to two great ladies in my life, Grom and Sally.

Light-headedness wasn't familiar to Ro...

But sitting next to Miles Mikowski made her feel as though the air had been sucked out of the truck's cab. The leather interior of the huge vehicle was roomy even by American standards. Except with Miles in the driver's seat. His long, lean yet muscular physique filled every inch of the driver's side. He had to be at least six-four. Whenever she stood near him, which wasn't often, he towered over her.

"You didn't ask in so many words, but being out on this bridge in these winds is begging for help, Roanna. Then to see you stopped at the high point like that..." He slapped his hand on the dashboard.

Guilt licked up her stomach, and nausea threatened to overtake her anger. She'd really frightened him. Miles, the man who'd already been through hell and back in the war.

"I know you like to run in the mornings, Ro, but maybe you should check the weather report before you run on the bridge in near gale-force winds."

His frequent use of her given name instead of her rank irked her. They were both officers, so of course it was okay to address each other by first name. Miles always called her "Lieutenant Commander Brandywine" in public. Privately he'd used her name—when he'd asked her out. And she'd refused.

It's not that he uses your first name. It's how he says it.

Dear Reader,

Navy Orders is only the second book in the Whidbey Island series and yet I feel I've lived with the characters forever! I hope they've become a positive part of your life, too. The romance between Miles and Ro in this story grew much hotter than I'd ever expected, and it was delightful to write about their journey.

Miles is a wounded warrior and exemplifies how veterans give back for all of us on a daily basis. Because of this, I wanted to give back in my own way and decided to come up with a great cause to support. Right around the time I started pondering this, I came across Delaware Head Huggers (www.delawareheadhuggers.org) on Facebook. I'd been looking for a chemo cap pattern to knit for a friend. Robin Agar, who runs DEHH with her beloved dog Schnapps (rumor has it that Schnapps knits, too!), generously donated a hat knitting pattern that you'll find at the end of the book. Please support Delaware Head Huggers by knitting a cap and mailing it to them. If you don't knit, Robin accepts other hats and monetary donations, as well. As of this writing, Robin is nearing the 9,000 mark for donated caps! Cancer affects too many of us, young, old and in between. While we fight for a cure, let's make those who are in the fight feel a little love with a hand-knit (or crocheted) cap.

Thanks as always for your support of my writing. I hope you enjoy spending time with Miles and Ro as much as I have. I'd love to hear from you via my Facebook page, website (www.gerikrotow.com) or Twitter.

Peace,

Geri Krotow

Navy Orders

Geri Krotow

HARLEQUIN® SUPER ROMANCE®

ISBN-13: 978-0-373-71865-8

NAVY ORDERS

This edition published by arrangement with Harlequin Books S.A.

For questions and comments about the quality of this book, please contact us at CustomerService@Harlequin.com.

Printed in U.S.A.

CHAPTER ONE

CHIEF WARRANT OFFICER Miles Mikowski was in no mood to save a life this morning. He'd driven across Deception Pass Bridge onto Whidbey Island countless times, and while it was common to see walkers or runners working their way across the pass, nearly gale-force winds usually kept the bridge clear.

Not this morning.

His hands gripped the steering wheel of his truck as the image of a lone figure clinging to the bridge's side rail morphed into the all-too-familiar Roanna Brandywine.

No, no, no!

"Christ."

Regret tasted metallic in his instantly dry mouth. Not another one, not another sailor lost to the aftereffects of the war. He never should have stopped asking her to go out with him.

How had he not seen the warning signs with her? He couldn't bear the loss of another warrior-in-arms to the war. No matter if the cause was a bomb, rocket-propelled grenade, bullet or PTSD.

Not on his watch.

Instinct took over as he floored his gas pedal to get to her. He slammed on the brake, unclicked his seat belt and burst out of the truck's cab in one practiced motion. He'd already checked his rearview mirror and knew he had a clear shot across Highway 20 to Ro.

WIND RIPPED AWAY any warmth from the early-morning sunlight as Lieutenant Commander Roanna Brandywine walked across Deception Pass Bridge. She'd run four miles and looked forward to the hot shower she'd get at the base gym. But first, she needed to complete a mission she'd planned for weeks. Poised nearly two hundred feet above the turbulent passage that connected the Strait of Juan de Fuca with Puget Sound, she fingered the engagement ring that lay in the palm of her gloved hand for the last time.

Her desolation loomed large and real as she paused at the bridge's midspan. The grandeur of Deception Pass never failed to make Ro feel at once small and insignificant yet able to conquer the world.

The small diamond that cut into her palm had been her link to what she thought a real, *normal* family life meant. Proof that she had somewhere else to go outside of the navy. That the navy wasn't the only thing she'd ever succeed at.

Her illusion of having a happy, fulfilling personal life was just that. An illusion she'd strung out over several years and half a dozen navy postings. Her relationship with Dick had been part of her fantasy life away from the military.

Face it—the only part of your life that's been real since you graduated from the naval academy nine years ago is your career.

She blinked.

No more.

She was done with pouring her emotions into the out-of-reach life that was never going to happen for her. Not in the way she'd planned it, anyhow.

So much of her pain was represented by this one tiny diamond.

She'd failed Dick. She should never have expected any man, especially a man who didn't understand her need to serve her country and see the world, to wait *years* for her.

Would she have waited years for a man who'd gone off like she had?

Dick knew her family as well as she did, and he'd loved her despite all its crazy ways. He'd fit in to her family so damn well, in fact, that he'd gone off and married her sister at the first hint of Roanna taking orders to Whidbey Island instead of getting out of the navy. Once her aircraft carrier pulled back into Norfolk, Virginia, they'd broken up.

Dick's timing had been unfortunate, since he'd told her he was breaking up with her at the same time he revealed he'd married someone else.

Her sister.

Their last conversation still replayed in her mind, over a year later.

They were at a chain restaurant in downtown Trenton, New Jersey. Dick's idea of a welcome-back-from-deployment meal. She'd been able to overlook his lack of planning even then. It was okay—he waited while she went off and fought wars and she put up with his not-so-desirable qualities when she came home. It was how they did things, both accepting less than what they deserved.

But then he'd revealed that their engagement was off. And, in fact, that he'd married the love of his life.

"Face it, Ro. We're more like brother and sister than a couple. Have been for years." He'd shot her a remorseful grin.

"I don't know of too many brothers and sisters who sleep together," she'd retorted.

Her bluster had been automatic, the reaction she knew she was *supposed* to have. In truth she'd been shocked at how little she'd cared. As if he'd done them both a favor. Maybe it was time for her to look at herself and even let go of whatever image she'd set out to achieve for her life.

But that would have meant she didn't know where she

was going next. Roanna always had a plan B, a safety net, and it had always been Dick. Plan A had always been whatever her navy orders said they were. The orders to Whidbey Island sent her three thousand miles from Dick. Did she really think he'd follow her out there and start a new practice in a strange state?

Again, her career was the one thing she'd been able to count on.

At Dick's silence, her cheeks had grown warm, and then she'd started to shiver.

"I'm sorry if it wasn't good enough for you, Dick." They both knew she was talking about their sex life. At its height it had been a release from months of separation, a simple youthful yearning that demanded fulfillment in their teens and had turned into an obligatory ritual.

"Ro, don't do this."

"Do what, Dick? Get upset that you got married before you dumped me? Or feel hurt that you've been less than happy with our sex life?"

She'd sighed. Dick's face bore an expression she'd never seen on him before—resignation. *Maybe it's time to grow up and move on,* she'd thought.

"I'm sorry, Dick. This isn't what I'd expected, but you're actually right. We've been kidding ourselves for a long time, haven't we?"

"I think so."

The waitress had come and taken their orders. Ro had picked her favorite fish and chips basket while Dick—previously the king of junk food—ordered a grilled chicken salad, dressing on the side.

"So who is she, Dick? I'm impressed that she's gotten you to eat healthier. She must be your soul mate." She'd felt genuine when she'd uttered that, too. Really, it had become clearer as their conversation went on that Dick had saved both of their lives by finding another woman.

Dick had stayed silent. She'd felt a flash of compassion for him then, and for his new wife. Poor dears must have tortured themselves over how she'd take the news.

"Oh, I almost forgot." She twisted off the small engagement ring they'd bought at the navy base exchange on one of his trips to Virginia Beach to see her. It had been inexpensive and tax-free, perfect for the young couple they'd been at the time.

"Here."

He waved her hand, and the ring, away.

"No, no, I can't take that, Roanna. Sell it or give it away, but it's yours to do with as you wish."

She'd held her hand out awkwardly for a few more heartbeats before she'd slipped the ring into the small front pocket of her jeans.

"So, do I know your bride, Dick?"

The guilt on his face had been palpable. She'd reached out to him and put her hand on his forearm.

"Dick, it's okay. Cross my heart. I know you must think I'm in shock or something—maybe I am—but deep down I know this is the best thing for both of us. And I really, *really* want you to be happy. So who is she?"

His gaze had stayed downcast on the plastic ketchup bottle. It had seemed an eternity before he looked back up at her.

"It's Krissy, Ro."

Finally the shock hit her, followed quickly by despair, betrayal and a sprinkle of good old-fashioned outrage.

"Krissy?" She'd tilted her head and tried to smile. Her lips had felt frozen. She only knew one woman named Krissy.

Dick had sighed and bitten his bottom lip, garnering more courage.

"Your sister, Ro. Krissy, your sister, is my wife."

Ro remembered that she stared at him for a good bit before she stood up without a sound and left the restaurant. She hadn't known what else to do—she'd never seen this in a movie before, hadn't practiced this type of exit strategy during any of her navy drills on the ship.

That was the last time she'd spoken to Dick. She'd refused Krissy's calls, too.

The Pacific wind tore at her cheeks and brought her thoughts back to the present.

That had been fourteen months ago. She hadn't spoken to her family since, except for holiday calls to her mother, and a brief visit from her a year ago. Mom had known all along about Dick and Krissy's relationship and had never bothered to tell Roanna. She'd been deployed to the Persian Gulf, in the midst of a freaking *war,* and her mother hadn't warned her.

No one had.

Why she'd kept the cheap ring this long was beyond her. Dick had certainly never offered her the family heirloom that her half sister, Krissy, wore on her petite left hand. Mom had let this tidbit drop last Christmas. It had been Ro's first Christmas willingly away from her family and it had been her best. A bit lonely but she'd dined in the chow hall on base with other single sailors who worked for her and it had turned out to be a wonderful day.

Ro was the strong one in her family. The natural leader with common sense. The one who broke the mold, got away from the hell she'd known as a child.

But strength was the last thing she felt as she battled the wind and her emotions. The moisture from the mist started to form drops.

The sorrow, sense of failure and complete emptiness she experienced in the driving rain belied the professional reputation she'd built for herself. Clad in only her running tights, athletic shoes and weatherproof jacket, she felt smaller than usual. Her runs often took her across this bridge. Usually it was a place of solace and exhilaration, mingled with consolation. She'd chosen Deception Pass for the closure she needed. No more waiting. Her new life, her new attitude, started today.

She looked out over the edge of the bridge. White foamy water resembled the froth on a cappuccino. It was so far below her it made her dizzy. She grabbed the cold metal railing to keep her balance.

This is it.

She ungloved her right hand while keeping her fingers wrapped around the ring that pressed against her palm.

"Goodbye, Dick, goodbye, old Ro. Hello, new life!"

Before she allowed herself to reconsider, she held the ring out, ready to release it into the wind.

A sudden strong gust of wind forced her to use all of her strength to keep from falling over.

The ring fell out of her outstretched hand, into nothingness.

For a horrible moment it looked as if the ring was going to blow right back in her face—the gusts were that strong. Instead, it made it only halfway back toward her before it pinged against the metal edge of the railing and ricocheted into oblivion. She visualized its descent past the massive fir trees that covered the cliffs on both sides of the gap. A lone seagull floated on the updrafts and she imagined the bird cocking its head at the sparkle of sun glinting off the gem.

The sense of empowerment she'd anticipated was mixed with chagrin and anger that a gust of wind had turned her grand gesture into no more than an accident.

IT TOOK EVERY ounce of Miles's explosive ordnance disposal training and prior experience not to scream at Ro to stay still and not—*please, God, no*—jump.

He was next to her in a few agonizing strides. He took in her stiff body, one gloved hand on the guardrail while the other lifted in front of her as if she were tossing her anguished thoughts away.

Only after he had his arms around her and they were falling toward the safety of the hard concrete sidewalk did he allow any words to escape his lips.

"Ro, it's over. I've got you."

RO REMAINED FROZEN as she tumbled with her assailant. The shock of being hit by a solid wall of muscle was as much to blame for her lack of response as her teeth-loosening collision with the concrete path.

The arms around her middle and shoulders, and the hand that cradled her head, kept her from a total loss of consciousness as sparks spewed in front of her vision.

"Stay with me, Ro. Are you okay?"

She blinked at the all-too-familiar baritone. A groan made its way past her clenched teeth. Only one man fit the bill of hero and rescuer, and had that deep sexy voice to match.

Navy Chief Warrant Officer and Explosive Ordnance Expert Miles Mikowski.

"Miles?"

"You scared the shit out of me, Ro."

Her breath came back in gasps. Anger began to warm her from the inside out.

"What the hell are you doing?"

His face was a mere inch from hers, his weight hard but hot in contrast with the frigid ground beneath her. She'd never seen his eyes this close—his pupils were pinpoints of black heat in his steel blue irises as his breath warmed her wind-burned cheeks.

"Ro, it's okay. I'm here, and you're not alone."

"Alone in what?" Their physical proximity started to register across all her senses and she squirmed. "Will you get off me?"

Had he lost his mind?

Slowly, as though she were a hand-blown Easter egg, he inched up and off her, all the while retaining a firm grasp on her arms, her hands. He rocked back on his heels in a crouch and pulled her up to a seated position.

The sound of car engines and the call-outs of drivers forced Ro's glance away from Miles and to the highway.

"What's going on, folks?" A uniformed state trooper stood on the street next to them. "Are you okay, miss?"

Ro looked at the officer, then at Miles.

"I'm fine, Officer. At least I was, until my…my colleague seemed to think I was in trouble. Miles?"

He shook his head.

"Tell me you weren't about to do something really stupid, Ro."

"The only thing I was going to do, I did. I tossed my old engagement ring." She stood up and ignored the sharp cries of pain from her battered bones. She was going to kill Miles when she had the chance.

He stared at her as if he was seeing a ghost.

"Sir, are you okay?" The trooper turned to Miles, a hand on his hip.

"Yes, I'm fine. Sorry about any confusion, Officer." Miles ran his fingers over his chin and Ro caught the grimace he was trying to hide.

Miles, embarrassed? This was new.

"I was in the war, and since I've been back a lot of vets have, ah—" he glanced past the trooper, to the vista of the Strait of Juan de Fuca "—I've seen a lot of vets with PTSD. I acted on instinct when I saw Ro on the bridge, in these winds, at this hour."

"That true, miss?" The trooper deferred to Ro.

"Yes, yes. Miles is my work friend. He's a good man, Officer, and wouldn't ever do anything to hurt me." She looked the trooper straight in the eye. No matter how much Miles drove her to distraction with his steady, determined attempts to date her, she knew he'd never act on anything other than honorable motives.

"Okay. I got a call from a concerned driver who saw you both take a tumble, and I had to ascertain that it wasn't assault or a suicide attempt." He paused, a slow grin overtaking his face. "Since you were just throwing away an engagement ring, we're fine. I won't write you a citation for littering, but toss the next ring into the trash can, all right?"

Ro smiled at him.

"No worries—there won't be another ring." Not for a very long time.

"GET IN BEFORE we cause an accident out here." His booming voice brought more goose bumps to her arms than the Whidbey wind ever could.

She skirted behind his red Ford F-150 pickup truck. Sure enough, the morning commuters were already lining up behind him. Most were headed to Naval Air Station Whidbey Island, where they would put in a full day's work for their country. They were going to start honking their horns at any moment.

Her fists ached to punch the tailgate, kick the tires. Instead, she pulled the passenger door open and slid into the leather seat.

She slammed the door shut, as much as one could slam such a heavy piece of metal, and turned to glare at Miles.

"Just drive to the pull-off and let me out so the traffic can get by."

"You're welcome."

"I didn't ask for your help, Warrant."

Light-headedness wasn't familiar to Ro but sitting next to Miles Mikowski made her feel as though the air had been sucked out of the truck's cab. The leather interior of the huge vehicle was roomy, even by American standards. Except when the likes of Miles took up the driver's side. His long, lean yet muscular physique filled every inch. He had to be at least six feet four inches tall. Whenever she stood near him, which wasn't often, he towered over her five feet six inches, normally a respectable height for a woman.

"You didn't ask in words but being out on this bridge in these winds is begging for help, Roanna. Then to see you stopped at the high point like that." He slapped the dashboard.

Guilt licked up her stomach and to her neck. Nausea threatened to overtake her anger. She had really frightened him. Miles, the man who'd already been through hell and back in the war.

"I know you like to run in the mornings but maybe you should check the weather report before you run onto the bridge in near-gale-force winds."

His frequent use of her given name instead of her rank irked her. They were both officers, so of course it was okay to address each other by first name. Miles always addressed her as "Lieutenant Commander Brandywine" in public. Privately he used her name but only when he asked her out. And she'd always refused.

It's not that he uses your first name. It's how he says it.

The way her name sounded on his lips made her think of sex. Her awareness of him annoyed her, to say the least....

"I'm not an idiot, Miles. I've lived here long enough to know I need to be careful. I'm on my way into the base, anyway. I've finished my run. I was cooling down." He stayed silent. "My car's right over here in the parking lot."

You're starting a new chapter today. Be nice.

"I didn't realize you live off-island." She referred to the fact that he was driving toward Whidbey.

"I don't."

No other explanations. She squirmed. What he did in his personal time was his business.

"Don't worry, I'm not courting anyone else, Roanna." He shot her a quick grin, an attempt at a return to their normal banter, while he waited for the car in front of him to inch forward. "I had to get up early to deliver a dog to a rescue group in Anacortes. It was the only time the volunteer could take delivery and get her out to Spokane today."

"You work with a dog rescue?" Chagrin struck her as soon as she said the words. She'd heard he'd lost his working dog in the war.

"When I can."

Miles swung off the right side of the highway and pulled into the small parking lot that heralded the start of Deception Pass Park. She didn't miss how easily he maneuvered the big truck among the smaller, more practical cars. Apparently EOD training included massive vehicle handling.

Her gaze went from his hands on the wheel to his legs. Clad in workout pants his prosthetic leg wasn't visible. But she'd seen him running in shorts on the naval air station jogging path, and working out in the gym. He had a titanium prosthetic for running and a more conventional one for his uniform.

"Looks like you're going to work out, too."

"Yup, every morning before I report to the wing. If I don't keep my muscles in shape I'll lose them." His left hand rested on the top of the steering wheel while he leaned on his right arm, which was way too close to her on the center divider of the cab. She could even make out the fine blond-tinged hairs that covered parts of his hand and fingers.

"Hmm." She wanted to tell him that his obvious strength

of character impressed the hell out of her, but that might make him think she cared. Or that she'd reconsidered his previous invitations to go out for a meal or cup of coffee together.

Not happening.

"Thanks for the ride."

"Sure."

She swallowed. "No, I mean it. You didn't have to stop, didn't have to give a damn. But you did. And I don't have to be such a pain in the ass to you all the time."

Now she had his attention. Bright sparks danced in his blue irises.

"So now, after almost a year, after I've made a fool of myself, you're willing to be nice to me?"

"I'm sorry for the times I was rude, Miles. Truly."

Before he made more out of this than necessary she pushed open the door, slid down from the high seat and got out of the truck. She was careful to appear casual as she shut the door and headed for her car. She noted that he waited until she was safely inside her car before he pulled out of the parking lot.

The drive into the base wasn't going to be long enough to get his brilliant blue eyes and shy smile out of her mind.

Miles's confident demeanor had pricked her bubble of I-don't-need-a-man denial since the moment she'd met him the better part of a year ago. They'd first come face-to-face when her mother's cat had decided to run up a tree. Miles had expertly scaled the tree and saved the cat. Unwittingly he'd also saved Roanna from her mother's emotional fallout. It would have been pure hell if Henry the Eighth, Mom's cat, had perished.

A week later he'd walked into the wing staff meeting as the new weapons officer and she'd been forced to acknowledge that he had an above-average physique. When she'd discovered he was an amputee she'd been in even more awe of his physical prowess, given the fact that he'd climbed such a huge tree.

But when he'd asked her out on a date she'd reeled in her drawbridge. No man was going to cross the moat she'd built around herself, especially not a man she found so attractive. Casually dating nonthreatening men was her modus operandi.

You played it safe with Dick and look where it got you.

Miles hadn't given up on her right away, but at least now he appeared to accept that they were work colleagues, period. Another point in his favor, damn it. He was a nice guy.

RO WATCHED AS her best friend, Gwen, carried two cups of coffee from the on-base fast-food restaurant's front counter. They had a standing appointment to meet each Friday morning, time permitting, to connect and see if they were going to do anything together over the weekend.

"Ah, heaven. Fresh hot coffee and it's Friday!" Gwen smiled at Ro and placed the paper cups with steaming liquid on the table. Ro reflexively smiled back.

They'd met at the academy on the sailing team and had been good friends ever since. Gwen was a few years older, ahead of her in college, and her senior in naval year groups. They'd both been happy when Ro's orders had come through for Whidbey—they hadn't been in the same area for the past ten years. Ro, especially, had benefitted from having Gwen available to listen to her vent in person instead of on Skype as she came to terms with her new life without Dick.

Gwen's frank gaze made Ro want to squirm.

"What? What is it you're dying to tell me?"

"You could do a lot worse than Miles Mikowski, Ro. I know you didn't want to go out with him, or anyone, when you first broke up with Dick and started this tour. But it's been a long time. You finally threw away your past today, even if you couldn't have chosen a stupider way to do it." Gwen's crooked smirk couldn't erase her classic beauty. A tall, wispy blonde, she'd been the envy of the other female mids when they were in school. She'd done everything they did and still managed to look like a porcelain doll no matter how sweaty or dirty she got.

"You could have just told me you needed a girls' night or weekend and we could have gone to Whistler for a spa weekend. There are plenty of high mountains to throw a ring off there, with no threat of being tackled by an EOD dude." Gwen stirred two packets of sugar into her coffee. "You're damned lucky the trooper didn't haul you off for a psych evaluation."

"Yeah, well, Miles could say the same. As for going on a trip, I had to do it on my own. You know that."

"I do." Gwen regarded her steadily with pine-green eyes. "This was better, wasn't it? Being in a hotel in Whistler with your best friend wouldn't have gotten you tackled by Miles."

Gwen leaned forward.

"Be honest—was it hot?"

Ro took a good gulp of her cappuccino to hide her smile. Gwen made her laugh but she didn't want to laugh about Miles. Not when every inch of her ached from the way he'd "saved" her this morning.

"How are you and Drew adjusting to the command tour?" She wasn't going to admit her feelings even to Gwen.

Gwen puckered her lips and raised her eyebrows.

"We're doing as well as we can, considering he's still upset I took the command tour orders. No, let me change that. We're doing horribly, and I don't know why we're still together. How's that for a depressing take on marriage?"

"And you want me to date Miles."

"Dating and getting married are vastly different. Miles

is perfect for you. If you think about it, it's pretty romantic that he pounced on you when he thought you were going to leap off the bridge."

"He was acting on instinct—he said it himself. He's been on too many battlefields, seen too many people in the throes of their PTSD. He did the right thing, I guess. Except that he should've taken a minute to ask me first before he assumed I was suicidal."

"Don't be so hard on him, Ro. Or on yourself. You said you want to let go of your past, open up your mind. Have you ever considered a more permanent change? Have you thought about getting out of the navy?"

No, but she knew this was the next area of her life that had to be addressed. At more than nine years in, she was nearing the halfway mark to retirement.

"I'm only willing to handle one life change per day, Gwen. You're the last person I'd expect to ask me about whether or not I'm making the navy a career. Where is this coming from?"

Gwen's glance strayed to the view of the runway the window they sat next to provided. She shrugged and looked back at Ro.

"With all the stress my new tour has put on my marriage, I'm wondering if I should have gotten out sooner, taken a job with the airlines. Drew's a good man. He doesn't deserve having to worry about me flying war missions all over the globe."

"B.S.! You're one of the most talented, proficient pilots in the whole navy! Drew needs to chill. After this tour you can get out if you want to, or take a shore tour and think about it."

Gwen shook her head.

"I just want you to consider that you have many, many options. You're an academy grad, you've served in wartime and you have a background in computer systems. You're eminently employable. But what about your knitting? There's more to your interests, lots of things I don't think you've even considered yet. This is your shore tour to do that."

"Gee, thanks, Mom."

"Cut it out." Gwen looked at her watch. "Gotta go. You've got an AOM today, too, don't you?"

Ro nodded.

"Suggestion—say 'yes' to Miles when you see him." Gwen smiled and gave her shoulder a squeeze before she walked out of the fast-food place.

Indeed.

CHAPTER TWO

TWO HOURS LATER Roanna straightened her khaki uniform skirt and put on her favorite tinted lip moisturizer before she left her desk to walk to the wing conference room. It was only a quarter to nine but she'd lived a lifetime since she'd left her house for her run on Deception Pass this morning.

Each week the wing staff, along with various squadron representatives, briefed the wing commander, also referred to as the wing commodore, on the status of all wing patrol squadron forces in the world that were under his command. A complete intelligence brief was part of the package, as was a weather brief, operations brief and maintenance brief.

Ro was responsible for the intelligence brief, but whenever possible it was presented by a squadron intelligence officer or one of her intelligence specialists. She'd had enough face time to last her an entire career. She believed in giving less experienced intel types a chance to improve their skills.

Ro entered the roomy air-conditioned space and glanced at the dozen or so seats around the huge wood conference table and the seats lined up at the sides of the room. Miles wasn't there yet and she let out her breath. At least she had a few more minutes during which she didn't have to worry about him looking at her.

Go ahead, tell yourself that. You'll be disappointed if he doesn't show up.

She was giving Miles way too much rental space in her head. She pulled out a chair three down from the head of the table, where the commodore would sit. He'd be flanked by his chief staff officer and the operations officer, followed by maintenance and intelligence. All rank-related.

Right after she sat down, the senior enlisted sailor came into the room and handed her a piece of paper.

"Good morning, Commander." The rank of lieutenant commander was often shortened to "Commander" in regular conversation.

"Hey, Master Chief Reis, how are you doing?"

"Fine, ma'am. The commodore wants to meet with you after the AOM." Master Chief Petty Officer Lydia Reis referred to the all officers meeting, AOM, as Ro took the small yellow slip of paper.

"Did his secretary say what for?"

"No, and it wasn't his secretary who told me—it was Commodore Sanders."

"Okay, thanks." She did her best to maintain an air of unconcern. Captain Leo Sanders, Wing Commodore, never made direct calls to any of his staff. They jokingly referred to him as the "CEO." He made sure everyone knew he was the boss, no questions, but was also more friendly and personable than the average high roller. Ro had worked for Commodore Sanders since she'd reported to N.A.S. Whidbey fourteen months ago. He'd been more than fair on her fitness reports so she didn't have a personal beef with him. But she'd also seen him slice and dice her colleagues for transgressions in front of the entire staff. He regularly broke the "reprimand in private, praise in public" rule of thumb. It was the epitome of how a leader *shouldn't* behave. But he was in charge and it wasn't her call how he acted. He gave her enough room to do her job as the wing intelligence officer without micromanaging her.

Besides, he had a great sense of humor that was most

welcome when the staff was under the gun for an inspection or unplanned mission.

Why does he need to talk to me?

Ro ran her fingers along the edge of the polished maple conference table. She hadn't screwed up on anything that she was aware of. She also hadn't done anything that merited a surprise award or commendation, either.

She felt a distinct ripple of unease. She'd never gotten into any kind of trouble as an officer, yet she knew from experience that when a high-ranking superior wanted to see you on such short notice it was usually for something pretty serious. Commodore Sanders was a busy man in a responsible job. He wouldn't be asking to see her for something he could have had his chief staff officer request from her.

Her apprehension was further piqued when Master Chief Reis handed Miles the same yellow slip of paper, with the same quiet request, right after he sat down in the chair opposite her. His expression remained unreadable as he read the note but when he raised his head and caught her staring, he grinned.

Oh, no. He thought she was looking at him for an entirely different reason.

"I got the same message." She blurted out the obvious.

Miles raised his brows. He didn't appear as concerned as she was. Of course, he was the weapons officer and probably got called into the commodore's office a lot more often than she did. Weapons cost a lot of money, hence they were right behind the costs of aircraft maintenance and fuel as the budget-driving concerns.

Ro rarely spoke to the commodore one-on-one; there was no need to. He received his daily intelligence briefings from her or her staff via a short classified memo, and if he required further explanation he called her in along with his

CSO to help explain and ask questions, too. The CSO served as the commodore's extra eyes and ears in most instances.

Ro thought about asking Miles if he knew what the summons was about when the ops officer barked out, "Attention on deck!" Ro pushed out her chair and stood at straight attention in one fluid movement, as did everyone else. Commodore Sanders strode in.

"At ease, everybody. Take your seats." He was always quick to put them at ease and get on with the briefings. Ro liked this about Commodore Sanders. He didn't have time to waste and he didn't want to waste anyone else's time, either.

She folded the admin message into fours and placed it in the front pocket of her khaki skirt. She'd worry about whatever the meeting was about later.

The briefings all went as usual with nothing significant to report from most departments. The meteorologist pointed out that the current gale-force gusts were from a Pacific storm that could make landfall on Whidbey over the weekend but would most probably break up before it arrived.

Ro had just finished her first full year here and had never experienced a major storm on the island. She looked around the room. No one else seemed too worked up over that piece of news.

She noted that the commodore was quiet this morning, which boded well for the junior officer who was about to give the intelligence brief.

The JO from Patrol Squadron Eighty-Six started up well and appeared to hold the commodore's interest throughout his brief spiel. He concluded his presentation with an overview of the current political situation in the Middle East.

"So you're telling me what I've already seen on CNN this morning, Lieutenant?" Commodore Sanders never held back on the intel types. Typical of most aviators, he liked to think that being a pilot was the only career in the navy worth anything.

Ro stifled a frustrated sigh. Sanders had been quiet so far. Why now, why *her* briefer?

"No, sir. CNN is open-source. What I'm providing is verifiable by multiple classified sources."

"The new data about the movement of the weapon sites is the salient point here, Commodore." Ro jumped in before the commodore could twist the skewer he'd lobbed into the junior officer. Let the big guy aim his ire at her, not one of her subordinates.

"I heard him, Ro."

Ro did her best to keep a grimace off her face.

"Sir, I can look up more information for you, sir." The red-faced lieutenant junior grade didn't get it. Ro shot him a look that she hoped conveyed her desire for him to shut up and sit down. The JO didn't move, caught in the clutches of wanting to make such a high-ranking officer happy.

"Thank you, Mike." She nodded at the row of seats behind the conference table as she spoke to the lieutenant. He shoved his pointer into the pocket of his uniform pants and sat down. Ro made a mental note to talk to him later, to tell him he'd done a bang-up presentation. It wasn't his fault that the commodore was in a prickly mood.

She knew his prickly mood could be the result of myriad things—but she hoped it didn't have anything to do with her meeting with him a few minutes from now.

The rest of the AOM was rocky in parts as the commodore grilled everyone from the admin to the ops officer about the particulars of their presentations. Everyone took it in stride; Commodore Sanders had a lot on his shoulders, and besides, it was the staff's job to inform and support the commodore, not wonder why he had his knickers in a twist.

After what seemed like hours but was only twenty-three

minutes from the start of the AOM, the CSO, also a navy captain and the commodore's right-hand man, wrapped up the meeting and everyone stood to attention as the commodore got up and left. The CSO paused and turned around.

"Miles and Ro, I need to talk to you."

Everyone else cleared out.

Ro liked the CSO. Captain Ross Bedford had been on the same aircraft carrier as she was during the war and they'd enjoyed a good working relationship. He was a solid guy who put his family first whenever possible. Ross and his wife, Toni, had Ro over for family barbecues and holidays from time to time. He served as a great counterpart to the commodore's often-serious demeanor, as Ross was always ready with a joke and liked to keep things positive. Despite the commodore's sense of humor, which made an occasional appearance, his job frequently required him to play the heavy or to convey an impression of gravitas.

This morning Ross didn't have any of his usual jovial spark.

"You two know you're meeting with the commodore now, right?"

"Yes, sir." Ro and Miles spoke in unison.

"Do you have any idea why?" He studied both of them as if looking for a reaction.

"No, sir," Miles replied, and Ro shook her head.

Ross sighed.

"Okay, that's a good thing, at least. Stand by for a major bombshell—" Ross grimaced at Miles "—sorry, Miles." His reference to a bomb only made Miles, an explosive ordnance expert, smile.

"No problem, sir."

Ro inwardly squirmed. Miles's leg had been blown off by an IED, close enough to a "bomb." She thought Ross could have been a little more aware of what was coming out of his mouth.

Whatever was going on was major. First, the commodore had been the crankiest she'd seen him yet, and now Ross was showing cracks in his usually professional deportment.

"Let's go." Ross turned and held the door open for Ro to go ahead, while he and Miles followed her down the carpeted hall. The commodore's office spaces were the nicest on all of N.A.S. Whidbey, even classier than the base commanding officer's rooms. The wing commander was at the helm of all patrol squadron operations on the island. If something happened in or to a P-3 squadron in the wing, Commodore Sanders was responsible and accountable. That included ugly repercussions from mishaps, such as last month when a pilot and his crew left their aircraft before completing all the items on the shut-down checklist. They hadn't noticed that the chocks under the front wheels weren't secured. When a gale blew across the island that night, it put the P-3 nose-first through a hangar door. The commanding officer of the squadron took a career hit but it was the commodore who'd had to brief Senate staffers on why his overall wing maintenance budget had increased by two million dollars in one operational cycle.

Ro's gut told her their impending meeting with the commodore was not going to be positive in nature.

The commodore sat behind his massive oak desk perusing his computer screen. He didn't look up, didn't acknowledge them at all on their arrival.

Ro noted how ridiculous the desk still seemed to her. The commodore had insisted on having it moved in here. He'd found it in a government surplus warehouse, he'd said. Ro guessed that the desk had originally been used by a politician from the area. It wasn't extra-fancy or anything, just massive. Too big for the office space. There weren't enough seats for them all to sit down so they stood, waiting for the commodore to look up from his screen.

Ro took in the vast number of diplomas and professional awards with which the commodore had basically wallpapered his office. She loathed when navy pilots lived up to stereotypes in any way, shape or form. While the commodore had his "I love me" wall, he never gave off the air of superiority conveyed by his accomplishments.

She supposed he was a good guy, overall. She couldn't fault him professionally, and who was she to judge? If she stayed the course and took navy orders tour after tour, to different jobs and places around the globe, she might want her own "I love me" wall in her office one day.

The silence stretched and Ro wondered why on earth Ross wasn't opening his mouth to get the commodore's attention. Whatever happened to dealing with the live body in front of you instead of an inanimate computer screen?

The commodore blinked before he looked up and studied all three of them. Upon closer inspection Ro saw that the lines fanning out from the corners of his eyes were deeper and more pronounced than usual. A lifelong golfer, the commodore had seen his share of sun and his skin reflected that with its perpetual tan. Today he looked pasty under his bronze.

Her curiosity swelled and she wished she had a cup of coffee to hold, something to cover her anxiety.

"Good morning, gentlemen." He always ignored the fact that women served in the navy—a fact that Ro didn't miss but didn't obsess over, either. She'd experienced worse discrimination over the course of her career to date. He probably thought he was paying her a compliment by considering her one of the guys.

"Morning, sir. I've gathered Ro and Miles as you requested. Are you sure you don't want Master Chief Reis in here, too?" Ross's tone was more conciliatory than usual.

"No, no, let's keep it close-hold as long as we can."

Whatever had them all in here at this moment wasn't something he wanted his senior enlisted sailor to know about, not yet.

The commodore pursed his lips and fiddled with the fountain pen that sat in a brass holder on his desk.

"We have a big problem, folks, and there's no easy way to tell you about it." He steepled his hands in front of his face and took a deep breath.

"One of our young sailors died last night. It's a clear case of suicide brought on by wartime post-traumatic stress disorder. Miles, I'm sorry to tell you it was a man from your department. Petty Officer José Perez."

The air left Ro's lungs.

"AMS1 Perez?" She referred to him by his enlisted rate—aviation structural mechanic—and rank—petty officer first class.

"You knew him?" The commodore's attention made shivers race up her spine.

"Yes, sir."

The commodore's hawkish gaze made her feel like she was the one under investigation. She wriggled her toes in her black patent uniform shoes. She'd be damned if she'd ever let anyone see her squirm, no matter the reason.

Her last conversation with the sailor flashed in her mind. Petty Officer Perez had been a friendly, easygoing type, no older than her—probably a couple of years younger, in fact. He'd had the fire in his belly that made her smile. It motivated her when a junior ranking sailor was so dedicated to the navy.

Now he was dead.

"When's the last time you saw him?" Ross's voice was

gentler than the commodore's but Ro caught the grim underlying tone.

"I had coffee with him on the hangar deck yesterday afternoon."

"At the gedunk?" The CSO referred to the snack shack that everyone in the hangar spaces frequented for decent coffee and greasy-spoon fare.

"Yes, sir. He wanted to ask me about switching rates to IS." *Intelligence specialist.* "I told him it was pretty much too late in his career as he's—he *was*—up for chief on his next exam." She winced at her word choice. Perez would never be promoted again.

The room was silent. It didn't matter what Petty Officer Perez wanted from his navy career—it was over. Ro felt a strong sense of sorrow and regret.

"He didn't work in the weapons office, sir." Miles broke the tension with his steady professionalism.

"No, but he was in maintenance. You're on the hangar deck a lot with weapons and no doubt worked with him." The commodore responded to Miles without any sign of a condescending attitude.

"This is going to hit the press before long, and when it does there's potential for it to turn into more than it is. At the very least, I expect the media will try to blame this command for not seeing the warning signs of Perez's PTSD. I need to have you—" he pointed at Miles "—and you—" he waved his hand toward Ro "—on the case. You are hereby appointed to the investigative team for the death of Petty Officer José Perez."

He turned to Ro. "I've picked you because you have experience handling classified information. You know how to put pieces of a puzzle together without added fabrication." The commodore ran his fingers across the top of his close-shaven head.

"Miles, I've picked you because Perez is—was—in maintenance and on the hangar deck, which you're familiar with. I can't have the maintenance officer doing this. Plus he's going to be busy enough handling the JAG, NCIS and possibly a higher-level investigation."

The commodore paused.

"Hell, Miles, I picked you because you've got the most recent wartime experience on the staff. I know you won't lose it over a dead body. I need your experience and stamina."

Ro looked at Miles. He was silent, his face solid and not yielding a clue as to his thoughts. A flash of envy hit her as she realized she'd never have that kind of demeanor.

But she'd seen past Miles's demeanor that morning on the bridge....

"What about NCIS?" Miles finally asked, referring to the Naval Criminal Investigative Service. "And the civilian law enforcement authorities?"

"They're all doing their job, but none of them are required to report back to the commodore. You are," Ross said. It was obvious he and the commodore had already hashed this out.

So why wasn't the command staff officer doing this investigation?

Ro didn't have to ask her question aloud. The CSO needed to handle the inevitable bombardment of message traffic and emails.

"Commodore, how often do you want to hear from us, and what kind of report are you looking for when we're done?" Miles's expression remained unreadable to Ro. Professional, cool.

"We'll worry about that later. For now, just call me if anything shows up other than what we already know—that Petty Officer Perez killed himself last night."

Ro suppressed a sigh. Her instinct was to take some time to mourn Petty Officer Perez, to see what she could do to help his surviving family. She needed a chance to go back over the few conversations she'd had with him these past few months.

Nonetheless, a mental list of the action items she had to clear off her desk, ASAP, rolled through her mind.

Her job wasn't going to involve her usual wing intel officer duties until the investigation was over; she was certain of that much.

Naval investigations often dragged on for months, and she'd seen firsthand while deployed to the Gulf and detached to Afghanistan that there was little chance she'd have any true influence over the outcome. If the civilian law enforcement agencies had already been called in, she and Miles, representing the wing, didn't even have jurisdiction to investigate. The local LEAs tended to be more cooperative in a close-knit community like Whidbey but she knew that if the feds got involved she and Miles would be out of luck.

"What about the JAG?" Ro referred to their staff lawyer.

"He's going to provide support to the deceased's family during this terrible time, and of course, he represents me for any official statements. He'll work continuously with the public affairs officer. I named a lieutenant commander who was supposed to join the wing in a month as the casualty assistance calls officer."

Ro was impressed that the commodore had the foresight to appoint someone who'd probably never met Petty Officer Perez as CACO. That made it easier on the CACO to do his job—to ensure the family was provided for and received all benefits due to them as surviving members of the deceased.

The commodore didn't even mention any concern over how the intel and weapons departments would run with Ro and Miles out of the office for an indeterminate time. There was no need to. They both had staffs that would fill in until their return.

This was an aspect of navy life Ro equally relished and despised. If she did her job right and delegated as much as possible, her subordinates were able to achieve their greatest potential and earn valuable experience. Ro had no doubt that she'd be able take on this unexpected mission and rely on the intel shop to carry on with its basic functions.

Miles stared straight ahead at the commodore. Why on earth did today have to be the day she'd decided to stop being so harsh on herself, to really let go of her past, to forgive herself for clinging to the idea of a fantasy fiancé for so long? Worse, why had she picked today to be more open toward a new man in her life?

This assignment would be so much easier if it were her and Ross, or her and any of the other department heads working together.

But it was Miles—the only man who'd threatened her vow to steer clear of any serious involvement with the opposite sex since Dick had dumped her. Ro harbored no illusions that working closely with Miles would prove to be anything but problematic.

This case was going to be a bitch.

CHAPTER THREE

MILES DIDN'T LIKE the feel of this. He wasn't a Commodore Sanders fan, per se. Au contraire. He found the senior navy pilot, like most navy aviators he'd met, to be pompous and a bit too free with his good opinion of himself.

The commodore was justified in wanting an officer or two from the wing to keep tabs, as much as possible, on the case. Miles would have done the same.

But Sanders had paired him with *Ro.*

It was hard enough seeing her almost every day, knowing she didn't want to go out with him. Didn't want much to do with him at all. The fact that she was the first woman who'd ever gotten under his skin to this degree didn't help matters. Nor did it assuage his ego, which she'd flattened last year with her repeated rejections.

Add his freak show of an overreaction this morning on Deception Pass Bridge, and his future with Ro was bleaker than ever.

A pang of longing to work with an operational team downrange hit him. In the fleet there wasn't time for personality conflicts or egos to get in the way. They had a mission and they accomplished it come hell or high water, often both. Even while clearing mines in a godforsaken field in Afghanistan, when he'd lost his leg along with his dog, he'd completed the mission. The SEAL team he'd been supporting had been able to go forward with no further loss of life or limb and successfully root out a group of Taliban.

"This is such a hard time for our wing, for the entire community. I don't want anyone who worked with Perez to think for one minute that they could have prevented this or that it's their fault. This is a horrible and perhaps inevitable outcome of war."

Commodore Sanders said all the right words but Miles relied on his carefully trained powers of observation. The commodore kept looking down and didn't make sustained eye contact with any of them. His speech pattern was faster than usual, indicating his excitement or anxiety over the prospect of being cast in the middle of a national news-making case. Miles suspected that guilt was eating at Sanders, no matter what the commodore said about no one needing to feel guilty. It was natural for a leader to feel responsible when one of his own came to injury. Or worse.

The bottom line was that they'd all failed Perez if he'd committed suicide. Miles didn't believe in anything except the team concept when it came to his shipmates.

"I need you two—" the commodore looked at Miles and Ro again "—to be my eyes and ears on this case. Get to the beach and survey the scene of his suicide. Make sure the local LEA doesn't turn this into anything overblown or sensationalize it. Sailors commit suicide. It happens. It isn't always because of PTSD or pressure from the military, but even if it is, no one deserves the disrespect of a magnifying glass on his own death. Not my sailor, not on my watch."

"Sir, it's not anyone's fault that Perez had PTSD, if that's what it was." Ro's emphatic pronouncement gave the old man pause as he stared at his intel officer.

Miles fought to not roll his eyes.

Why did she have to be such a master of the obvious? This was what was wrong with support staff like intel. Ro was going to have to learn to toughen up and only worry about the investigation. How the commodore felt about the loss wasn't the issue.

The commodore's glance strayed again, but just for a moment.

"What are you waiting for? Get the hell out of here." He finished his last sentence in a low growl, Sanders's way of making a tough order less emotional for all of them.

Ro left first and Miles followed her. She turned around to wait for him in the hallway. For the first time he saw the cracks in her "work" face that revealed her frustrations and her questions about what had happened.

Ro was obviously as thrilled as he was that they'd been paired to do the investigation. He was surprised she hadn't said so to the commodore, or simply refused to work with him.

Her blue eyes widened in query.

"What—"

"Not here." He held up his hands and nodded forward. Ro clamped her mouth shut and turned around. It afforded him a wonderful view of her backside as he trailed her down the hall. Judging by the pronounced swing of her hips she was working up to a good fight.

He'd rarely looked twice at the few military women he'd worked with. EOD teams still didn't have many females, although he'd worked alongside his share of operational and staff officers who were women. He knew he'd been in the midst of intense operational situations during those times and he could blame that for not being distracted by the opposite sex—he'd had a war to fight.

He also knew that was complete bullshit. He'd be aware of Ro if they were both in the Arctic bundled in cold-weather gear with only their eyes showing through tinted goggles. Even in the midst of a firestorm he'd want to kiss Ro like he'd dreamed of since he'd first laid eyes on her.

He'd noticed her the day he'd met her, the weekend before she reported to the wing. She'd been wearing tight jeans that revealed just how curvy her ass was under her khaki uniform. She'd been spitting mad that his friend Max's dog had chased her mother's cat up a tree. Her anger had boiled over when she realized he was perfectly certain he could rescue her mother's cat from the sixty-foot fir tree. When he climbed back down the trunk with the fuzzy creature under his arm it had only ticked her off more.

He suppressed a grin at the memory.

They exited the plush corridor into the utilitarian part of the hangar, above the main aircraft parking area. Ro turned to face him again and he fell in step with her.

"Let's go outside. We can take my truck to the beach."

"I have to get my purse."

"Do you have your identification on you?"

"Yes, of course I have my ID," she snapped.

"Then you don't need anything else. Not for now. Let's keep walking and get out of here."

"Aye-aye, sir." Sarcasm tinged her words and Miles smiled. He knew he sounded like a jerk to a softie like Roanna. It was clear to him that she was already bored at the wing after being there for not even half of her assigned tour length. Like him, she'd been out in the fleet fighting the war until circumstances brought her home. Like him, she wasn't a native of Whidbey Island or Washington State. Unlike him, she showed no indication that the beauty and mystery of the Pacific Northwest had seduced her.

You haven't seduced her, either.

He wanted her, all right. From the moment he'd watched her get her back up about her mother's precious cat that was stupid enough to climb so far up a tree that it needed rescuing. A laugh escaped him as he remembered Ro's face after he'd handed the bundle of white fur back to her mother.

"What's so funny?" Ro's mouth was set in a grim line. Her tension had been palpable in the commodore's office and he'd wanted to squeeze her hand. Of course that would not only have been unprofessional, it might very well have earned him a smack to the head.

"Tell you in a sec." He unlocked the truck.

They slid into his truck in silence. Only when they cleared the main gate did he speak.

"I was remembering the expression on your face when I climbed up and got Henry out of the tree for your mother."

"It's Henry *the Eighth.* You have to use his entire name." She was sitting up straight, tense as a scared cat herself. But he saw the muscle twitching at the corner of her lip.

"You were so pissed off."

"I was *stressed.* My mother is not the easiest person to please, and her cat is everything to her." Ro relented and smiled. "I realize now how much I owe you. I had no idea you were an amputee. I get that, for a weapons expert like you, scaling a tree is no big deal. But you did it with one leg. For my mother's stubborn cat."

"Two. I have two legs, Ro, as long as I'm wearing my prosthetic."

"I'm trying to give you a compliment here, Miles. Let me."

He glanced at her and not for the first time was blindsided by her huge eyes. Her chestnut-brown hair floated around her face in a pretty cloud of spikes and curls. Her gaze, a sexy blue laser, conveyed so much more than her words ever had—at least to him.

He put his gaze firmly back on the road.

"If we need to work together on this, we need to agree to have each other's back."

"That's a given, Miles. But it's not about us—it's about

seeing that Petty Officer Perez is treated with respect and dignity."

"Come on, Roanna. You're naval intelligence. Do you really believe everything is as it looks?"

"I saw you watching the commodore," she said, and he felt her shrug next to him. "He's not the best I've ever worked for, either, but certainly not the worst. Either way, he's our boss. We have orders."

"To get to the truth. The truth may not be what he wants to hear." He needed to keep his misgivings to himself; he sounded paranoid. The collateral damage of a life spent expecting an explosion at every turn.

She sighed as if she'd read his mind.

"This isn't a Hollywood movie, Miles."

"No, it's not, Roanna. It's for real—and we need to be on the same page. For Petty Officer Perez, for his family and for each other."

ROANNA HELD ON to the handle above the passenger's side window as Miles drove them to the area known as West Beach. They'd learned that AMS Perez's body had been discovered by a dog walker early that morning.

"Good thing they found him while the tide was still out."

"You're not kidding. An hour or two later and he would've been shark bait." Miles was a guy all the way.

"That kind of comment's not necessary, is it?"

He flashed a glance at her, then brought his attention back to the road.

"No, but it's important that we stay detached enough to do this right. Neither of us knew him that well, correct?"

"You heard what I said to the commodore. I was talking to Perez about switching rates, just yesterday afternoon." Hours before he took his last breath. "But no, I didn't know him that well."

"He'd understand that we're doing what we need to do to keep our sanity."

Ro didn't reply because that meant looking at Miles and whenever she caught a glimpse of his profile she got that funny hitch in her chest. Not from discomfort, but from realizing how natural, almost familiar, it felt to be with Miles.

She was even getting used to her body's hormonal response to him, damn it.

"You have to admit this is pretty funny, Ro."

"How so?"

"It's taken a death for you to come to your senses about spending more time with me."

She bit her lip and gazed straight ahead.

Just focus on the case in front of you.

She peered at the house numbers.

"Up there, that's the one, isn't it?" The sun had burned off any remaining morning fog, which was common on Whidbey Island. The house stood at least two hundred feet back from the road, and Ro knew the island well enough to know that the backyard led to a precipitous cliff a hundred feet above the stone-strewn beach. All the homes along this route backed up against the cliffs.

"Let's check it out."

They weren't headed to the house—it served only as a landmark as it was the first home on the road, next to a large open area that residents used for picnicking and whale-watching. Ro was grateful she'd worn her uniform skirt with oxfords today. She usually preferred pumps with a skirt, but since she'd been putting in a lot of running miles her back was sore and she needed the lower-heeled shoes. Her pumps would never have survived tramping through gravel and across the windblown timothy grass to the edge of the cliff, not to mention the rocky shore.

There were still a handful of LEA agents wandering

around the beach four or five feet below them. She and Miles needed to climb down the rough path to the tide line. This was the lowest point of the western island, punctuated by tsunami warning signs.

The LEAs were distinguished by reflective vests and evidence collection kits. A small area had been cordoned off with yellow crime scene tape.

"What will we tell them we're doing?" They needed to be in concert with their story if they hoped to appear credible. "We can't say we're investigating officers, not really."

"No, but we can say we're with the wing and we're here to help." Miles reached over and squeezed her hand. It was a brief, warm reassurance, but her reaction was so electric Ro felt as if he'd just kissed her. She glanced around to see if anyone else had seen his gesture.

"Relax, Ro, it was a friendly squeeze. Not a public display of affection. I'd never put your career at risk with a PDA. You aren't affected by my charms so we're good, right?" His flirting made her want to sneer at him. Kind of.

You're starting new today. Remember?

"Um, yes." She took in the scene in front of them one more time before she turned back to Miles.

"Let's go."

They started the climb down to the scene of AMS1 Perez's untimely death.

RO HAD NEVER seen a dead body before. Except for at her great-aunt Ruby's funeral, during which her seven-year-old self wondered why Aunt Ruby's eyebrows weren't their usual dark color. They'd seemed so odd to her, all thin and high-arched, giving Ruby an expression of extreme surprise. Even as a little girl she knew that someone at eternal rest probably didn't look so startled. That was before she'd learned the nuances of eyebrow pencils. In retrospect Ro had figured out that the funeral parlor's cosmetologist had mistakenly assumed that Aunt Ruby's eyebrows should match her beauty parlor bleach job.

The sight of Petty Officer Perez wasn't as bad as she'd expected, not at first. At least that was what she told herself. There wasn't any blood; that much she could see from several paces out. Except for his face, he was clothed. As they approached his body and moved around it, she decided that first impressions were overrated.

The angle of his head was at once unnatural and revolting. It signified death as clear as any pool of blood would have.

As if a huge sasquatch had taken his head and twisted it around, his head faced into the beach gravel while his body faced skyward. She saw mostly the back of his head, but the large, black beach rock kept his head tilted at just the right angle to see his face with its bulging eyes in their final death stare.

Vomiting in public while in her uniform wasn't an option, but she really wanted to. She averted her gaze and took deep, practiced breaths through her nose. Navy training paid off in so many different ways. How would she have guessed that learning to control her panic while doing swim qualifications in the helo dunker would keep her from throwing up at the sight of a dead sailor?

"First time seeing it this raw?" Miles's voice wooed her back from the edge of her panic.

She let out a short gasp.

"Not all of us are in the field as much as you."

"Not all of us sit behind computers and analyze data as much as *you.*"

His sharp words startled her. Anger replaced shock.

"Please don't slip into your Cro-Magnon persona now, Warrant. You actually had me thinking that maybe you respected me as a partner in this investigation."

"I respect hard facts and someone who knows what facts I need."

The fact that they were actually sparring over the difference in their military occupations while Petty Officer Perez's body lay yards away catapulted Ro from nausea to anger.

"You didn't have a problem with my career choice when you asked me out." There, that would shut him up.

"I wasn't asking *LCDR Brandywine* out on a date. I was asking Roanna, the woman whose mother has a crazy cat, and who was new to Whidbey. I knew we could be friends."

She met his eyes and steeled herself to outstare him. "You didn't know anything about me when you asked." He still didn't.

"I'm good at reading explosives."

With her eyes still locked on his, her anger started to melt into something more visceral, more sensual.

Desire.

In front of Perez's body. Self-loathing made her stomach churn again.

"This is sheriff's business only, people."

Miles broke their stare-down and turned to the man in civilian clothes who was flashing his Island County badge at them.

Get a handle on yourself, girl.

The detective was tall and blond like Miles but with longer hair and not quite as muscular, and his physical appeal wasn't missed by Ro. Obviously he noticed her, too, as his gaze lingered a bit longer on her than Miles as he checked them both out.

"We're from the wing, Detective. We're just here to observe and make sure Petty Officer Perez's remains are handled properly." Miles spoke with authority. It was clear he didn't expect much resistance from the detective.

"IDs?"

Miles and Ro whipped out their military identification without comment. Before September 11, 2001, a uniform was enough identification. Not anymore, as it was too easy for a terrorist to get a uniform and try to pass himself off as a good guy while attempting to take down a military base.

"Okay." He handed them back their IDs. "I'm Detective Ramsey. You can stay as long as you don't get in the way. Don't ask questions, and for God's sake don't contaminate any evidence. Stay out of the taped-off area. Perez has already been assigned a CACO, as I'm sure you know."

The detective was trying to push their buttons. Searching for a hole in their explanation.

"Yes, he has, but the CACO's job is primarily with the surviving dependents, as I'm sure *you* know." Ro didn't want to start off under the shadow of the Island County sheriff's doubt. They'd most likely need information from him at some point, and would have to build trust with Detective Ramsey right from the get-go.

She offered him a smile.

"We appreciate what you're doing here, Detective Ramsey."

"Do you, Commander Brandywine?" He looked over his shoulder at the water for a brief moment before he resettled his ice-blue gaze on Roanna. The man knew the navy and he'd memorized her name already.

"Then you'll appreciate it when I tell you that if you hear anything in the next few days about Perez, his friends, family, whatever, you'll bring it to me."

"That's a job for NCIS, isn't it, Detective?"

Miles's voice held an edge. Ro got it. First the detective had told them to be impartial, uninvolved observers. Now he was asking them to provide him with information, possibly privileged if not classified information.

"Of course. And my team is questioning everyone, as well. But since you're both insiders, and here to 'represent the wing—'" he paused, his brow raised as if he knew exactly what they were doing "—there's a good chance you'll stumble across something I won't. People may be more willing to open up to you. And since I'm allowing you to stay and observe this part of the investigation, it's only fair that you make me privy to whatever insights you glean."

"We report to the wing commander, Detective." Ro's anger bit at the back of her throat. She was willing to play nice but she had her limits. This civilian really thought they'd enter into some kind of private deal with him? That they'd tell him something before they told their chain of command?

"LCDR Brandywine is correct, Detective, but of course we're open to information sharing. We're all after the same results." Miles was smooth and unemotional.

Detective Ramsey nodded.

"Good."

They exchanged business cards before the detective walked away. No doubt his mind was already back on the case. Ro waited until Ramsey was out of earshot before she faced Miles.

"Are you crazy? I'm not going along with your method of doing business, Miles. You're going to get us both a court martial!"

"Get a grip, Ro. All Ramsey asked is that we help him out if we can. There's no harm in that. Plus, in your usually overanalytical manner, you're missing the big point here."

She sighed.

"Which is?"

"On the off chance that this isn't a suicide, then someone at the wing may have killed Perez. The detective knows that the navy will circle its wagons if this becomes evident. He's pegged us as his way in."

Someone they worked with, killing Perez in cold blood?

She shook her head.

"Doesn't matter. It is a suicide and, bottom line, we report to the commodore."

"Of course we do. But it doesn't hurt to make friends when we can. No matter how certain we might be that this is probably a suicide, we're not the experts with the evidence. The sheriff's department is."

MILES HAD TO hold back a smile three times while he spoke to Ro.

She was the überprofessional she thought she should be, and she was shit-hot at her job. But she was too uptight, too by-the-book. His operational background was going to have to be what got them through this, especially if the case turned sour and wasn't a suicide.

His one gripe with navy intel had always been that it was so easy for the spook types to do a slick PowerPoint presentation on enemy territory and weapons stats. But they weren't the ones on the ground with zero visibility from a sandstorm, fighting off Taliban who'd grown up in the area and knew it like the back of their hands.

He watched her expression as she took in the whole grisly scene. It was normal to feel sick the first time—hell, every time—you saw a dead body. Especially one that had recently met its violent end. Suicide made it more emotional, too. If a young sailor who was apparently happy with his job and life was willing to kill himself, how close were they all to this kind of despair?

"You dealt with this a lot in Iraq and Afghanistan." She didn't ask, but assumed she was right.

"Probably not as much as you, or someone else who hasn't been there, thinks. Some of the folks I worked with didn't see anything too rough. Some saw way more than their share of death and destruction."

"And you?"

He didn't look at her. Couldn't look into her rich violet-blue eyes and tell her the worst. She didn't need it, not today.

"I'd say I was somewhere in the middle."

Ro took out a notebook from her jacket pocket and began writing notes.

"What are you afraid you'll forget?" From what he'd seen of her briefings, she had a near-photographic memory.

She shot him a quick glance. "As you said, it's my first time doing this, seeing this." She motioned at Perez's body. "My emotions are running higher than usual so I don't want to risk forgetting simple details."

"So even when you're upset, you control it? Is there anything you *don't* try to control, Roanna?"

Her nostrils flared and her mouth set in a determined line. He'd pushed too far.

Oh, he'd love to kiss her until her annoyance with him turned into something more enjoyable....

"Just keeping it professional and giving Perez my best effort, Warrant."

"Right."

He wanted to tell her that no matter how many notes she took she'd never get the image of Perez's body out of her mind, not entirely. He wanted to shout at her and tell her to put the notepad away and rely on her gut. Let her emotions do whatever they needed to and allow the bigger picture to come into focus.

Instead, he shoved his hands in his own pockets and looked out toward the sea.

CHAPTER FOUR

RO ENTERED HER small foyer with a deep sigh of gratitude. It had been a long day and wasn't over yet. From the AOM to the meeting with the commodore and then the awful scene at the beach, she felt like she'd been at sea—as though one day was really a week long. Time seemed immeasurable.

She only had an hour, tops, before she had to meet with Miles again. Her years at the academy had taught her the value of power naps as well as power breaks. She'd have to make the next fifty-eight minutes feel like a weekend.

Her home wrapped its arms around her and her shoulders let go of the weight they'd carried since Miles had tackled her this morning. She didn't have many people over, and that was by design. This was her oasis from all things navy-related. When she'd returned stateside after her last wartime deployment she'd decided it was the right time to purchase a house, no matter where she ended up via her navy orders. The fact that Dick had dumped her, and she'd accepted that she was truly alone, only hastened her quest to find her own home.

Oak Harbor, Washington, was a long way from Virginia Beach, Virginia, where she'd rented a condo while assigned to the aircraft carrier. The wilds of the Pacific Northwest contrasted sharply with the crowded suburban sprawl she'd grown up with in New Jersey.

She was thousands of miles from her family and childhood friends.

It was exactly what she needed and still wanted. Each month when she paid her mortgage, she was above all else grateful that she was a homeowner, free and clear of anyone else's emotional tentacles.

She dropped her fitness and lunch bags onto the bench she'd reupholstered last Saturday. Had that only been a few days ago? Less than a week?

Her whole life had changed this morning.

She'd thrown Dick's ring away. Let go of the shame, self-pity and sorrow she'd worn like out-of-date costume jewelry.

Finally.

Guilt tugged at her conscience as she untied her oxfords and slipped out of her uniform skirt. The investigation needed to be first and foremost on her mind.

Except it was the image of Miles, as he drove his big blue pickup truck, that flashed across her mind. The way his hand caressed hers for that brief moment on the West Beach cliff. The promise of heat in his eyes.

Why did all her emotions have to rise up at once? It was as if she'd cursed herself the minute she'd gone to throw that ring away. Miles had shown up and, ever since, she hadn't been able to control her attraction to him the way she had for the past year.

Even the gruesome death of a good sailor wasn't enough to take her mind off Miles and what it might be like to actually get to know him.

"Stop it." She whispered the request to herself as a form of prayer.

While she and Miles were at the scene of Petty Officer Perez's death, his body had been moved to the morgue. They spoke to the coroner and asked about a timeline for his investigation and the need for an autopsy. The coroner had been cryptic but respectful as he'd relayed that he would be required to do an autopsy even though the preliminary investigation pointed to suicide, just as the commodore had said. The coroner had made it clear that his business didn't involve the U.S. Navy.

Still, Miles told her he was hopeful they'd get into the autopsy, which would probably be performed tomorrow or Sunday. Time was of the essence.

Miles suggested they take a break for dinner and regroup in a couple of hours. They needed to keep the commodore appeased, yet the reality was that between NCIS and the local LEAs, there wasn't much wiggle room for two non-JAG naval officers to glean extra information. They'd have to track down every possible lead they could within the first twenty-four to forty-eight hours, before sources shut down.

As soon as she had pulled on her jeans and cream-colored nubby wool sweater, she went into her kitchen and got a bottle of sparkling water from the refrigerator. She slid her feet into plastic gardening clogs and walked out onto her patio.

The cottage-size home afforded her a wonderfully wild garden area out back, nourished by the moisture and rain-forest climate of Puget Sound. Her patio was the only level spot in her entire backyard. The ground sloped up to her neighbors' wooden fences—fences she never saw except when she did her annual cleanup of brambles and fallen branches.

Ferns, junipers and other low-climbing evergreen growth blanketed the yard, offset by random patches and containers of flowering plants. Roses thrived in the upper left corner of her garden, while the half dozen whiskey barrels she'd planted with fuchsia and seasonal bulbs gave the green carpet pops of vibrant color.

She took a swig of her water and smiled when the bubbles tickled her nose. Even if she only had five minutes of free time in a day, she spent it here.

With her knitting needles, of course.

Her fingers itched to go back in the house and get the chemo cap she was working on but she wasn't convinced she had enough time. She looked at her sport watch. Miles had said they'd "connect" after dinner; she assumed he'd call her on her cell within the next half hour or so. She made a mental note to go out to Whidbey Fibers, her favorite yarn haunt on the island, as soon as her work schedule cleared up. Which, judging from today's events, wasn't going to be until the commodore felt the entire investigation was over. She'd completed a few of the knit hats she was donating to the yarn shop's charity drive. The owner collected hand-knit or crocheted hats for chemotherapy patients who'd lost their hair. Ro heard they donated the caps to head trauma patients, too, down at Madagen Army Hospital in Fort Lewis.

If nothing else, focusing on someone, *something,* other than herself gave her a sense of belonging in the community. Plus it kept her close at heart to her deceased Aunt Millie, her mother's sister, who had died much too young from cancer. She still missed her, fifteen years after her passing.

Knitting also took her mind off her job.

Impossible at the moment.

It bothered her that the commodore had basically assigned her and Miles to be his lackeys. His orders to them weren't by any means illegal or unheard of; commanders used their staff subordinates to be their proverbial eyes and ears all the time. It was an effective way to make sure nothing slipped through the cracks. But this could turn into a freaking murder investigation and, for the life of her, Ro didn't see any reason the commodore needed to put both her and Miles, two of his busiest staff officers, on the case.

Of course, he was probably worried about political fallout.

Being politically correct had become *ingrained* in the navy and other armed forces in the fourteen years since Ro had graduated from the naval academy. Every commander, no matter how morally upstanding he or she was, needed to be very careful when it came to personnel matters. One mistake, one instance of even the *appearance* of a mistake, could and did end otherwise stellar careers.

Of course, she'd witnessed commanders who should have been fired and never were. And she was justifiably proud of her service to her country and the navy. The great majority of her bosses had been of the highest integrity and served their nation well.

There had been a few jerks, too. Some got their due.

She couldn't say the commodore here was a bad leader and certainly not a bad person. She just didn't respect him with the intensity she had other leaders. Maybe if she'd worked with him earlier in her career, she'd have witnessed a more enthusiastic leader when it pertained to the operational side of their missions. She knew him now, when he was gunning for flag rank, and she found it difficult to see past her impression of him as a bit self-absorbed and career-motivated. Again, nothing surprising given his rank and résumé.

The commodore wanted her and Miles to cover his ass, period. So the wing wouldn't be sullied by unfair comments in the press, sure. But she couldn't help assuming that the commodore wanted to ensure that he made the next rank.

Wasn't that what they were *all* aiming for, no matter where they were in their careers?

Wasn't she?

"Good girl, Lucky." Miles scratched the boxer-mix behind her cropped ears. She rolled onto her back and bared her belly for a proper rub.

"It's okay. Sorry I was gone so long today, gal."

Lucky was staying with Miles while her owner, another staff officer, was deployed to Afghanistan. Brad had never stated it aloud but Miles knew that leaving Lucky with him had been more of a favor to Miles than anything else.

Miles's explosive ordnance partner when he'd been in combat had been Riva, a Belgian Malinois. Riva had lost her life saving Miles's when a land mine detonated in an area they were sweeping. She'd received a hero's burial with honors, as she'd so valiantly and selflessly earned.

Her death had nearly crippled him emotionally. He'd known the odds were against both of them when he went into that godforsaken field but it didn't make losing her any less painful. His counselor and doctors told him his extended grief for Riva was how his mind kept him from focusing on the loss of his leg and his operational career. On a mental level, he knew that. In his heart, however, there'd always be a special place for Riva.

He figured he'd get his own dog in time. He wasn't ready yet. It wouldn't be fair to compare a new pup to Riva.

"Woof!" Lucky gave him the sign that she needed more than a belly rub.

"Okay, let's go for a little walk. You can't come with me tonight, okay, gal?" The boxer possessed nowhere near Riva's mental acuity but Lucky's ability to perceive his mood changes rivaled that of anyone—human or canine—he'd ever met. He allowed himself to wonder what Lucky would make of Ro.

Miles never had a problem focusing on a mission—it was a vital result of the rigorous ordnance disposal training he'd had. Lose focus, lose your fingers, a limb, your life.

But today he'd been distracted by Ro ever since he'd seen her standing in the middle of Deception Pass Bridge. He'd instantly known it was her—he could recognize her petite, well-toned body, not to mention her wisps of sexy curls, even under a knit cap, anywhere. Although she'd turned him down when he'd asked her out all those months ago, he didn't harbor a grudge. It wasn't as though he'd been looking for anything serious. He found her attractive and figured it was mutual, judging from the way she got her back up whenever he was around.

He laughed as Lucky gave him a sharp bark.

"Hey, girl."

Lucky butted her head into his thigh, seeking another belly rub.

As he rubbed her chest he thought about the animal shelter where he volunteered on weekends. He needed to call and let them know he wouldn't be in tomorrow morning as usual. He had a feeling his time at the no-kill shelter was going to be limited until this investigation was put to bed.

THE CHILLY SPRING evening proved too much for Ro's cotton sweater. She closed the sliding glass door behind her, cheered by the bright colors of her family room while she waited for the warmth of the house to chase away her goose bumps.

She didn't remember when she'd started, but sometime during her carrier tour she'd begun knitting decorative accessories out of the brightest hues she could find. She'd collected skeins of lush yarns in fibers she relished and brought a box of them on her deployment. Her downtime on the ship was basically nil, but every now and then she'd find a moment to pull out the yarn and start a pillow cover. The bright colors perked up the drab navy-gray and olive hues of her carrier stateroom, and gave her mind a brief escape from the pace of wartime carrier operations.

Once she'd returned stateside, the pillowcases turned into afghans, and then she found herself working on the wall hanging that hung over her bed. Her knitting wasn't anything she shared with others—she knew there was a group of knitters and crocheters that met every week in downtown Oak Harbor because she saw the flyers whenever she shopped for wool. But what if one of those women was the spouse of someone she worked with? What if it was another active duty person she saw every day? She valued her privacy and didn't want to share her hobby with anyone else.

The guys at work would have the ultimate weapon to tease her with if they knew she knitted. This super girly side of her belied the warrior image she wanted to project at work. Regardless of how good-natured her colleagues were, she didn't need them prying into the one thing that gave her peace of mind no matter what was going on around her.

She looked at her watch again. Still forty-five minutes until she had to check back in with Miles. Unless he called sooner, it was certainly enough time to get in a few rows on the chemo cap she'd started last night.

Last night.

It seemed a lifetime ago. Before she'd finally pitched the diamond. When Petty Officer Perez had still been drawing breath.

The repetitive motion of her fingers began to work their magic. Fifteen minutes was all she needed….

Her doorbell sounded through her reverie.

"You've got to be kidding me!" She quickly finished her row and shoved the project back into the cloth drawstring bag she used to stash her works in progress. It was bright neon green and had an equally neon pink sheep printed on the side.

If Miles had found out from the wing roster where she lived and had come here early—instead of letting her meet him—he was going to be sorry. But then it occurred to her that something critical might have happened regarding the investigation.

She opened the front door.

"Miles, I—"

The words lodged in her throat.

"I'm leaving Richard. Who's Miles?"

CHAPTER FIVE

RO GAPED AT her younger half sister, Krissy. Her shoulder-length hair was its regular dyed platinum blond, but had unusually long, dark roots. Krissy *never* let her roots show. Ro took in the rumpled hair, the circles under her baby-blue eyes, the complete lack of makeup. Krissy was dressed in a wrinkled sweatsuit and looked nothing like the fashion plate she usually resembled. And she was…heavier. Fuller.

Heavier? Krissy—who put the skinny in skinny jeans—heavier?

Upon further inspection she concluded that Krissy was plumper in one particular area.

"Did you have a boob job?"

"Great way to greet your only sister after you cut her out of your life for over a year. Nice going, Ro."

"You're my half sister. And you married my, oh, what was it? Yes, that's it—my fiancé. While I was at war. No biggie."

"It's time to get over it, Ro. I'm pregnant and I don't have anywhere else to go."

"You're pregnant?"

"Didn't Mom tell you? I'm due in February."

"So you're…four months along? I haven't spoken to Mom since Christmas, really." She left out Mother's Day—she'd had a very brief conversation with Delores then.

Anger-induced tears welled in her tired eyes. Of course Mom hadn't told her. Why would she? In her usual meddling manner Mom probably thought she was protecting Krissy from Ro's jealousy and disappointment that *she* wasn't the pregnant one.

That she wasn't the one married to Dick.

"Can I come in? I'm exhausted. I've flown all day and then the drive from Seattle was *sooo* long. Why can't you live somewhere more civilized?"

Ro stepped back.

"You can come in, Krissy, but just for a minute."

"You're kidding, right? I don't have anywhere else to go. I'm almost five months pregnant and my baby's father is an ass. You're all I have!"

She'd been there all of thirty seconds and already Ro's forehead pounded.

"What about Mom? What about all your girlfriends? Why didn't you just kick Dick out?"

Ro walked ahead of Krissy, toward the kitchen.

"I couldn't kick Richard out. I didn't really talk to him about this, you know."

Ro stopped in front of the refrigerator and turned back to face Krissy.

"What are you saying, exactly, sis?"

Krissy played with Ro's knitting-related refrigerator magnets. Ro put her hand on the fridge door.

"You didn't tell him you were leaving?"

"I don't owe him anything! He's been staying at work late and when he comes home all he does is eat, sleep and then go right back to work!"

Ro sighed.

"Of *course* he does, Krissy. He's a surgeon. His work is his life."

Krissy wouldn't make eye contact while she pouted. The sight of her spoiled, immature sister with a burgeoning pregnant belly made Ro's blood boil. She'd been getting Krissy out of jams for far too long. After Krissy and Dick got married she'd promised herself she was free of Krissy's neediness, Mom's conniving and Dick's constant demands—whenever he wasn't in the O.R.

It had worked for almost a year and a half.

Almost.

"You can stay here until you get on a plane and go back to New Jersey. I'm not your safety net anymore, Krissy."

"You have no idea what I'm going through! You've never had to worry about anyone but yourself." Krissy's eyes widened when she realized what she'd said.

"I didn't mean it in a bad way, Ro. But you *said* it was a relief when Dick broke up with you."

"What else was I supposed to say? You'd already married him!" Ro shook her head. "You're right, it was a relief—to be free of that relationship. It wasn't going anywhere. But that doesn't erase the lying and deceit you and Mom pulled."

"You hadn't even seen him for over nine months!"

"I was *at war,* Krissy. You know, keeping the world safe so that people like you and Dick could find each other and fall in love."

"Touché, sister." Krissy pronounced it "touchy."

Ro rubbed the back of her neck.

"Look, Krissy. I wasn't expecting you. It's the end of a very long week. I'm in the middle of a project at work that's just begun and I won't even be home this weekend. You need to catch a flight back to Newark. Now."

"I don't have any money."

"You had money to get here. Surely you didn't buy a one-way ticket?"

Ro was proud of herself. Not too long ago she would've paid for whatever Krissy asked for or needed. That all stopped when Krissy became Mrs. Richard Brewster.

"Well, not exactly. I bought a nonrefundable ticket but my return flight isn't until next month."

"Next month?" Heat crept up her neck and Ro was grateful she'd put the knitting needles away. If they were in her hands she didn't know if she'd stab her sister or herself from sheer frustration.

Krissy had never grown up. Ever. And now she was going to be a mother. She was carrying Dick's baby.

Dick and Ro had never planned on having kids. It would have been too difficult with both of their demanding careers. So why did seeing the evidence of Krissy's baby make Ro want to go to her room, slam the door and knit an ugly sweater?

The doorbell jerked Ro out of her rumination.

She looked at the clock on the microwave.

"Crap."

She strode to the front door and, for the second time in ten minutes, opened the door.

"Hey, Miles. I thought you were going to call."

Ro stared at Miles and thought his face was too damned handsome for someone who'd had as long a Friday as she had.

"I did, but you didn't pick up." Belatedly, Ro realized she'd left her cell phone in her car. "I thought I'd stop by—you realize we only live two neighborhoods apart?"

"No, I didn't know that. Come on in."

"Who's there, Roanna?"

Ro turned and looked over her shoulder as Miles stepped into her tiny front hall and Krissy poked her head around the corner from the kitchen.

"A work colleague." She sighed. "Miles, this is Krissy. Krissy, Miles."

"Hi! I'm Ro's sister." Krissy walked over to Miles as she held a dish towel in front of her belly and gave a flirty little wave with her free hand. Did she really think Miles wouldn't see she was pregnant?

Why did it bother her if Krissy wanted to flirt with Miles, anyway?

"Krissy's my half sister. She dropped in for a quick visit. Unfortunately, she'll be gone by tomorrow."

"Nice to meet you." Miles smiled at Krissy, and the resulting stab of awareness in her midsection made Ro take notice. She'd never seen that nice a smile on Miles's face before. God, was he flirting back with her pregnant half sister?

Wish it was you?

His gaze jolted her back from her unwelcome revelation.

"We need to go. It's going to be a late night." He held up his phone. "I got a text from Ross. This is a good time for us to head over to the house."

"Who's Ross?" Krissy inserted herself as though she were working the case with Miles.

"He's our CSO, the wing's number two guy." Ro was not in the mood to explain the navy staff system to Krissy.

"Don't worry about me here, Ro. I'll be fine." Krissy was only too cooperative when it suited her needs.

Ro gritted her teeth.

"I'm not worried about you, Krissy, not at all. You're an adult, and I know you need the time to make sure your travel arrangements back to New Jersey are squared away for tomorrow."

Krissy ignored her and kept her gaze on Miles.

"Is she always this serious at work, too, Miles? Ro's never learned how to lighten up."

"Ah, Ro is the consummate professional at work. I don't really know how she is outside of work." He offered Krissy a placid enough expression, but Ro saw the muscle twitch next to his mouth. He'd love to add that she wasn't the most cooperative woman he'd ever known, she'd bet a skein of cashmere on it.

To his credit, Miles kept his trap shut. Ro reluctantly gave him more points.

"I've got what I need—let me get my backpack." She squeezed past Krissy into the kitchen. Ro's home was the perfect size for her but with Krissy and now Miles inside she found it claustrophobic.

The fact that Miles towered over her and was built like a rock didn't help matters.

He'd barely fit in your sleigh bed.

No matter how professional she was, she couldn't stop herself from being human.

She just hoped she'd keep her most human instincts under wraps.

When she felt the door latch behind her she let out a deep breath and went into the still night with Miles.

THE IMMEDIATE, PALPABLE quiet was rare for Whidbey Island. Since it was perched on the most northwestern corner of the continental United States, every weather formation that came in from the Pacific or down from the Artic passed over the island. Ro often imagined her cottage was at the very edge of the earth. The winds had a habit of being unforgiving and brutal to anything but the native fauna.

It was so quiet she could hear Miles's breathing as they walked down her winding drive to the road where he'd parked.

His motorcycle.

"Where's your truck?" She bit her lip. She'd have to go back to the garage and get her car—no way was she riding on that bike.

He sent her a mischievous smile. "Left it at home. Too many people know my truck. This way we'll be more under the radar."

"'We'? I'm not getting on that. Besides, can you, uh, are you able to manage two people?"

"Two's as easy as one, Ro. It's my thighs that grip the seat, not my calves. And my prosthetic leg does what I need it to, even on a motorbike." He eyed her with restrained patience in the still-light evening. Whidbey Island was so far up north that the sun stayed up until nine or so on a spring evening.

"I've had the bike outfitted to my specifications." Of course he had. He was an amputee, not an invalid.

She put her palms to her shame-heated cheeks.

"I'm sorry, Miles. I'm not questioning your ability."

"Yeah, you are, Roanna."

"It's not you, it's me, really—I'm not the motorcycle type. Besides, isn't there some navy regulation that prevents us from riding motorcycles?"

"The only reg that says anything about it is that we can't drive recklessly. I don't do that." He cocked one eyebrow at her. "As for not being the bike 'type,' you may surprise yourself. You look like you'd adapt in no time."

Shame turned to desire and inflamed her face, her throat, her stomach. Just the briefest flirtation with Miles set her on fire.

This investigation needed to get wrapped up fast or she risked breaking the one promise she'd made to herself and had always kept.

Never date a man in uniform, especially one you work with.

Unfortunately, the population of single men in Oak Harbor who *weren't* on active duty greatly diminished her chances of finding someone to distract her from Miles.

And what will you do when you prove that no one tempts you as much as Miles does?

MILES KEPT HIS revelations to himself. The expression on Ro's face when she spotted his bike had been priceless. She tried to be so tough and was quite the naval officer, but he was learning that she'd forgotten that it was okay to be a girl, too.

Girl, hell. More like a woman of amazing beauty. Her large, round breasts couldn't be hidden in her khaki uniform blouse. The formfitting hoodie she had on tonight left even less to his imagination—in which he'd already held Ro's breasts and—

He groaned.

"What's wrong?"

Shit. He thought his sexual frustration had been silent.

"Nothing. Nothing at all." He flipped up the top of the storage box and pulled out a helmet, which he handed to her. "Put this on and make sure the strap is snug, like a flight helmet."

"I'm not—"

"You already told me. Frankly, Ro, I've never seen you as a pussy. Don't start now."

Anger threw sparks out of her irises that almost made him laugh. But her anger wasn't the passion he really wanted to spark. For now, it'd have to do.

His strategy appeared to work as she shoved the helmet on her head.

"You win this one, Miles, but if you pull any crap on the road—" she adjusted the neck strap "—like speeding or making crazy turns—" she snapped the buckle on the strap into place "—or making me feel at all uncomfortable—" she pulled down the visor "—I'm done."

He hated not being able to see her eyes.

"Got it."

He put on his own helmet and lifted his good leg, his right leg, over the bike. It was one of the many adjustments he'd had to make since losing the left leg. He used to mount bikes and horses alike with his left leg first. He still could if he really wanted to, but he felt much more stable doing it the new way.

Ro remained next to the bike.

"Get on."

She complied, although he understood beyond any measure of doubt that she did so only because she, too, was convinced this was the best way to travel at the moment—light, fast and basically undercover.

His abdomen quickened when her hands reached around his waist and clasped in front of him. The fact that she didn't even try to hold on to the back handle inexplicably pleased him.

Despite her refusals to see him on a social basis, she trusted him on some gut level. She wouldn't be on his bike, much less with her arms around his waist, unless she did.

That insight was enough to make him pray she didn't allow her hands to wander any farther south or she'd know just how much he wanted her to trust him.

Miles smiled broadly under his helmet and revved the engine.

He'd enjoyed an active, commitment-free sex life before the accident. It was the only kind he'd felt safe having; with worldwide missions that took him away often and unpredictably, he hadn't wanted to settle down. He especially hadn't wanted to worry that he'd left a widow or, heaven forbid, orphan behind.

That was then, this was now. He'd had some time to think about his life and the fact that he wasn't immortal. He'd known he could die while he was out on deployment—half expected it. It was part of the package when he signed on for explosive ordnance, and then again when he'd joined efforts with the SEALs on his last set of missions.

He'd faced the possibility of his own death head-on.

He sped the bike past the fir tree-lined streets in Ro's

neighborhood and eased them onto the main highway that bisected Oak Harbor and the island. They were headed north to where Petty Officer Perez had lived with his wife and two young children.

Miles turned on the motorcycle's communications system and filled Ro in on the brief meeting he'd managed with the CACO.

The Perezes lived off-base. Mrs. Perez was a nurse and had a good job at the base hospital, so they could afford to purchase their own home. This wasn't the case for most navy sailors who, once they had families, had to live in base quarters just to make ends meet. Living on base meant no rent, no utilities other than telephone, cable and internet. Quarters were often cramped but very livable, especially on Whidbey Island with the abundant natural scenery. It was easy to enjoy most weekends outdoors year-round, which made up for the tiny homes.

The Perezes had done well for themselves.

He pulled the bike into a small cul-de-sac in the Perezes' neighborhood, then took his helmet off and motioned for her to do the same.

They were still on the bike.

"Why didn't you just pull up to the house?" Ro's voice was low and he liked how he could feel the faint timbre of it.

"I could have—they'll assume we're here for a condolence visit either way. But I'd rather not run into anyone who knows us if we can help it. Discretion being the better part and all that, right? I thought it might be a good idea to walk around the neighborhood and get a feel for the area first. Plus we might get some information out of their neighbors."

"I really hate that we have to do this like we're creeping around." In his peripheral vision he saw her raise and then lower her helmet onto her thigh.

“We aren’t ‘creeping around,’ Ro. We’re officially non-official, working for the commodore.”

“You never call him ‘boss’ or ‘Captain,’ either, I notice.”

“No, I don’t.” He wasn’t going to elaborate. It was rare for him to respect any leader as much as he did his EOD colleagues, but that wasn’t what was at issue here. The reality as he saw it was that Commodore Sanders was, plain and simple, out for himself and his promotion. Miles didn’t let his own opinion take up too much space in his head, though. The commodore stayed out of Miles’s business and always made it clear that he respected Miles’s weapons expertise.

“Can you slide off first, please? It’ll be easier for both of us.”

“Oh, I’m sorry—of course.” He regretted the loss of her body heat so near his the moment she broke contact with him and slid off the bike.

“Nothing to be sorry about.” He took off his helmet, then accepted hers and put both of them in the storage area under the seat. He pocketed his keys and looked around.

“I get it.” She sighed softly.

“Get what?” He saw her expression and held up a hand. “No, wait. I haven’t said anything about the commodore. My opinion is just that—mine, and it’s irrelevant. He’s our boss, we’re following his orders. Did I miss anything?”

She smiled at him.

“Nothing at all.”

Damn, her smile made him forget what she’d asked. Why they were here, his own freaking name…

“Let’s go.” He turned and headed up the street, away from the cul-de-sac. Perez’s family home was just around the bend, on the other side of the woods that separated the neighborhood streets.

“Aye-aye, Warrant.” Ro mock saluted him as she fell into step.

"Knock it off, Ro. We're in this together."

"Yes, we are, aren't we?" She giggled. "I think it must be my nerves. There's nothing funny about this."

As they continued to walk together, he turned his head to watch her.

This was the closest he'd been to Ro in or out of the workplace. Her hair was a riot of spikes—the helmet hadn't been able to squash it down. Her lashes were long and at this distance he saw that the tips were golden, so they were even longer than he'd realized. She filled out her jeans as though she were a lingerie cover model. He stopped himself from hanging back a pace—just to catch a glimpse of her ass as she walked.

It's turned into your favorite hobby.

"What?" She'd caught him staring. She stopped and turned toward him, ready for a fight.

"It's you. You distract me." It was true. She'd caught him and he saw no reason to hide his interest. It had always been there and he'd told her as much when he'd asked her out.

She rolled her eyes.

"Knock it off, Warrant." Was she purposely repeating the expression he'd used a minute before? "We're on a mission, remember?"

"Yeah, I remember."

He studied her face for one more heartbeat before he looked over her shoulder and saw a group of wing staffers walking away from Perez's home.

It wouldn't matter if they recognized him and Ro, but his gut told him it was better to stay under the radar.

He didn't need a reason to kiss Ro, but this was good enough for him.

IT SURPRISED HER that he didn't try to come up with a lame-ass excuse as to why he'd been staring at her. But of course he didn't—he was Miles. Over six feet of solid EOD and dedicated warrior. He wasn't going to prance around any issue, especially his attraction to her.

And she was attracted to him, too. But he wasn't the right guy for her to date casually. No way was she ready for anyone as intense as Miles. Besides, he wasn't her type.

She worked with him.

"We have to stay on task, Miles. It could get dicey enough without you looking at me like this every time we're together."

"You're right."

Already, he was distracted. She saw his gaze wander and catch on something over her shoulder.

If egos made noises, she heard hers let out a huge protest.

"Ro, we need to—"

Before he finished his sentence, he grasped her shoulders and pulled her close. The shock of his body against hers sent crazy signals to her brain and then back to her most sensitive areas.

"Um, Miles?" Her voice came out in a whisper and she should have been perturbed that it didn't sound more forceful.

"I'm going to kiss you. Relax and see where it goes, will you?"

CHAPTER SIX

HER MOUTH BELIED her thoughts. It opened to meet his lips as they covered hers. Warmth, excitement and curiosity collided and months of speculation came to an end.

This was what a kiss from Miles felt like.

Sparks of delight jumped across her tongue as his tongue flicked at hers.

Her hands uncurled from their fists and she raised them to his chest, his shoulders, his neck. She sighed into his mouth and reached around his neck, pressing her pelvis against his. She liked Miles's idea of letting go.

He reacted to her enthusiasm by running his hands over her back, to the small curve of her spine, where he pressed her even closer to his body, his erection.

God, it had been too long for her. *Way* too long. His touch was like the most delicious chocolate bar, the first sip of rich red wine, the hot bath after a ten-kilometer run.

A groan deep in his throat was her only warning before he drove his fingers through her hair and cupped the back of her head, deepening the kiss to an all-out sexual campaign.

MILES HAD NO choice. Well, okay, he could have just pulled Ro into an embrace, no kiss included. But she was too close and he'd wanted to touch her, to kiss her, for too long.

Her lips didn't hold back. They were soft and still but her mouth was open in her surprise.

He used her open mouth to his best tactical advantage.

He tasted her with a confident lick, and then fully engaged her tongue with his. Her sigh vibrated against his lips and whatever tactical reason he'd had for kissing her went out the window. He placed his hand on the small of her back and pulled her hips into him. It didn't take much pressure at all. His other hand was on her nape, under her short waves that were much softer to the touch than he could have imagined.

His skin throbbed with the touch of her hands on his chest. When her hands reached up around his neck he couldn't help groaning.

Focus.

Still kissing Ro, he opened one eye and looked behind her. The officers he'd recognized from the wing had gone. He heard the slam of doors and the revving of car engines as the group drove away from the neighborhood.

With that distraction gone, he should have ended the kiss. But Ro was at once soft and insistent beneath his lips. She quivered when he left her mouth and placed a well-targeted kiss on the side of her neck, then let go of a sexy sigh as he trailed his tongue on her throat.

Her mouth demanded satisfaction as she put her hands on either side of his head and guided his lips back to hers. He was gone—diving deep into the hot sensuality that was all Ro.

The sound of a screen door closing followed by a dog's high-pitched barks brought him back.

He lifted his mouth from Ro's hot lips and rested his forehead on hers.

Their breath came in light gasps and he found himself enthralled by the thought that the two of them were breathing the same air.

You've got it bad.

"That was a surprise," Ro whispered.

He traced her cheek with his fingers. "I'm not sorry I had to kiss you."

"You did it to keep the wing staff from seeing us, didn't you?"

"Yes."

She sighed again, and her shoulders rose, then lowered. The arms around his neck fell and she took a step back. Reluctantly, he allowed his hands to leave the sweet curve of her lower back and drop to his sides.

"Is this how you usually run an explosive ordnance op, Warrant?"

"Out in the field the guys and I don't do much kissing."

He saw her lips twitch but no way in hell was she going to let him see her grin. Ro was so damned strong. He knew it killed her to let go of her professional demeanor, even in civvies. He'd heard some of the other staff joke that she had a stick up her ass but he knew they were as bemused as he was that she was able to stay so solid no matter what the circumstance.

Dealing with aviators on a daily basis was never easy, yet she made it look like a jog through City Beach Park.

"No wonder, since that would be distracting, to say the least. I hope you don't plan a repeat maneuver, Warrant."

"I do whatever duty requires, ma'am."

She glared at him. She didn't usually show this kind of heat, and it took all of his control not to haul her onto the bike and take off for his place.

"What we're doing will not call for that kind of tactic again, get it?"

"Got it." She'd enjoyed it as much as he had, he was sure of it. But this discussion was for another time, if at all.

He looked toward Perez's house. It was modest and neat, at the end of the cul-de-sac one street over, easily visible through the grove of fir trees that separated the streets. Only the trunks of the tall, thin evergreens were visible at eye level as the trees towered over a hundred feet above the homes.

"It's time to get to work, Commander."

ROANNA STEPPED BACK and looked up at Miles. With the glare of the sun's lingering rays behind him she couldn't read his eyes the way she needed to. But she knew he could read hers and it pissed her off. What did he see—her pupils dilated from the intensity of it all?

Damn it.

"I didn't want the group of wing sailors to see us. But if they did, they'll just think we were a couple out for a walk."

"And a grope to go with it?"

Miles winced.

Score.

"I didn't grope you. And a kiss may not have been a great solution, either, but can you name a better one?"

She couldn't. She was impressed, in fact, that he'd acted so quickly. She'd been all wrapped up in simply walking next to him, trying to keep her mind on the case. Who was behaving more like a resourceful naval officer at this point?

"No, it was quick thinking." She shrugged. "You were smart to act."

"Was it that bad?"

"Cool it, Warrant."

His chuckle warmed her shoulders as if he'd reached out and put his arm around her.

She'd gone months—more like *years*—*without* reacting so strongly to a man. Now when she finally did, it was at the worst possible time.

With the worst match possible for her. She had enough difficulty keeping up her expert persona at work. If she ever dated a colleague, no matter how "legal" it was in navy terms, she risked losing the tenuous control she had over her emotions.

That control had slipped when she'd admitted to herself that her engagement was a sham. When she'd realized she'd created a fantasy to cling to as she gave her energy and life to the navy. Even though she'd been nothing short of relieved when she and Dick called it quits, he'd gone and married Krissy, her *sister,* for God's sake.

Cool it. You know your real hurt is from Mom and Krissy lying about everything while you were gone.

At least it had all been out of sight of her navy colleagues.

"Don't worry, I don't think that necking with you is part of our investigative duties." His tone was cool but the way he said "necking," such an old-fashioned term, made her belly feel warm with anticipation.

Face it. Necking with Miles wouldn't be the worst of your problems.

But it was still too much of a problem.

"Are you ready to go knock on the door?"

"Of course. The CACO's already done the hard work. We're just going to offer our condolences, see if we can help, right?" She looked at him and was gratified by his reassuring expression.

"Yes, he did." Miles was silent for a moment. They both knew what the CACO's duties entailed and understood that this had probably been the worst day in Mrs. Perez's and her children's lives. The knock at the door, the group of uniformed men and women on her porch, the terrible pronouncement that Petty Officer Perez was dead.

"All we're trying to find out is whatever we can about their marriage, reasons he'd commit suicide and if there were any extra life insurance policies." Miles ticked off the list they'd already agreed upon. It had made perfect sense after they'd visited the beach scene but seemed so insensitive in the hours after the Perez family had been devastated.

"Right. And we're going in tonight, before she has too much time to think about it and decides to withhold information that we could use, or that the press could use against the wing." Ro needed to voice her justifications for adding to the Perez family's burden.

He nodded. His brusqueness irked her. She wanted to be detached from her emotions, too. It wasn't happening for her.

Her usual manner of coping with stress at work by throwing herself into the situation wasn't coming as naturally as it had before this morning.

"For the record, I think you're watching too much *NCIS*. It doesn't matter what we find out—if the press wants to slander the wing or the navy, they're going to." They walked up the last half block of the street and stood at the edge of the Perez driveway.

Miles groaned. "Please. I don't watch anything military unless it's a documentary. Do you?"

"No, but I had to yank your chain about something."

"Whatever, Ro, but I disagree—I think the commodore's right. We might be the only line of defense that keeps this whole case as private as possible for the family and allows Perez to rest in peace."

"You don't think we're out here to simply protect the wing, and by turn, the commodore, from bad press?"

He turned to her.

"The commodore's motivations aren't my problem, Ro. Giving a navy sailor the dignity he deserves in death is our job here. Don't you agree?"

"Yes, of course. But it's naive to think we're not somehow looking out for the wing, too."

They were at the front door. She glanced at Miles and he nodded. Ro pressed the doorbell.

Silence.

She looked at him again.

"Maybe they don't want any more visitors."

"Ring it once more."

She did, and this time the door opened before the last dong sounded.

A tall, bronzed goddess of a woman swept her gaze over Miles before giving Ro a brief, cursory nod.

"What do you want?"

"Mrs. Perez?"

"Yes?"

"We're from the wing. We worked with Petty Officer Perez and we've come to pay our respects."

"Sure you have." She eyed Miles with what Ro could only surmise was interest and shot a hard look at Ro.

"Who are you?"

"I'm Lieutenant Commander Roanna Brandywine. This is—"

"I'm Miles Mikowski, a warrant officer on the staff."

Anita Perez's attention was focused on Ro, and from the blank but intense look on her face, it wasn't because she was interested in getting to know her.

"May we come in?" Miles kept things moving, bless him.

"Yes." Anita took a step back. "You first." She nodded at Miles. Miles didn't hesitate and stepped over the threshold.

Ro knew from her CACO training that family members in grief and shock over the loss of a service member often behaved in a less-than-polite manner. Ro had faced discrimination while in the navy but never so blatantly from a civilian. She wasn't going to take Anita Perez's rudeness personally.

It didn't make her initial gut reaction of mistrust and dislike of Mrs. Perez any less.

Let Miles run it if that means getting the information we need.

Ro stepped onto the small throw rug in the entryway. The entrance to the home was modest, a modesty inconsistent with the interior. Rich colors on each wall and large, stately pieces of what appeared to be antique furniture complemented the vaulted ceilings and elaborate crown molding.

Certainly not what she'd expect from a first class petty officer's paycheck.

"Didn't you know I'm a surgical nurse at the base hospital?"

Anita had caught her gawking. So much for behaving surreptitiously.

"No, he never mentioned it." She didn't refer to her earlier conversation with Miles on the motorcycle.

"Did he mention I'm a kickboxing instructor?"

This was Ro's only warning before she registered Anita's closed fist in front of her eyes.

MILES TURNED AROUND from his brief perusal of the house just in time to see Anita's fist connect with Ro's left eye socket.

"Hey!" He immobilized Anita in two movements he hadn't needed since the war. Since he'd lost his leg.

Anita struggled against Miles. She was strong for a woman but nothing he couldn't handle, even with a prosthesis.

"That bitch has been sleeping with my husband!" Anita all but spit as she tried to lunge at Ro's still form again.

"Anita, what's going on here?" A man Miles judged to be in his fifties came into view from where the kitchen must be. He could neutralize him, too, if necessary.

"Just taking care of unfinished business, Dad."

Miles grew increasingly concerned as Ro lay motionless on the floor.

He frowned at Anita's father. "Can you please restrain your daughter for me? My colleague needs my help."

The man scratched his chin as he looked at his daughter, then at Miles and Ro's sprawled body.

Ro's hand rose to her head and relief washed over Miles. She was coming around.

"I'm not sure my daughter needs *restraining*."

Miles knew how to manage his anger. He was an expert at it, in fact. But he wasn't convinced he *wanted* to manage his anger, not when an old man fired off verbal potshots and an Amazonian widow had just taken out Roanna with a single punch and behaved as if it was all in a day's work. No matter how sad a day it had been.

He felt Anita's shoulders relax.

"I'm okay. Let me go."

He didn't tell her that he didn't give a shit if she was okay, he just released her, but not before he gave her shoulders a knowing squeeze. "Try to hit her again and you'll be on the ground next to her." He'd have a quick ticket to a court martial, too, but hoped none of it would come to pass.

He bent down to Ro, who had maneuvered herself into a seated position. Blood poured from her cheek, between her fingers.

"Let me see it, Ro."

She studied him with her good eye and he maintained a neutral expression as she lowered her hand. Her eye appeared okay but the gash under it, just on the edge of her cheekbone, was going to need stitches.

"It looks worse than it is. Here, press on it with this." He shrugged out of his pullover and cotton T-shirt. He folded his T-shirt into a wallet-size lump and placed it over her gash. He guided her hand to where she'd been hit and held it there for a moment.

"Keep it here, okay?"

"Okay." She should have looked defeated or shocked.

Instead, he saw anger like molten lava in the depths of her good eye.

"You're not going to try anything, are you?" He didn't see Ro as an instigator, but he wouldn't blame her for wanting to kick some ass. All they needed was to add battery to their list of complications. They'd already triggered a scene, negating his wish that this would be a low-key way in which to find out any loose ends about Petty Officer Perez.

"No, don't worry. I'm okay."

"Good girl," he whispered for her ears only. He put his pullover back on over his bare chest.

He stood up. Ro needed to sit for a few more minutes.

"Do you have any ice, Mrs. Perez?"

CHAPTER SEVEN

AN HOUR LATER, Ro saw Miles look at his watch. They all sat at the kitchen table. Anita Perez was next to her father, who kept squeezing her hand. Her children were upstairs with her mother, getting their baths and being read to.

Since Anita was a nurse, she'd taken a look at Ro's gash but only after they'd both calmed down and Ro wasn't afraid Anita would use the proximity to hurt her again. Anita validated Miles's take that Ro was going to need a stitch or two to close the wound and give it a chance to heal without scarring.

Ro didn't give a squirrel's butt about a scar.

She knew that she was seeing things through a haze of pain and anger, but she had to hand it to Miles. He'd kept his cool through all of it and was still managing to get information out of Anita and her father. Ro had no doubt that Anita wouldn't even have opened the front door if she'd come alone. Miles had saved the day.

"As I told you, I know LCDR Brandywine very well, and she's never been involved with anyone on our staff, much less a subordinate." Ro gave Miles points for backing her so staunchly. How did he know she hadn't screwed every guy on the hangar deck?

"Why were you so sure she was the one your husband had the affair with? Are you sure he *had* an affair?"

"He told me that she was the only woman on the wing staff. That she was single, and that he was leaving us for her."

"Anita, there are other women on the wing staff. But there are only a few at the top—and he may have been referring to a senior enlisted woman on the staff. When did he tell you about the affair?"

"Last week. He'd moved out a few months ago. He was barely scraping by on his own. In case you can't tell, I'm the major breadwinner. It worked for us for a long time—until José didn't make rate on the last exam and I got a big raise the same week."

Anita referred to the exam required by enlisted sailors to make each pay grade. The biggest leap was from petty officer to chief, and it wasn't unusual for that to take a few tries. Not making chief could have been a contributing factor to Perez's death, if it was indeed suicide, Ro thought, but unlikely.

"Bessie, our youngest, had just been born, and José was feeling the weight of needing to be the big provider." Anita clenched her fists in front of her on the table. "It never bothered me. I didn't care how much he made. He was doing what he always wanted to do—serve his country. I was doing what I wanted to do—helping heal people." She hugged her shoulders and her father placed a hand on her back.

"I told him I was thinking of taking a better-paying job in Seattle—that we could move there if he wanted to get out, or stay in and take orders to Bremerton or Everett. He flipped. He couldn't deal with the fact that it was my job driving our family life and where we'd live. He's from a very traditional family and it didn't sit right with him."

"Are you in debt for any reason?"

"No, we're not, *I'm* not. But he bought himself a fancy car and started bringing the kids really expensive gifts. Nothing he could afford on a petty officer's salary, which is all he had after he moved out. I cut him off from any bit of my salary. I was protecting the kids and myself—I had to. Judging by his spending sprees he had to be living off his credit cards, maybe even payday loans. I was afraid he'd blow through our life savings if given the chance. I had to take precautions for me and my kids."

"I'm sorry to be asking you these questions now, Mrs. Perez. Roanna and I are very sorry about your predicament."

She cast a sheepish glance at Ro.

"I apologize—I reacted out of pure anger. I think it's been building up in me for a long time." She stared down at her hands. "This isn't the first time he strayed, you know. It's never been an easy road with him."

"I'm sorry." Miles was the comforter, the investigator, the medic.

Ro sat with frozen fingers holding a bag of frozen corn to her eyeball. They'd traded Miles's blood-soaked T-shirt for a clean kitchen towel wrapped around a plastic bag full of ice cubes. After the ice melted they'd switched to frozen vegetables.

She couldn't complain, not at the moment. But when she got out of there, she was going to allow herself to spew a decent string of obscenities. She couldn't remember the last time she'd felt so physically uncomfortable.

"I'm fine." Ro tried to smile but wasn't sure if it came out that way. Her muscles felt as though they were straining to create even the simplest facial expression.

Ro had heard of CACOs taking punches from bereaved family members. Emotions ran untethered during such tragic circumstances. The death of a service member more often than not involved a young person. A death that was unexpected and brutal in its suddenness.

She berated herself for not being more prepared for Anita's fist. There'd been warning signs from the minute Anita had opened the door. The way her eyes had narrowed, the way she'd looked at Ro like a lioness looks at a jackal—it had been pretty obvious she'd seen Ro as an adversary.

Anita seemed to buy into Miles's explanation that Ro was not Petty Officer Perez's lover. If Ro could have mustered a glare at Miles she would have. Smooth as honey on peanut butter, he calmed Anita and her father down. He had them both captivated.

As I sit here with my eye swollen shut.

This was the refrain of Ro's life. She worked her ass off trying to show she was half as good as any man in the same uniform, only to have her efforts stalled whenever a decent officer came into the picture. Her intel colleagues told her it had nothing to do with male versus female issues. It was an ops versus intel dynamic. It was the way it went for their navy branch—all support, none of the glory.

Ro didn't want glory. She wanted answers and respect. Unfortunately, Miles had never given her anything less than respect, so she couldn't take her resentment out on him. But she so badly wanted to that she could envision punching Miles the way Anita had punched her.

Was it because he was doing what she'd wanted to do for the investigation—developing a rapport with Anita Perez? Or because she was still annoyed by how attracted she was to him?

Miles definitely fit the bill of a "decent" officer. Unlike most of his single peers, he didn't seem to have a need to brag about his sex life at work. Ro had never seen anything but pure professionalism from him. Even when he'd tried to get her to go out with him, he hadn't pushed it and never took it out on her in the hangar. Miles was the consummate officer and a gentleman.

She respected him, too.

"Ro, didn't you want to say something about Petty Officer Perez?" Miles's eyes flickered over her face. She knew he didn't miss one ugly bit of it, either. His powers of observation spoke for themselves since he'd worked EOD, but it only took a few minutes in his presence to realize this was a man who lived fully in the moment, ready for whatever came his way. Essential for working with explosives, unnerving when that attention was focused on her.

"Yes, Mrs. Perez—"

"Anita."

"Yes, of course, Anita." She moved her bag of corn to the other hand so that she could look at Anita with her good eye.

"I had a couple of conversations with Petty Officer Perez in the past few weeks about his career options. Did he ever mention to you that he wanted to switch from aviation maintenance to intelligence specialist?"

Anita's hands shook but she steadied them by folding them in front of her on the farm table.

"He mentioned that he wanted to go back to school and finish up his master's degree. He already earned his bachelor's. I thought he wanted a commission. He'd always wanted to be an officer." Anita sighed. "What I haven't told the police, because it's irrelevant and private, is that José came to me last week and told me he was sorry for all he'd done. That his affair had been stupid and a one-time deal. He missed the kids so much. He wanted to reconcile."

"What did you say?" Ro had to know.

"I told him to go to hell."

Silence settled over the four of them.

"What was his reaction?" Miles continued.

Anita gave them a wan, sad smile.

"He was visibly upset, but told me he'd wait for me to come back—wait forever if need be. Said he was going after a commission when his current enlistment was up."

"Which was soon?" Ro asked the question Petty Officer Perez had given her the answer to last week—his enlistment was up in three months. He needed to make a decision to "reup," reenlist for a number of years, or get out and try for a commission.

"Just a few months away." Anita confirmed Ro's understanding. She unwittingly also confirmed that Perez had been communicating with her right up until his death.

Not necessarily the mark of someone isolating himself before a suicide.

"Did he say anything else that indicated he was upset enough to take his own life?"

"It wasn't suicide, trust me." She shook her head. "The sheriff said he couldn't rule it out due to the epidemic of PTSD-related suicides in the navy, but he thought it looked like an accident—that José fell off the cliffs. Check his medical records—José was never diagnosed with PTSD."

Ro turned to Miles. Did he realize this was in direct contrast to what the commodore had intimated? His gaze remained on Anita.

"I don't appreciate you coming in here and upsetting my daughter, Warrant." Anita's father spoke up, his voice steely, his fists clenched.

"I apologize. We're just trying to make sure all the angles are covered. The civilian law enforcement has to do its job, but to us this isn't a job or an investigation—this is about seeing that our fellow sailor gets the justice due him as a last gesture from the U.S. Navy."

"Isn't that what the CACO is for?" Anita eyed Miles, then Ro, with a wary glance.

Ruh-ro, Scooby. Busted.

"Yes, of course. But the CACO is more for you and your children, to ensure that you get every benefit and financial consideration due you. To see that Petty Officer Perez is laid to rest as he wished, as *you* wish. You are still legally married, correct?"

Ro hoped she'd be able to keep Miles and herself out of hot water here. All they needed was to get accused of interfering with the CACO and they wouldn't be allowed to come anywhere near Anita or her kids. Their effectiveness would be completely compromised.

"Look, José had no reason to kill himself. I don't think I helped him feel better, if he was truly depressed, when I told him to go to hell. But when he left the house he was still very positive about trying to win me back. He'd had a wonderful day with the kids down at City Beach and then took them for ice cream. He wasn't a man about to commit suicide."

"I'm sure he wasn't. Again, we're so sorry for your loss, Anita." Ro's voice sounded smooth, despite the effort it took her to speak through a swollen face.

"Thank you." Anita bowed her head.

"I think you've been here long enough. Anita and the kids need some peace and quiet," her father said.

"Of course."

"No, wait—I have to tell you one more thing." Anita's plea cut the tension in the room.

Miles rested his hand on Ro's forearm to keep her from standing up.

Anita's eyes were red-rimmed and tears trickled down her cheeks. Quite a difference from the stone-faced woman who'd clocked Ro with a right hook only thirty minutes ago.

"There's no way he was responsible for his own death. First, he hikes around the island all the time and knows the paths like the back of his hand. He wouldn't get that close to the edge, ever. Plus it sounds like he fell at night—they said something about him drinking and walking it off."

Anita shook her head.

"No way," she repeated. "He's been sober for five years.

This affair was his first emotional slip that I'm aware of since he sobered up. I don't know what state he was in when he was walking, but he wasn't drunk."

Ro hoped she kept her gasp silent. This was a big admission from an estranged, wronged wife. She looked at Miles.

"Thanks, Anita. We're doing our best to get to the truth," Miles responded.

His gaze met Ro's with equanimity. "Let's go."

Ro nodded.

"Thanks again, Anita, and—" she smiled at Anita's father "—thank you for being here to support your daughter. Again, I'm so sorry for your loss." She left the pack of corn and dish towel on the kitchen counter.

Ro didn't wait for another verbal attack, which appeared to simmer behind the man's expression. She'd had enough.

Miles waited for her to walk in front of him. As they neared the front door, the doorbell rang.

"Son of a bitch, when will people figure out that you don't need this, Anita?" the father growled with pent-up rage. Ro knew it was from the rush of adrenaline that any trauma caused. She didn't, however, want to stick around for it to abate.

Miles reached the door first and opened it.

"Oh! I thought the CACO team was gone." Karen Sanders, the wife of the commodore, stood on the porch with a large picnic basket in her arms.

"They are. We're just here to offer our condolences." Miles answered for both of them. Ro was grateful. Karen Sanders had never taken a shine to her. They had nothing in common. For all the years and sweat Ro had poured into making herself a successful career officer, Karen had used the same energy to become the perfect naval spouse. It made Ro sick. Not that the job of a naval spouse wasn't important and welcome. Ro knew and enjoyed spending time with a good number of her colleagues' spouses, male and female alike.

Ro had issues when any woman gave up her identity for her husband. She'd seen more of it in the navy than her friends in the civilian world experienced. Constant moves across country and often the globe curtailed a spouse's civilian career no matter how proficient they were at their job.

Some spouses simply stopped trying to eke out a separate vocation for themselves. Too often that led to the spouse assimilating the active duty member's career as if it were his or her own. As if they wore the rank of their spouse.

Karen Sanders was "Mrs. Commodore" to a T.

"Hi, Karen."

"Roanna, what happened?" Karen's eyes were large, incredulous at the appearance of Ro's face. Too late, Ro wished she'd kept the bag of corn, even though it had gone soggy and was useless as a healing tool. It could have hidden her ugly eye from this diva's gaze.

Ro tried to strike a nonchalant pose. "I ran into a tree on the way here. It looks worse than it is." Miles remained silent but she felt his laughter emanate silently from him. Even Anita's father snorted from the kitchen.

"If you say so. Still, you might want to get it checked out." Karen bit her lip. "Is Anita in?"

"Right here." Anita stepped in between Miles and Ro.

Karen held out her basket.

Just like freakin' Little Red Riding Hood.

"I won't stay, I just wanted to give you my condolences and bring you this meal. You can heat it up whenever you need it." Karen sent Anita a motherly smile.

Karen was petite, her blond hair in the process of being expertly replaced by silver in its impossibly smooth bob. Her outfit under the open swing raincoat screamed "prep" from her white blouse down to her chinos and expensive loafers.

Stop it. She's just the commodore's wife. It's her job to come and play Florence Nightingale. Mind your own business.

"We're just leaving," Miles said and Ro let out a sigh of relief. She wasn't convinced she would have said anything as innocuous.

She stepped out and brushed past Karen. No words were necessary at this point.

MILES STAYED BEHIND her until they reached the end of the driveway. The darkness of night enveloped them as the limited streetlights spilled pools of white every so often.

"Ro, wait up." He grabbed her hand and spun her around.

"I just want to get home, Miles." Exhaustion and a distinct chill pervaded her whole body.

He lifted her chin up until their faces were a whisper apart in the dark.

"You're a real trooper, Ro. You stood your ground in there, and I know this hurts like hell." His fingers lightly touched her swollen face.

"It's nothing, you'd do the same." She didn't take praise well and from Miles it was too much. The warmth she felt at his words was yet another reason she'd avoided him for so long.

Miles turned her on like no one she'd ever met. In her pain and distress she still had to fight the urge to jump him.

"I'm here for you, Ro, and I mean it when I tell you we're in this together."

He leaned toward her and brushed her lips with his. The sparks of sexual attraction were there, but more insistent was the comforting warmth from his mouth.

Ro stood still and allowed him to pull away.

She let out a shaky breath.

“Right. Can we go home now?”

“Only after we get that cut taken care of.”

CHAPTER EIGHT

CAPTAIN LEO SANDERS, Commodore of the Patrol Wing, N.A.S. Whidbey Island, took off his khaki cover as he entered his family's house in the residential area of the base. The minute it came off and the metal silver eagle clunked against the foyer table, he became "Leo," "honey" or "Dad." And no one in the Sanders household was impressed with his rank or success in the navy.

He walked into the kitchen that had a bank of windows with a sweeping view of Puget Sound. He and Karen often enjoyed their morning coffee out here—when Karen wasn't already up and gone to the gym. She prided herself on her schoolgirl figure, as evidenced by the small fortune she spent on her clothes.

"Anyone home?" He called out to what he suspected was an empty house. Karen's MINI Cooper hadn't been in the driveway when he pulled up, and after school, their teenage daughter spent most of her time with her friends. Still, a father held out hope.

He knocked lightly before he cracked open Stefanie's bedroom door. She looked up from her laptop and yanked her headphones out of her ears.

"Hey, Dad."

"Hi, honey." He walked into her room, deliberately ignoring the piles of laundry and papers that lay in wait, invitations to trip or sprain an ankle. He kissed her on the forehead.

"What are you doing?"

"Just talking to my friends."

"Facebook?" He prided himself on keeping up with current technology. He'd been a navy pilot for twenty-four years, after all, entrusted with the most advanced technology in the fleet.

Stefanie's pretty face twisted in a scowl.

"*Skype,* Dad."

"My bad."

She rolled her eyes but didn't comment.

"Where's Mom?" He asked Stefanie the million-dollar question.

"I have no idea." She maintained a blank expression but he knew his daughter. She was too used to having her mom do these disappearing acts.

"Okay, I'll give her a call on her cell. I'll get dinner going in a few, okay, kid?"

"Sure." She poked the earbuds back in place, effectively slamming the door on him.

Leo changed from his uniform into jeans and a white polo shirt that bore the wing's logo on the left breast. The wave of sadness at the end of a workday was a familiar companion of late. He'd been so wrapped up in his work at the wing, trying to make sure he didn't miss a trick. His fitness report was due and it had to make an impression on any future selection boards. Leo's goal had been the same since he was a junior officer: become an admiral like his father, grandfather and great-grandfather had.

Today had been the absolute worst. The mess of AMS1 Perez's death was one complication he could have done without.

He sighed as he slipped his feet into the soft lambskin slippers Karen had given him this past Christmas.

That had been only half a year ago, and their lives seemed

so different now. Karen spent more and more time away from home. She'd always been the quintessential navy wife—to a fault. Leo had tried to encourage her to find something that was all hers—go back to school and get a master's degree in teaching, or start her own business.

Karen always pointed out that the constant moving and often heavy social schedule that his assignments required made it foolish for her to do anything else. The fact that the new generation of military spouses, increasingly both male and female, often had careers separate from their active-duty spouses hadn't influenced her.

He'd caught a whiff of the fact that Karen drove the other squadron wives crazy at the spouse club meetings. She liked to be involved in everything to a degree that intimidated and downright annoyed the other volunteers.

Leo popped the cap off a bottle of beer and took a long drink. His relationship with his wife had cooled over the years, but these past few months he'd started to wonder why the hell they stayed together, other than for Stefanie.

He pulled out two steaks and some fresh veggies. At least Karen kept their kitchen well-stocked.

He heard the front door open and close, the tinkle of her keys as they landed on the tray by the door, the click of her heels.

"Hey, sailor, what are you doing home so early?" She smiled and walked over to him. He was wrapped in the cloud of her perfume before she gave him a full kiss. Her lips tasted of peppermint.

"It's past seven o'clock, Karen. Stefanie didn't know where you were. Neither did I."

Her eyes widened slightly and he noticed that they seemed puffy, even red.

"Stefanie knows that if I'm not here I'm at the gym or the commissary."

He stared at her, hard.

"You don't look like you just worked out, and unless there are groceries in your car, I'm going to go out on a limb and say you weren't at the commissary, either."

She bristled.

"No, as a matter of fact I was out doing my job as the commodore's wife. Which I wouldn't even have known about if I'd counted on you."

His gut hardened.

"Where were you, Karen?"

"I was at Petty Officer Perez's home. I took a casserole and a plant to his family."

"Goddamn it, Karen. I didn't tell you because Mrs. Perez had made it clear on her 'in case of an accident' request form. She didn't want anyone from her husband's staff to visit—only the chaplain and CACO. Few things are sacred in the navy anymore but the request form for spouses' wants in their hour of greatest need is one of them."

"She wanted only the CACO and command chaplain there when she was informed, yes. But I found out the wing staff went over late this afternoon. Even your intel officer and Miles were there. You never told me he'd died, Leo. I had to hear about it at navy relief."

So the word was out on base. He raked his fingers through his hair, a stabbing pain behind his right eye. He'd never had headaches until he was transferred back to Whidbey.

"I didn't tell you because it's none of your business. Of course I was going to tell you about Perez before it hit the press, but this is a highly sensitive situation, Karen. And being the commodore isn't the same as being a squadron CO. You're not the CO's wife anymore. And as the commodore's wife, no one wants you mucking around in their affairs."

She looked as though he'd slapped her, and he felt guilt in addition to his anger.

"If you'd taken my suggestion and found something for yourself to do, you wouldn't feel the need to get so involved with *my* job."

"Sure, I get it, Leo. It was great in the early years, when my involvement helped your career. And don't tell me it didn't—I threw every hail and farewell party for every CO's wife we ever knew. There wasn't a spouse club I wasn't heavily involved in, if not running. But now you think you'll make admiral on your own. You haven't gotten *anywhere* on your own, Leo. You'd have nothing if I hadn't sacrificed my career for you."

He wanted to point out that she hadn't had much of a career to sacrifice, but wasn't in the mood for her familiar tirade about how she'd had "amazing" offers to travel the world with her international relations degree from Tulane University. How she'd sacrificed it all for him, for their family, once Stefanie was born.

The way he saw it, she'd traveled the world with him and the navy. Saw things she never would have if she'd stayed in that godforsaken Podunk town she came from.

He was determined not get into the subject of Karen's martyrdom for his career.

"So you went over there? To the house?"

"Yes." She sniffed. "It was very tragic. I'm glad I took over my lasagna—God only knows when Mrs. Perez will be up to making a meal again."

This was completely different from what the CACO had told him earlier today. He'd made it clear that his first impression was that Anita Perez had been upset but not to the point of physical collapse. She was a trauma nurse by trade and was used to dealing with high stress. The CACO reported Anita had been holding her own.

"I think you should have gone over there, Leo." Karen's accusation wasn't even veiled by politeness. She never thought anything he did was good enough.

"We'll have to differ on this, Karen. You did a nice thing. Thank you." He knew he had no other option than to assuage his guilt and smooth her ruffled feathers.

She breathed deeply, smelling the air.

"What are you cooking?"

It was so typical of her to change the subject and shut him out of her thoughts. He did find it curious that her face was so haggard. Granted, going over to the surviving family's home after a mishap of any kind was never pretty, but the aftermath of a suicide had to be the most horrible.

If everyone buys that it's a suicide.

She shouldn't be so upset over this. Karen hadn't known Perez's family; neither did he. He only knew Petty Officer Perez—he'd never met the wife or kids. They hadn't shown up at the annual wing picnic and he'd taken his time to grip and grin at each department and hangar deck workshop.

You could have missed them.

He had a lot of people to speak to at any event, and he'd relied on Karen to hold court for him—it was her favorite pastime.

"I thought I'd grill the steaks you bought, along with some mushrooms and zucchini." He considered that a conciliatory gesture—an olive branch.

"Stefanie will love it." Karen held out a small branch in return.

"Would you prefer something else?" He didn't want to talk to her anymore. He wanted solitude.

"Oh, no—my appetite is kind of flat, you know? A cocktail is more what I need."

He shrugged and she sent him a look of complete reproach. "I honestly don't understand how you can be hungry at a time like this, Leo."

He wanted to tell her to save her pious nun act for the kids she taught at the Sunday school on base.

"Karen, I know it must have been rough at the Perezes', but you didn't know them. You can't take on their grieving and sadness. If I did that with every domestic violence case I'd be a nut job."

"Leo, this wasn't domestic violence. A young man killed himself and left behind a beautiful wife—" she put her hand to her mouth "—and two children. His wife won't even accept that it's a suicide." Her voice turned into a whisper. "He had every reason to live."

"Honey, come here."

She remained stiff and unresponsive in his arms but he held her, anyway. "The wars have taken their toll. We don't know what horrors that young man saw over in Afghanistan. His mental health wasn't completely readable—nobody's is."

A shudder racked her shoulders.

"I just feel that if I'd known him, their family, maybe I could've made a difference."

Aww, here it was. Karen the all-powerful.

"No, Karen, not even you could have changed this."

He certainly hadn't been able to change much during his past eighteen months as commodore. And now the issues he'd taken steps to control—to make sure he'd be a shoe-in for flag rank—had blown up in his face.

Karen only knew the half of it.

KAREN EYED LEO through the sliding glass door. He had his beer in one hand and the barbecue tongs in the other as he grilled their dinner.

When she'd agreed to marry him almost thirty years ago she'd known he was her match. A good person overall but not afraid to go after what he wanted in life. Like her, he'd learned at a young age to keep himself on top of his list of priorities.

But at least they'd kept each other up there on their respective lists, too. Until Leo started amassing career accolades and paying less attention to their marriage. He was the golden boy of the P-3 community. She'd loved being on his arm, knowing that all the other women were watching her for their example.

But then the surprise that was Stefanie showed up. Of course Karen was so grateful for her daughter, these teenage years aside. But having kids hadn't been in the plan. So it'd thrown them for a bit. Their reunions after long deployments weren't the two of them holing up for a weekend of reacquaintance sex anymore. It became all about Stefanie and Leo. Their father-daughter bond was unbreakable.

Karen had thrown herself into being the best navy wife ever. For a long while, it had kept her so busy she didn't even think too much about the fact that they spent less and less time together in bed. At least their morning coffees were one constant routine she appreciated.

This past year Karen had realized she needed more than she was getting from Leo. She needed a confidante, someone who appreciated her for *her,* not just her volunteer organizational skills.

She'd discovered parts of herself that she'd long ago buried. For that, she owed Leo a thank-you for checking out of their marriage.

But it hadn't played out the way she'd thought it would.

THE LAST THING Ro wanted to do was place the hard helmet over her face. Her tender face.

"Let me look at that cheekbone before we get going." She didn't resist as Miles ran his fingers over her skin. They were under the glare of the hospital parking lot lights and

Miles's pupils were dilated as he studied her face. She kept her gaze on his in hopes that it would distract her from the urge to lean her head against his chest.

Her cheek was still fairly numb from the anesthetic used by the plastic surgeon, so it didn't bother her to have Miles probe around as though he knew more than a doctor. Until his finger pressed the place that hurt the most.

"Oww!"

"Sorry. That *should* hurt—it's the precise spot she clocked you. Good thing you didn't shatter your orbital lobe. Did you lose consciousness?"

"No. Just my pride."

His grin took her by surprise.

"Your pride will heal. So will your eye. Do you have to come back here this week?"

"No, the surgeon said the stitches will dissolve on their own, and the scar will fade within a year or so."

"You're beautiful no matter what, Ro."

"Spare me, Miles." She was too tired to call him "Warrant." "I just want to go home to my own bed."

"And that you shall do."

He put his helmet on only after he'd gingerly helped with hers.

"I'll go as easy as I can back to your place."

"Thanks."

Roanna didn't even bother trying to hold on to the bike's back handle. It had been a long day, and if it foreshadowed the way the rest of their assignment went, it could be a long few weeks. She hooked her arms around Miles's waist and rested her head against his back.

She resisted his hard-core EOD demeanor, but in this moment it meant the world to her to be able to trust him to get her home as smoothly as he'd promised.

And he did. He seemed to possess a magic ability to hit

all the stoplights just right so the most he had to do was slow down. He coasted them up to the front of her house and cut the engine.

"Thanks for the ride. Next time, I'll drive." She slowly rose from the bike's seat and eased her helmet off. She hissed, but didn't see the stars she had when Anita hit her.

"You don't like the way I drive?" Miles slid off the bike and hung his helmet on the handlebar.

"No, that's not what I mean. It's only fair we divvy up the driving responsibilities and whatever other tasks show up."

"Sure. But if we get into any kind of trouble, I'm driving." His authoritative tone should have annoyed her but she didn't care—whether from acceptance that he had more experience at high-risk driving than she did or plain exhaustion.

"Trouble? I'm the one who got punched in the face, remember?" Keeping things light wasn't difficult. It was a nice change from the heavy conversation at the Perezes'.

"How's it feeling?" He laid a hand on her shoulder.

"Sore. It'll be brighter than any eye shadow I have by morning. I'm so tired right now I don't give a mouse's butt."

Miles's laughter reached across the night to her. It was warm, rumbling, genuine. In spite of herself, Ro smiled back at him.

"Oww." She involuntarily winced at the sharp jab of pain in her cheek.

"You're a surprise around every corner, Ro." He released her shoulder and let his arm hang down at his side.

"I am so sorry you took that hit tonight. You have no reason to believe me, but I do have your six on this, Ro. I won't let you take the brunt of anything again."

"Chill out. We're not in the field. There aren't any bombs or mines to defuse." She heard her words too late.

"Crap, I'm sorry, Miles." How obtuse could she be?

Miles held up his hands.

"Whoa, drop it, Ro. This won't work if you're constantly walking on eggshells about my mishap. I almost stepped on a mine. If not for my dog, who got the worst of the explosion, I'd be dead. As it is, I lost a leg below the knee. Do you realize how lucky I am to be alive and functioning at full capacity?"

She couldn't speak. How could he talk calmly about such a devastating event?

"Ro, you with me?" He took a step toward her and grasped her upper arms.

"Focus on me for a minute."

She tilted her face up, peering at him with her uninjured eye, and saw the mirth in his.

"I can still get it up, if that's what's concerning you."

Ro shook off his hold and placed her hands on her hips.

"You can still be a pig, Warrant."

He moved so fast her only impression was of his face near hers before he kissed her. Unlike the kiss in front of Perez's house, this wasn't hurried or such a shock. She already knew his lips, and her own lips responded before her mind could click into gear.

When the kiss ended she stepped backward and he dropped his arms but continued to hold her hands. They let the silent night weave between them, their breath visible in the cold air.

"I think we need to keep our noses to the grindstone on this, Ro. The trail's still hot. Hopefully we'll get into the coroner's office tomorrow."

"Are you kidding me? We'll never get in there, and really, why would we want to?" She had no desire to observe an autopsy.

"You don't have to be a doctor to know if someone was murdered, necessarily. We can learn a lot by listening to the coroner and his team while they do their job."

"No, but you have to be a doctor, LEA or at least NCIS, to get that kind of access."

"We managed at the beach this morning. Surely a coroner's office will be a piece of cake, especially if we let Detective Ramsey know that we had an interesting meeting with Mrs. Perez today."

"I don't like this tit-for-tat stuff. Nothing is worth our careers."

"You don't have to worry about it, Ro. I'll call Ramsey in the morning. I owe you, remember? You took a hit for the team tonight."

His words met her silence.

"Doing the right thing is always worth it, Ro. Navy orders are to be carried out to the best of our abilities. Sometimes it doesn't happen in black-and-white."

Her breath caught as she realized that he was talking about his time downrange.

"I'm sorry about your leg, Miles."

"Me, too. But I'm used to it now, and besides—" he waved his hands around him "—I'm getting to do administrative work at a P-3 wing in the remote Northwest."

She opened her mouth to offer some kind of consolation, but he raised his hand again.

"Contrary to what that sounded like, I'm not about to have a pity party for myself. Been there, done that. And I'm honored to be on this case, to fight for Perez and find out how he died. Perez, while I didn't know him, deserves as much effort from me as any of my wartime missions did."

Of course Perez deserved their full attention. Of course Miles had his priorities straight—he'd had the toughest training the navy had to offer, survived the war minus a leg and still remained on active duty. He certainly could have opted out on a medical disability discharge, but he'd stayed.

And, dang it, he was in better shape than she was, hands

down. Not just because he was a guy, either. His dedication to his physical fitness made her six-mile runs look like sandbox play.

"I've never been in the kind of danger you have."

"No, but that was a mean punch you took back there. You don't seem to have a concussion, but some symptoms can lie low until they broadside you. Your body needs rest."

"Spoken from experience, I take it?"

He shrugged. "There's a risk of injury in every navy job."

Just like that, he was humble Miles. She'd seen his beribboned uniform. Under his gold EOD warfare insignia, a torpedo with lightning bolts crossed through it, he wore some of the rarest combat awards, including a Bronze Star. He was a war hero, for heaven's sake. She'd never know it from anything he ever said. Typical of the nation's greatest heroes, Miles was silent when it came to his wartime achievements.

"So how did you lose your leg, exactly?"

"Like so many others—an explosive I wasn't expecting."

"IED?"

"No, a field mine. I was clearing the area for the team to go in and do their mission."

He'd lost his dog. She couldn't imagine the feeling of hopelessness.

"Do you miss it?"

"The adrenaline? The fear? Or the glory?" His grin belied the harshness of his words. He sighed. "I miss the team. The sense of accomplishment. I miss my dog."

Compassion gripped Ro.

"I'm so sorry," she murmured. "I'd be a mess if I'd lost my pet, even though I don't have one right now."

"Yes, you would. We all are when it comes to our pets. But Riva wasn't a pet—she was a working member of the team as much as you and I are."

Silence settled around them in the darkness. The lights in her front room glowed through the tree line, and Whidbey's winds sighed overhead.

"You handled yourself well back there with Anita Perez." She owed it to him to tell him that.

"You would have, too, if you hadn't gotten your eye bashed in."

She was as surprised by the laughter that bubbled up her throat as she was delighted.

"Trust me, I didn't plan it." She grasped at her composure, swollen face and all.

She had to ask him the question she didn't want to contemplate on her own.

"What do you think about the idea of Perez having an affair with Master Chief Reis?"

Ever since Anita told them that Perez had confessed to being involved with the "most senior female on staff," Ro couldn't get Master Chief Reis, the most senior *enlisted* woman, out of her mind.

Miles gazed up at the stars and let out a breath. He still had her hands in his and she marveled at the warmth of his rough palms.

"Anything's possible. People never reveal themselves fully at work, especially in a shore duty command like ours. But I have to admit I'd never have expected it from Master Chief Reis. She's never been anything less than the epitome of a great command master chief around me."

"She's great at motivating the young sailors, too."

"Now I have to wonder exactly *how* she motivated them."

Ro grimaced. "Wait a minute—maybe this is the one time she's ever screwed up. Maybe she *is* a great professional who got involved in a bad scene."

"Come on, Ro, you don't believe that, do you? If she was junior to Perez, sure, but she's…she was—" he corrected himself "—his superior. She's been around forever, a lifer. She knows the deal and if she indeed had an affair with him, she knew exactly what the hell she was getting into."

"I doubt she expected to find her lover dead, though."

"How do you know she didn't push him over the edge?"

"What edge—do you mean mental, so that he'd kill himself, or literal?"

Miles was silent. Ro absorbed his words, his determined stance.

"You really think MC Reis could have killed Perez?" She gaped at him with her good eye. "Holy crap, I sure hope you're way off on this."

"And if I'm not?"

"We have a lot of work to do to see that justice is served. And to protect the wing and the commodore from any blowback."

"I'm not saying it happened that way. But we can't rule it out. Unless Anita was right the first time."

"What?"

"That it was you having the affair with Perez."

CHAPTER NINE

MILES WATCHED HER good eye under the streetlight as it first widened in shock before it narrowed in total agitation. He wanted to hug her, to calm her down and tell her it was all going to work out. But *why* did he want to do this? He wanted to date her, have sex with her. Not become her freaking boyfriend. Boyfriends comforted. He was more the hook-up-and-enjoy-the-ride type.

Sure you are.

"You have to know how ridiculous that accusation is. Or did the land mine blow some of your brains out along with your leg?"

He sucked in his breath. Damn, she played hard.

"I'm such a jerk," she muttered.

"Yes, that was a shitty thing to say. But I deserved a good hit. Of course I don't think you were having an affair with Perez."

Because I would have found out about it. I'd sense it.

He couldn't explain why but he was always aware of Ro whenever she was near him. He'd have a gut feeling she was at the gym and bam! He'd see her there twenty minutes later. He'd let his mind drift to his thoughts of her and she'd show up on the same jogging path as if she'd materialized from his dreams. She wasn't ready to admit it, but there was some kind of connection between them. Something drew him to her fire. Even though she did her damnedest to smother that fire under layers of naval officer bravado.

"We need to verify that *a)* he was having an affair and *b)* that it was with Master Chief Reis…or whomever. Then we need to find out where they were last night."

"True, but there's a good chance the cops are already on it."

"Not necessarily. Anita said she hadn't told them all the details. She didn't see the point, at least not when she believed he'd had an accidental fall off the cliff."

She saw his thoughts play across his features, and a thrill went through her at the unexpected intimacy.

As if sensing her awareness of him, Miles's expression turned to concern.

"Ro, I can't tell you how much it kills me that you took that hit tonight. I'm dead serious. I will not let anyone hurt you again. Not while we're in this together."

"I appreciate that, Miles. But you're not responsible for me—I am." The beginnings of a dull headache were made worse by her annoyance that she felt her arousal through the pain.

She'd been smart to avoid him until now.

"Ro, do you ever stop fighting?" He tugged gently on her hands.

It would be nice to let the fight go, if just for a little while.

When he leaned in this time, she was ready for him. His lips touched hers, and whether it was because she was too tired to resist or needed comfort after a hellish few hours, she wasn't going to turn down another kiss from Miles.

His hand cradled the side of her jaw, his touch gentle as spring rain. He had his other hand on the small of her back, making circles with his fingers at the base of her spine.

Ro relished the contact of their hips, pelvis to pelvis. Miles was leaning into her and it felt so right, so safe. She marveled at the way he was able to keep kissing her so thoroughly while working magic with his hands and hips.

She pulled back.

"Miles, you have to be tired, too. It's been a long day for both of us."

He laughed, a low rumble.

"Save it, Ro." His lips hadn't moved more than a millimeter from hers. His breath was hot and she craved more. She wrapped her hands around his head and angled hers so that her eye wouldn't get in her way as she kissed him back. Deeply and with lots of tongue. She'd been with other men but this was nothing like that. It wasn't a simple attraction, a means to work out sexual frustration. She felt it in the hum of her skin at each touch of his fingers, in the way she longed for him.

Twigs and brush crackled and popped just over Miles's right shoulder, in front of the house. Before Ro could react, Miles was in front of her, standing with his feet apart, blocking her view.

In an instant he sprang toward the source of the noise and Ro heard him grunt as he grabbed someone by the collar and whipped him around to the side.

Ro's stomach sank.

"Whoa, hey, calm down, dude."

A rush of air blew out of Ro's throat.

"It's okay, Miles."

"You know this guy?"

"Yes. It's just Dick."

"Dick who?"

"Dick as in her former fiancé, dude. Back off." Dick pulled out of Miles's grasp and shook his shoulders as if he'd initiated the break-off. Ro forced down a giggle. If Miles had wanted to choke the crap out of Dick, he could have. With one hand.

"Richard as in my half sister's husband."

"You're Krissy's husband?" Miles was still in full interrogation mode. Ro didn't see a need to ask him to chill.

"Yes, I am. I take it you've met my wife. She's hard to forget." Dick turned his attention to Ro. "Your sister won't let me in the house. I came three thousand miles only to have her say I can't stay here without your permission. Will you please talk some sense into her?"

"*Former* fiancé?" Miles's gaze was on Ro, his hands at his sides.

"Ancient history." Ro was so not going to tell Miles about Dick or any other aspect of her personal life. Miles was too smart, too observant, and he made it too easy for her to forget how much she needed, wanted, solitude.

"It wasn't that long ago, Roanna." He took a step closer. "What on earth did you do to your eye, girl?" His surgical instincts were evident in the angle of his head.

"It's been long enough since we split, Dick. My eye is fine. I've already seen a doctor about it." Like she'd ever let Dick touch her again.

She turned to Miles. "I'll see you in the morning."

"I'll meet you at the wing for our briefing with the commodore at 0800." Miles had his helmet back in his hands, ready to slide onto the bike and drive off.

"Fine." She wasn't going to fight him over who'd drive.

"You." She turned to Dick. "Come with me. You can stay here one night, then you're out. I told Krissy the same thing."

She didn't look at Miles again. She couldn't. There was too much of a risk that he'd see the defeat, the regret, in her expression. Dick, however, seemed to be fascinated with Miles.

"Watch out, dude. She's a ballbuster."

"So I gather." She barely heard Miles's reply before he gunned his engine and sped off.

"When did you start dating him?" Dick was beside her

now, all buddy-buddy. Of course. He wanted a bed to sleep in tonight.

With her sister.

She opened her mouth to refute his assumption, and shut it so sharply her teeth clicked together. She owed Dick no explanation.

"We have more important things to discuss, Dick. Like the kind of father you plan on being to my niece or nephew."

RO KEPT HER conversation with Krissy and Dick short and to the point. She was exhausted and needed her wits about her for work. For honoring the memory of Petty Officer Perez.

"You two, um, *three,* are your own family. Figure it out. Leave me out of it. Be gone by tomorrow."

Even as she issued the eviction notice she knew it wouldn't be followed. No one in her family had ever respected her boundaries—why would they start now?

"We can't get flights that soon, Ro. Give us at least a few nights—we'll help you out." Krissy was all smiles now that her knight had showed up.

"Help me out with what?" Ro glared at Krissy. Yes, Krissy was still her younger sister but she was twenty-six and pregnant. An adult.

"Krissy doesn't deserve your ire, Ro." Dick put a protective arm around Krissy's shoulders. "Direct your anger at me."

"My *ire?*" A short bark that four hours ago would have been a hearty laugh popped out of Ro's throat. "You are too much."

She glared at them both now. It wasn't helping her self-esteem that she looked like Popeye the first time she'd had to face them since they'd gotten married.

"You deserve each other. Now, if you don't mind, I have

a real job and I have to be up and at it in—" she checked her watch "—five hours."

She turned on her heel, scooped her knitting bag from the hallway table and went upstairs to her bedroom. They could find the guest room on their own.

ROANNA COULDN'T REMEMBER a time she'd been so exhausted. Plebe summer at the naval academy came to mind, as did seemingly endless mid watches on the carrier. Neither of those had involved the emotional intensity she experienced now. Because even in wartime situations, fighting for every shred of intelligence that would be needed to keep the air-crews alive, she hadn't had Miles next to her, step for step.

It had been hard enough to keep saying "no" to his requests for a date last year. She'd found him attractive from the moment she'd met him when he'd scaled the tree for Henry the Eighth.

But she hadn't been ready to date anyone. Then he'd been assigned to work on the same staff as her, at the same command. Nothing said they couldn't date except Roanna's determination to always present the appearance of complete propriety.

She'd had so many reasons, good reasons, not to let her guard down around Miles. Their attraction was mutual and hot. She couldn't imagine anything less than a full-blown affair with him—he wasn't the kind of man to ask for half of anything.

She rolled over and punched her pillow under her head.

A relationship with him wasn't worth it. The entire wing staff would learn about her personal business. When she and Miles stopped dating, which they would, the awkwardness of seeing him at work would be too much. More than she was willing to deal with.

She curled her fingers under her pillow, wishing that the

part of her she never showed anyone else hadn't revealed itself to Miles when he kissed her.

The sound of muffled conversation seeped through the wall of her bedroom, which adjoined the guest room—usually her yarn room. She'd lovingly created a hobby haven with shelves for skeins of yarn and wooden dowels nailed to the wall on which she hung her hanks of the more artisanal fibers. Long primitive shelves, whitewashed in a pale cream, lined the walls on three sides of the room.

She'd arranged the skeins by color so it was like walking into a rainbow every time she went inside. A futon folded into a comfortable sofa that she spent hours on while she pored over patterns or matched fibers for one of her custom designs for furniture covers. She'd had to move the sofa cover she was in the process finishing up—a soothing aquamarine knitted center with a crocheted picot edge in coffee-hued alpaca—in order to flatten the futon into a bed for Krissy.

Krissy and Dick.

She stared at her ceiling. It would be too easy to blame her angst on her surprise guests instead of her restless ache for Miles.

CHAPTER TEN

RO ROSE WITH the sun the following morning, atypical for a Saturday. It had taken her a while to unwind but once she did she fell into a deep slumber. She woke without an alarm and it took her a moment to remember why her eye hurt. The previous day's events streamed across her mind. Her lips still tingled at the mere recall of Miles's kisses. She allowed the back of her hand to linger on her mouth as she looked at her face in the bathroom mirror.

"Now, that's the definition of fugly."

She was relieved that her eye was starting to open but stitches sat on the puffy purple circle around her eye and over the rise of her cheekbone. The surgeon had done an excellent job; except for the tiny butterfly bandages, she could barely make out any stitches.

The memory of how tender Miles had been with her when he drove her home warmed her in the cold bathroom.

"Enough." She forced herself to get showered and dressed before she grabbed her mobile and headed downstairs.

It was a relief to see there were no messages on her phone.

Getting out of her house and to the base without waking her uninvited guests became her top priority.

She almost made it, too. Her gym bag was slung over her shoulder and she held a newly cleaned and pressed uniform in her hand. She didn't plan on wearing her uniform today but she'd be able to leave it in her office, ready for Monday morning.

"Roanna." Dick's voice made her jump as she reached the landing. How long had he been up?

"I'm already late for work, Dick."

"On a Saturday?" He stood in front of her in flannel pajamas. Not the type of outfit you packed if you were in a hurry to get somewhere. Her gut contracted as she recognized his complete disregard for her, her life.

"My job is 24/7, Dick. You know that." She wasn't getting into the details of the investigation with him.

"I'm glad I caught you, Ro. We need to talk." As if she hadn't just stated she didn't have time.

"Can you let it go? All I ask is that you and Krissy lock the door behind you when you leave."

He stepped into the dim hall light. He looked older, more somber than she'd ever seen him.

"That's just it, Ro. Krissy and I have worked out our fight, don't worry. We're good. But we agree that we can't go back to New Jersey until Krissy makes things right with you. What you think of me is one thing, but please don't take your disappointment and anger out on your sister." He ran his hand through his longish dark hair.

"Krissy and I share something you and I never did, Ro."

"Um, yeah, like, a *baby*." She sighed. "Dick, I don't want to get into this with you. Not now."

He shrugged, his face compassionate. Another first.

"Sure, I get it. But you know how crazy your mother can be. She's been doing her best to make life a living hell for Krissy. Delores calls her every day and tells her she needs to mend fences with you. I don't disagree, but Krissy deserves to be excited about this time in her life. She needs your strength to help her see that it's okay to enjoy her own goddamned life."

A sucker punch right to her emotional gut. As if Dick had

planned to make her feel like even more of a loser. So now she was supposed to make both their lives easier?

Remember, you're starting over.

Why couldn't she have tossed that ring off the bridge with a few profane words of release? Why did she have to be willing to change, to keep a more open mind?

"Fine. We'll all sit down together. But I can't promise when—it might not be until tomorrow or even next week."

"No worries, Ro. We'll wait as long as it takes."

She knew they'd wait. In her house, on her time.

Damn it.

COMMAND MASTER CHIEF Lydia Reis glanced at her dossier. She'd cleared everything off her desk except any documents having to do with AMS1 Perez and his surviving family.

Her hands shook as her fingers poised over her computer keyboard. If she had to stand up she wasn't certain her knees would support her.

The tears welled and the heaving sobs she was sure had run dry last night threatened a reappearance. This wouldn't do. She was the senior enlisted sailor in the wing, the person all the other enlisted were looking up to. How she handled this would either be an honor to Petty Officer Perez's name or make the wing seem like a circus.

She had to put her broken heart on hold.

Her phone rang.

"Master Chief Reis."

"Master Chief, do you have a minute?" Commodore Sanders was in this morning, too. They all were.

"Yes, sir." She stood up and pushed away from her desk, her office only steps from the commodore's.

Usually, he emailed her when he needed a meeting. The seriousness of the Perez case drove through her heart as she walked into his office. She prayed she'd be able to do whatever was asked of her, if only for Perez's family.

"Have a seat." He motioned for her to sit down, as he all but fell into his own leather desk chair.

She waited for him to speak.

"Master Chief, you've done a bang-up job for this wing since I've come aboard. I can't thank you enough for the hours you've put into rebuilding morale as the tired squadrons come home from deployment and your troops have to put their planes back together, as they get ready to go again."

She shifted in her seat and hoped her expression remained detached.

Sanders leaned forward, his elbows on his massive oak desk. Her fingers itched to curl into fists but she controlled herself.

Don't let him see you sweat.

"There's no easy way to put this, Master Chief. I happen to have caught wind that you and Perez shared more than a professional relationship."

The son of a bitch. To put this in front of her, today, this week.

She crossed her legs. "May I ask where you heard this, sir?"

Sanders leaned back, the satisfied gleam in his eyes underscoring his confidence that he had her number.

"Perez had a hard time keeping his mouth shut when it came to his philandering. You were a prize trophy."

He's bluffing. He would've been able to see Perez come into her office if he wanted, but she was positive that was all he'd seen.

"He came in and talked to me a lot, yes."

"I'm referring to more than idle conversation, Master Chief."

"I didn't know him outside of the office, if that's what

you're getting at, Commodore." The lie was so easy when it came to protecting someone she cared about. Protecting his surviving family.

"Then why does the scuttlebutt put you in the center of his supposedly estranged relationship with his wife?"

She forced down the rage that wanted to stand up and deck the self-serving captain.

"I can't control hangar gossip, sir. Of course anyone I give any extra attention to is bound to get flak from, or be questioned by, the other sailors. I counsel dozens of different sailors each week, one-on-one. Just like a lot of the others, Petty Officer Perez was looking to change rates to intel, or go back to school so he could become a warrant officer at some point. He was motivated to provide for his family."

The last was a stretch of the truth but she'd never let the commodore know everything Perez had told her. She wasn't that stupid.

"This is where you have to come clean, Master Chief. I'm willing to go to bat for you but if I find out you're lying to me, I won't be able to help you."

"I understand." She'd be damned if she told him again that she hadn't had an affair with Perez. The truth hurt too much, and Commodore Sanders was the last man she'd ever share her heart with.

"Okay." He paused. "I'll assume it was all gossip. I have to put my trust in you, Master Chief."

She remained silent—she didn't trust herself to say anything that wouldn't land her in a court martial.

"Have you heard any more news about the case this morning?"

"No, sir. Only that they're performing an autopsy sometime today, and that the coroner plans to reveal the cause of death soon thereafter."

Commodore Sanders scratched his chin.

"Good. It seems the coroner isn't interested in waiting for body fluid test results—so he must have enough reason to think it's a suicide."

The commodore shook his head. "How many good men do we have to lose to PTSD?"

The military had also lost women to PTSD and other wartime causes, but Lydia wasn't going to point that out to the commodore. Not today.

For Perez she could do what was right, no matter how much it pained her.

"SIR, IT WAS REALLY clear to Miles and me that Anita Perez was upset, but it seems she and Petty Officer Perez had been having marital difficulties."

The commodore nodded at Ro and grimaced. "I'd figured as much from what I heard on the hangar deck. Unfortunately, marriage issues aren't uncommon in our profession, are they?"

He looked more haggard than he had yesterday. Was this why he'd seemed subpar? Was the commodore having marital problems? A dead sailor on his hands would certainly stress him to the maximum.

The commodore gave Ro a closer examination. "What the hell did you do to your eye, Roanna?"

"Mrs. Perez mistook me for someone else."

"You don't say." The commodore rubbed his eyes. "Who did she mistake you for?"

"I have no idea, sir." Ro should have been galled at how calmly she lied but she and Miles had agreed to keep any personal accusations and discoveries to themselves until they could be verified. It was their job to protect the commodore from political fallout and the less he knew about these things, the better. Until anything proved vital to the investigation, they were only going to report pertinent, validated facts.

Sanders shook his head. "Strange things happen during times like this. You okay, Ro?"

"Yes, sir. Miles kept things even over there."

"We'll go back to the Perez home again, sir, if needed. I do think it's a good idea that you followed Mrs. Perez's wishes and didn't go out there." Miles looked at Ro.

"She seemed to trust us, didn't she? After she hit you." Miles gave her a wink that Sanders couldn't see. Ro wanted to hit *him*. "That's the most we can hope for under the circumstances."

"Absolutely." The commodore, also in civilian clothes, pushed back from his desk. "You two keep on it. I can't tell you how much I trust you with this. If you get any information about the autopsy, let me know ASAP."

"Yes, sir." They responded in unison and left his office.

It was almost scary how well she and Miles worked together. How they both refrained from mentioning to the commodore that Anita Perez thought her husband had been having an affair with one of the commodore's senior female staffers.

Ro wondered if they were doing anyone a favor by keeping information from the commodore, but she was going to listen to her gut for once, instead of all the navy rules she'd lived by for more than half her adult life.

Miles stopped when their paths diverged. "I'll call you as soon as I hear back from the sheriff's department."

"Okay." Ro wasn't going to hold her breath. Miles seemed so certain they'd get in on the autopsy but he failed to realize he wasn't in a U.S. war zone. He was on Whidbey Island and Perez's death had taken place in civilian territory—not on base. They weren't going to come anywhere near Perez's body or any sensitive results without the sheriff's say-so.

They went their separate ways.

AN HOUR AFTER they'd met with the commodore, Ro sat at her desk, more comfortable in her civilian clothes than she'd thought she would be. Normally, she only wore her civvies to and from work or the gym. The office was uniform-only. But this was Saturday and it was more important that she be able to head into town without taking the time to change.

She'd managed to get through over half her classified message traffic before her desk phone rang.

"LCDR Brandywine. This is an unsecure line."

"Ro, it's me." Miles's voice startled her. They'd never spoken on the phone before. Odd, she realized, since they'd known each other for nearly a year. His voice sounded close, intimate.

"Yes?"

"I got us in with the coroner. Meet me in the parking lot in five minutes."

The line clicked off as he hung up.

"Damn it," she swore under her breath. Miles had talked to Detective Ramsey as promised and now they were going to the autopsy. Was there anything he couldn't accomplish?

"Everything okay, boss?" The petty officer who worked with her poked his head into her office door. Ro never swore at work. Not audibly, anyway.

"Yes, Petty Officer Rossignol. I'm afraid I'm going to be out of the office for the rest of the day." She pushed away from her desk, stood up and walked out to IS2 Rossignol's desk. "I'm doing a collateral duty for now and I may be away more often than not over the next week or so."

"Does it have anything to do with Petty Officer Perez?"

"Officially, no." She'd let Rossignol fill in the blanks. "But suffice it to say that my assignment is a top priority for the commodore."

"I've got your six, boss. We have the reservist coming

on board next week, so there'll be real work for her to do if you're out."

Ro smiled at her subordinate. They were a good team, she had to admit. Rossignol kept the other ISs in line and she knew she could count on him to manage the entire shop if need be. Had, in fact, on a couple of occasions.

"We're going to treat the reservist with as much respect as any active duty sailor, right?"

"Yes, ma'am. I'm just saying—sometimes there isn't enough work for everyone if it's a quiet time operationally."

"And when's the last time we were in an operational lull?"

"Point taken. Don't worry, boss, we've got it."

"I know you do. Just don't overwork yourself while I'm out, okay? Don't be afraid to delegate, and that includes the individual squadron intel officers—I'll call them in for a quick update in the next day or two."

"Are you going to tell them why you won't be here?"

"Of course not. I didn't even tell you, did I?" She winked at her right-hand sailor and went back into her own office. She only had a minute to get out to the parking lot to meet Miles.

CHAPTER ELEVEN

MILES HAD SEEN his share of gore during his wartime assignments, but never an autopsy. He wasn't sure how he was going to feel about seeing Petty Officer Perez's, but it didn't matter—he'd procured himself and Ro a front-row seat in the mortuary. Smoothing the waters with Detective Ramsey, he'd scored points for him and Ro. While he didn't think the autopsy would reveal anything major, one never knew. And it would help the commodore rest easy to know that he and Ro had witnessed the procedure. Miles was privately grateful that they'd be there, if only to accompany Perez's body through this hurdle. It was customary for the military to remain with the deceased until burial.

He cast a glance at Ro. She was quiet and beautiful in the afternoon light, black eye notwithstanding.

She looked out her window in the passenger seat of his truck as he drove them down to Coupeville.

The coroner's office was located in the heart of the little town that was situated south of Oak Harbor and twenty minutes from the naval air station. The beauty of Puget Sound's deep blue waters and majestic Cascade Mountains was so contrary to what went on in the nondescript office building.

"Have you had any new insights since last night?" All he'd thought about was why he'd let her go home when all he'd wanted was to spend the night making love to her.

Ro didn't answer at first but kept her eyes straight ahead. "Nothing other than conjecture on my part."

"Such as?"

Did he have to pull everything out of her?

"I don't know if I should be saying anything without facts to back me up."

He tightened his grip on the steering wheel.

"Ro, this isn't an operational intelligence brief. This is what we're supposed to be doing—digging around and inspecting it from all angles. We're just brainstorming here. I'm not going to hold you to a sworn oath."

"And here lies the difference between you and me, Warrant. I don't just shoot my mouth off to get what I want. I wait until I have all the facts."

"You're right, *Commander.* You sit around to the point where you miss out on a target of opportunity simply because you don't want to say anything that can come back to haunt you." He shook his head. "Typical intel—you're so afraid to say 'boo' that the ghost escapes out the freakin' front door every time."

"Not every time, Warrant." Her voice was quiet, her hands clasped in her lap.

"You're right. Every now and then one of you—" again he referred to navy intel types "—makes a great prediction, a great early warning about potential enemy offense. But more often than not, it's what I already said. You've got to let go of that training, Ro, or we won't get our job done right."

"So it's all on me as to whether we do this unofficial official investigation correctly?" She took her turn to shake her head in mockery of him. "So typical of an operator, and especially an EOD type. You're willing to take all the credit and glory for a job well done, but at the first hint of a screwup you blame intel. Nice."

"I'm not blaming you for anything. You have to admit that if you can't share your thoughts with me, no matter how impossible they seem, we stand less of a chance of knowing how Perez died."

She snorted.

"So I'm supposed to tell you what *I'm* thinking and you hold all the cards? What about you, Miles? What do *you* think is most likely responsible for Perez's death?"

"I'm thinking this seems like an awful lot of rigmarole for a straightforward suicide. Usually the coroner calls the cause of death if it's obvious and an autopsy isn't necessarily required. But there's definitely going to be a full autopsy, and when I drove by the beach this morning there was a full team of Island County sheriff's staff still sweeping the scene."

"You were already there this morning? Why didn't you call me?"

"I was taking my friend's dog for a run, and I needed a long one today. West Beach was as easy as any other route, and I figured I might get some information. I would've called if I'd known you wanted to get up and run that early, honest. I thought you needed some rest after getting yourself clocked last night."

He would've loved to be the one who woke her up while she lay next to him in his bed....

"I was up early." She let out a low chuckle. "I did sleep like the dead, though. Solid until the sunlight started peeking through my blinds. I didn't even remember I had a black eye or stitches until I'd been awake for a few minutes."

"You don't have blackout curtains for this time of year?"

"No—I know I should get some, at least in my bedroom. But I do like getting up early and watching the sunrise. They're always so beautiful here, at least when the fog's not in."

"Yes, they are. I have to admit I haven't lived in a more

beautiful place, and I've seen a lot of places in this country and the world."

"I've been thinking the same thing."

The Island County government offices came into view. Their small talk was over.

RO WANTED TO hold Miles's hand during the autopsy, it was that bad. She'd worked through the most intense wartime scenarios while on board the aircraft carrier, had been inside the most secure communications buildings in the world, working out ways to keep U.S. and Allied soldiers, airmen and sailors alive.

She'd never felt the need to grab anyone's hand or receive physical assurance that she was going to get through it. She'd pressed on and done her duty and, when all else failed, prayed.

But Miles had opened something up in her gut. In her heart. They'd been on this case together for less than forty-eight hours, but he'd been in her mind's peripheral vision for the past year. As if he was waiting for her to crack.

Anita Perez's punch to her face hadn't cracked her. Krissy showing up, pregnant, on her doorstep hadn't put her over the edge. Even having to deal with Dick first thing this morning seemed trivial to this.

Seeing a body that was alive only a day ago, splayed open like a gutted fish—that did it.

She breathed through her mouth, refusing to allow her nostrils to take in a whiff of the air. She thought they'd have to smear stuff under their noses like she'd seen in the movies but nothing had been offered.

Nausea wasn't imminent, but passing out was.

She kept her knees loose, rocked back and forth on her feet. She and Miles were only observers, period. Neither of them had any kind of medical expertise to chime in with, anyhow. She knew Miles had no doubt seen worse—his friends being blown to bits by enemy IEDs was a horrifying reality for him. In truth, she had no idea what he'd seen, how much he'd suffered.

She was out of her league when it came to near-death experiences.

You aren't impenetrable.

It was so difficult for her to admit she was wrong, or that she'd made a bad decision, and she wasn't proud of it. Equally difficult was facing the fact that she didn't know it all—even as a scrupulous intel officer. Things got overlooked. Miles was right; she and her intel cohorts didn't have the last word on everything.

She didn't have the same type of wartime experience as Miles.

Not too long ago that would have bothered her. Today, it felt more like a relief to be able to admit, if only to herself, that this autopsy—maybe even this case—was beyond her capabilities. Certainly it was beyond her training.

"Hang tight."

It was a soft whisper spoken under the din of the coroner's nearly constant dictation into the digital voice capturing system. She turned her head and met his gaze.

If it was possible to convey strength, compassion and pure grit through a glance, Miles did it. She gave him a slight nod and turned her head back toward the surgical table.

You don't have to look at the body. Just listen to the coroner.

It took several minutes, but by the time the coroner started describing the inside of Perez's thorax, she was able to home in on his voice and listen for anything that sounded out of the ordinary. She might not have a medical background, but she was a pretty good judge of others' emotions. Growing up with her emotionally abusive mother and the constant chaos that had been her home had trained her early to pay attention to the slightest change in cadence or tone of a speaker's voice.

"The neck bones are fractured, combined with a blunt trauma wound to the base of the skull, consistent with death due to immediate respiratory cessation."

Ro heard that. So the fall had killed Perez—not some mysterious killer. Most of the coroner's description droned on like the buzz of a worker bee. *Blah, blah, blah.*

He'd gone up in pitch at the end of his last word, and now paused as he looked at an area behind Perez's right upper arm.

"There are two visible marks that indicate mosquito or similar insect bites. Definitely not injection sites." The coroner held the arm up and studied it more closely. Then he let the arm drop and went back to the heart that he'd left on a metal tray.

"The heart muscle appears normal and healthy. Cardiac disease is not an apparent cause of death. This is consistent with death by broken neck/spinal cord and subsequent respiratory cessation. Must be cross-checked and validated with blood and urine samples but appears victim died from the effects of a fall from twenty feet or more."

Great. So they had nothing more than what they'd walked in here with. Ro studied Miles. His expression was fixed on Perez's face, pale and otherworldly under the fluorescent lights.

In the midst of her own anxiety she'd forgotten that this could trigger Miles if he suffered from any kind of PTSD. She honestly didn't know anyone who'd survived a war tour who didn't have PTSD in one form or another. She'd had nightmares to deal with for her first few months back. They'd faded, as had her initial overreactions to orders from the commodore for more detailed intelligence. This was a shore tour, and she wasn't providing direct, actionable intelligence to operators in the fleet.

Miles had been there for a much more prolonged time. It was feasible that he was still living with the aftereffects.

He didn't appear anxious or upset. With his relaxed profile and intent gaze on Perez, he looked like a man paying his last respects to a shipmate.

"COME ON UP to my office, folks." Detective Ramsey motioned at Ro and Miles after the autopsy concluded.

They followed him up a short flight of stairs and into a modernized, spacious work area. He led them to his small but classic office and pointed to the break counter just outside his door.

"Help yourselves to coffee or tea. I think there might even be some of that good hot chocolate from the shop down the street."

"Thanks, Detective." Miles went straight for the coffee machine.

There was no use talking to each other as everything they said would be overheard by Ramsey. Besides, words failed Ro at the moment.

Ro used the time it took to brew her tea to mentally review what they'd found out.

While it was clear that the fall had indeed killed Petty Officer Perez, it wasn't common for someone who wanted to commit suicide to do so by jumping, unless it was from a high bridge that would guarantee no chance of survival. Because of this fact, the sheriff had dispatched his homicide detectives, and upon inspection of the area from which Petty Officer Perez had supposedly jumped, several sets of footprints had been found.

Most of the prints were too eroded by the rain and wind

from the storm that passed through the morning after he'd died, but Detective Ramsey said they hadn't given up hope yet.

"I don't know how much you two know about suicide, but it's highly unlikely that Perez killed himself." Ramsey sipped from his mug of coffee as they sat in his office.

Miles drank his own coffee while Ro had ginger tea. She'd been grateful to find the bag in the box next to the hot water tank. Ginger was her go-to herb for nausea, ever since she'd experienced a bout of sea sickness on the ship.

"The coroner said the fall is what killed Perez. There were no indications of any other foul play," Ro pointed out.

Ramsey looked at her as though she was twelve years old.

"The coroner can determine the cause of death—yes, the fall was the cause of death. To be specific, the impact of Perez's head on the beach boulder is what killed him. But how he came to fall off a private cliff in the middle of the night is the question I want answered."

Ramsey put his mug down. Ro noticed that he didn't have any piles of paperwork on his desk—just a huge computer screen and an iPad. She'd be willing to bet he had endless notes stored on both.

"We're going to have to wait for the toxicology report, but I won't be surprised if there was some sort of substance in his blood. It doesn't make sense that a man who was asking about career possibilities turned around and committed suicide within twenty-four hours. He hadn't shown any indication of PTSD in his medical evaluations, either."

"Most sailors don't volunteer that they're suffering from PTSD until their symptoms get unbearable, Detective." Miles set his mug on the edge of Ramsey's desk. "It is feasible that he was struggling with it but didn't tell anyone."

"True." Ramsey nodded. "It's been a tough time for all of us. A good number of the men and women on our detail are reservists—they've all seen combat action in one form or another. Combine that with the stress this kind of job can bring and PTSD has become all too common right here in Island County."

Ro and Miles were quiet.

Ramsey leaned back in his chair.

"I'm going to need help from both of you when we get more definitive information from the forensic scrub at the top of the cliff. Neither of you are leaving the area anytime soon, are you?"

"No." They responded in unison, and then looked at each other.

"I suppose you're both stuck here until this is all resolved, huh?" Ramsey's expression was unreadable but Ro had a definite sense that he thought they were more than a professional couple. At the least, he was poking around to see if they were.

Why should he care?

"Good. I'll be in touch. And as I told you on the beach, what we say to each other stays here, among the three of us. I know you're reporting to your commodore, and I know you work for Uncle Sam. But we're all working to get Petty Officer Perez any justice he may deserve."

"Got it." Miles answered for both of them. He stood up. Ro finished her last swallow of tea before she put down her mug and also stood.

"Please call us if you get any new information, Detective." Ro felt like herself again. All she needed was a good lunch and she'd be back in fighting form.

"One more thing, folks." Ramsey got to his feet. "Have either of you heard anything to the effect that Perez was a problem drinker? More specifically, that he was out drinking the night he died?"

Here it was. The payback for getting them into the autopsy.

Ro smiled at Miles.

He ignored her.

"Yes, we heard from Anita Perez that he'd had a problem with alcohol years ago, but had been sober for a very long time. She didn't believe he committed suicide, and made it clear that if anyone said it was an alcohol-related death she'd take it as a fabrication."

Ro felt a twinge of betrayal toward Anita Perez but Ramsey had asked the question, and they were all out for the truth.

Ramsey looked at Miles, then Ro.

"That's interesting, because I have a witness who saw Perez leaving the base club and he appeared to be intoxicated."

Ro shook her head. "I know you can't tell us who your witness is, but I'd consider the source, Detective. Anita Perez had no love left for her soon-to-be ex-husband, but she was adamant about his sobriety."

Ramsey nodded thoughtfully.

"Could you ask around at the local AA meetings?" Ro felt her idea was a stroke of genius.

Ramsey shot her down faster than the thought had entered her brain.

"No, it's not something that's done. Yes, I could poke around a bit, but I'd be asking a group of people who value anonymity at all costs to talk about one of their own. But thanks for the suggestion, Commander Brandywine."

"Sure." She felt like a girl who'd thought dressing her cat up in baby doll clothes was a good idea.

"We'll be in touch if we hear any more, Detective. Thanks again for getting us into the autopsy." Miles brought the meeting to a neat conclusion.

Ro's mind was numb as she and Miles left the building. The autopsy had taken only a few hours but their brief conversation with the coroner afterward, followed by the meeting with Detective Ramsey, had given them both a lot to think about.

They could work for weeks, months, on this and never have an answer. Meanwhile, Perez was dead and his children had lost their father.

CHAPTER TWELVE

AS THEY EXITED the Island County government offices, Ro and Miles were hit by the strong rainstorm that had whipped up from the north.

Ro shivered.

"Ready?" Miles stood under the awning with her. They were both poised to make a dash for his truck.

"Yes!"

They ran into the rain—which was virtually horizontal—and didn't speak until they were both inside Miles's truck.

"Heat, now!" Ro shivered and hugged her arms. One thing she loved about Whidbey Island was how rapidly the weather changed. Some groused about it, but Ro enjoyed the constant sense of change and movement that the various weather systems visited on one of the longest islands in the continental United States.

"Aye-aye, ma'am." Miles turned on the ignition and pressed the corresponding dashboard buttons for the heater and seat warmers. Ro couldn't keep herself from staring at his long fingers as they accomplished the task. He had blondish hair on his knuckles, and the healthy amount of hair that sprinkled his wrists made her wonder if he had a lot of hair on his chest, too.

She stared at his fleece jacket next and the long-sleeved thermal under it. Her fingers itched to lift the hem of his shirt, to take a peek.

"Ro."

She moved her gaze from his torso to his face. His eyes blazed in their intensity. Her shivers melted into a flush of heat that started in her midsection….

"What?" Her voice was steady but her heartbeat wasn't—she swore he could hear it pounding erratically.

"I'm proud of you. You did great in there."

He gave the compliment as one professional to another, but the way he stared at her mouth wasn't the least bit professional.

She'd never felt such a pull of attraction, of downright longing, for another person. Not even on the most romantic dinner dates with Dick, or one of her "sexy" dates with men she never intended to have a long-term relationship with.

Yet here, in her wet clothes, after a gruesome morning, she was hotter for Miles than she'd ever been for any other man.

"Thanks." She swallowed. If he kept looking at her like this she'd be a puddle of hormones in thirty seconds. "So, um, lunch? What are you in the mood for?"

"Ro." He lifted his hand to her ear and stroked along its edge, down to her jaw. He tilted her chin. "You know what I'm in the mood for. What I've been hungry for since the day I met you."

"Miles, this isn't the best idea either of us has ever had."

"Did my kisses last night bother you? Did you enjoy them as much as I did?"

Maybe if he hadn't stroked her face so tenderly, if his voice wasn't so sexy and needy, she'd have been able to keep the subject on a culinary menu.

Instead, she leaned forward.

"Last time I didn't give you much of a choice, Ro." His lips were next to hers, his breath redolent of coffee. "Can I kiss you this time, Ro? Do you want me to?"

He was teasing her and it was excruciatingly wonderful.

"Yes."

She didn't wait for him to lean in farther. Bridging the tiny gap between their mouths, she closed her eyes to fully appreciate the feel of his lips on hers. He waited for her to deepen the kiss until she was tugging at his lips with hers, before he opened his mouth wide and sucked her tongue against his.

She moaned with pleasure as the kiss developed into something more than a kiss. The only part of their bodies that touched was their mouths, yet Ro felt Miles's imprint on every inch of her skin. Her breasts swelled and she thrust her chest forward, begging him to hold her, caress her nipples.

Miles anticipated her before she made any physical moves. His hands were stroking her nipples through her blouse, her bra, and the friction made her frenzied. She leaned into him, needing him to press against her, to fill the ache between her legs with a decisive touch.

Their tongues licked, their mouths sucked and their breath grew ragged and indistinguishable, one from the other. Ro heard gasps and moans but didn't know and, more important, didn't care if they were hers or Miles's.

His hands grasped her hips, pulling her toward him, to straddle him. Ro was grateful she'd worn jeans to make the journey easy, but just as frustrated that there was still so much clothing between them. As she shifted and was about to allow her pelvis to rest completely against his rock-hard erection, her buttocks hit the steering wheel.

The blare of the truck's horn made her jump and she banged her head on the sunroof.

Miles groaned.

Ro looked down. Miles's head was between her breasts. He showed no indication of moving as she felt him breathe in her scent.

"Oh, Miles." She swallowed a giggle. "This is…most

inappropriate. Crap!" She wiggled off him and swung her legs around, over the dashboard, and sat back in the passenger seat.

"Shoot, woman." Miles's voice sounded like the gravel they'd walked over on the beach. She risked a peek at him. One arm rested on the steering wheel and the other was propped on the divide that should have kept them from making love in the front seat. As if he felt her gaze, he turned his head toward her.

Their eyes met and Ro was shocked at how naked his need for her was. It was all she could do not to throw herself at him again.

"This was, could have been—"

"A disaster if anyone had seen us." Miles wiped the condensation off the driver's side window and peered out. "No one's around—we're alone." He turned back to her. "And anyone walking by wouldn't have been able to tell who it was with the steam on the glass."

"I'm sorry, Miles. I never want to put you—either of us—at risk. This is why I don't date people I work with!" Her heated desire threatened to blow into full-fledged shame. What the hell had she been thinking? She'd never let her guard down like this before.

"Hang on, Ro. I can see you're off to the races. First, we weren't doing anything wrong. It's our legal right to have a relationship. Making out in uniform in a public parking lot, well, that would've been very poor judgment. But we're in civvies and I don't regret a moment of this. I do think it's time you took me up on my offer to go out together and do this properly—in civvies and at a place far away from our daily routine."

She didn't answer him. Her actions made it clear how badly she wanted to be with him, all common sense and self-drawn rules to the contrary.

She caught a peek at him as he got his clothes back in shape in the driver's seat. Yeah, he wanted to be with her, too.

MILES DROVE ALMOST all the way back to the base before he pulled off into a residential area.

"I thought we were going to lunch." She'd done her best to make her hair lie as neatly as possible in the humidity after being so thoroughly mussed just moments ago.

"We are. My place is here and I have food for us. I'll take you back to base to get your car after that."

"I don't think we should be alone together now, do you?"

He shot her a wide, relaxed grin.

"You're probably right. I promise I'll keep my hands off you if you'll do the same, okay? I have someone I want you to meet. We won't be alone."

He maneuvered the truck into the short driveway that ran alongside an A-frame home.

"This looks like something you'd see in the Swiss Alps." White-splashed plaster was framed by dark wood beams. A porch encircled the entire building, at least from her vantage on the left side of the house. She got out of the truck.

Just across the street from the house was another row of homes, but beyond that, she caught glimpses of the sound and the Cascade Mountains.

"Can you see the Cascades from the upstairs windows?"

He'd walked around to stand next to her.

"Yes, and the balcony off my bedroom opens out to the best view in town."

Heat ran up her face. "I wasn't fishing for an invite."

Miles laughed. "It'd be like fishing when the salmon are running, Ro. All you gotta do is reach down and pluck up a big, pink juicy one."

"Stick to dismantling bombs, Warrant. Your double entendre intention is an epic fail."

"Fine." He motioned to the steps leading to the front door. "Go ahead. I've got your six."

"I never doubted that, Miles." She smiled at him as he used the common navy vernacular to indicate he was guarding her backside, the six-o'clock position.

She walked ahead of him, fully aware that he was checking her out. She stepped aside at the top of the steps so he could unlock the solid red door. The black wrought iron detail work on the lock, handles and door knocker impressed her. Whether Miles had added these touches or simply maintained what had been here before, he'd done a wonderful job.

"Stand back." He issued the warning just as he opened the door.

A huge brown dog launched itself toward Miles, and jumped high enough to give him a lick on his lips. Miles laughed and rubbed the dog on either side of its face before he stood back and raised his right hand.

"Sit, Lucky."

The dog sat, and Ro was mesmerized by the complete adoration that radiated from Lucky's eyes.

"You can pet her if you'd like."

"I'd love to." She bent over and held out her hand for Lucky to sniff. "You're a pretty girl, aren't you?"

Lucky replied with a *thump-thump* of her tail on the tile entryway and licked Ro's palm. Ro was smitten and promptly gave the dog a good scratch behind each ear, which Lucky in turn responded to by immediately rolling over on her back to reveal her belly.

"She's a sucker for attention." Miles beamed and Ro bit back a giggle. If he could only see himself.

"What's so funny?"

"Nothing—well, okay." She stood back up and faced him.

"Seeing you so tickled over a dog is a far cry from the big, bad EOD dude who struts around the hangar."

His smile faded and his expression grew serious.

"Whoa, what did I say?"

He shook his head. "It's not you, Ro, it's me. I get the humor in what you're saying, but you've got to understand that a dog saved my life. She took the mine explosion for me so I could stand here in front of you."

"Miles, I'm so sorry." What he'd shared with her about his bomb-sniffer dog last night came rushing back.

He absentmindedly rubbed the dog's head. "She isn't even mine—I'm watching her for a friend who's downrange." The wistful note in his voice told her he'd love to have a dog of his own again.

Crap.

"Miles, I feel like an idiot. I wasn't belittling you or your love of dogs, honest."

"I know you weren't, sweetheart. Let's go eat."

Sweetheart?

CHAPTER THIRTEEN

"DO YOU WANT any more eggs, Ro?" Krissy looked like a Julia Child midget with Ro's Hello Kitty apron wrapped around her slightly rounded tummy.

"No, thanks." Ro drank her coffee and eyed Dick as he wolfed down Krissy's breakfast feast. Even though it was Sunday she half expected a call from Miles or the wing to inform her that they had some work to do.

Until then, she longed to enjoy her usual Sunday morning routine. Sleep in, drink gallons of coffee or tea while she knitted a chemo cap, get in a run, maybe peruse the ceramics shops in La Connor, the artsy town just off the island.

But Dick and Krissy had thrown a big rusty wrench into her dreams. She knew she had to be an adult and deal, but she had no desire to.

Worse, Dick and Krissy seemed content to stay as long as they wanted at her place.

"Don't you have a large caseload of patients who need you back at work?" She put her mug down on her oak table and waited for Dick to shovel more pancake into his mouth.

Had she ever really thought he was attractive?

"I have two weeks off."

"You told me you came out here in a hurry after Krissy." Ro turned toward her sister.

Krissy held up her spatula as though it were a crucifix and Ro was a vampire.

"He did come out here in a hurry. Right, Dick?"

"You two were fighting. You said you were leaving him." Anger bubbled under Ro's composure. "That was real, right? This isn't one of Mom's stupid ideas, is it?"

"Calm down, Ro." Dick held up his hand in a wave befitting the queen of England. "That's what's wrong with this family. You women overreact to everything and none of you communicate effectively. We can work this out."

Ro slammed her hand down on the table and winced, which made her bad eye start to throb again.

"I don't believe this! You two planned this—you actually thought it was okay to come out here and bunk down in my house?" She focused her full energy on Dick. "Just for the record, you may never, *ever* tell me how to behave in my own home. And you may never, ever say things about my family, no matter how fractured or messed up it is, in front of me. Got it, bucko?"

Dick had the elegance to at least appear mollified. She suspected it was simple incredulity at her outburst.

"Ro, it's okay. Do you need to talk about it?" Krissy slid into the chair across from Ro and put her spatula down. "You haven't been yourself since we got here. Half the reason we came is because you haven't returned any of Mom's calls. My calls, I get why you didn't answer them. But Mom—you know she's fragile, Ro."

"Mom is fragile when it's convenient for her to be fragile, Krissy." She drummed her fingers on the table.

"You may be right, Ro, but she's still our mother."

"I can't get over her showing up here in an RV with her hair that awful shade of blue-gray. She had everyone who met her thinking she was some poor, pitiful widow." Ro shuddered at the memory. Her mother had insisted on parking that RV in front of the house for nearly two weeks, and drove it almost daily down to City Beach to get a cup of coffee and go for a walk.

"To top it off, she brought that stupid cat with her and used him as her excuse for going into town every day with that house on wheels." Ro's allergy to cats had always been ignored by her family. They loved cats and her medical issue was an inconvenience in their eyes.

"Please let's keep it real, Krissy. Mom wanted to find some of her old boyfriends along the way, maybe meet some new ones. She never made a trip in her life just to see me." It was always about Mom's need for a new man, the man who'd fulfill her every need and take care of her for the rest of her life. What Ro's and Krissy's respective dads hadn't done.

"Ro, Mom loves you. She wanted to see where you live and she's earned the right to travel however she wants to. Why shouldn't she take an RV across country?"

"It's not that she did it, it's that she showed up, unannounced, just like you. When you all know I treasure my privacy and like to be able to plan for your visits."

"You don't know how to relax, Ro."

"Your sister's right," Dick chimed in.

Ro grimaced. "Shut up, Dick."

"Ro, you have to learn to accept Dick. He's my husband and he's the father of your future niece or nephew."

"Oh, joy." Ro flicked her finger against her ceramic mug.

Krissy reached her hand out to Ro.

"We're worried about you. We just want things to be the way they used to be."

"What do you mean?" Ro cocked her head to imply that she actually gave a crap what Krissy thought.

"It was so much nicer, before, when you lived closer and you'd come home at least once a month whenever you were in port. You were happy, Ro."

"Was I?" She turned to Dick. "Was I happy, Dick? How about when you broke up with me in a Denny's, for God's sake? What about all the times I came home hoping we'd have some nice, quality time alone and you never once got off your butt and made a reservation anywhere for us?"

She stood up. "It doesn't matter at this point. You two are together. You're having a baby. I wish you well, but you can't possibly expect me to be overjoyed at your happiness."

"Ro, wait." Dick stood up. "I owe you an apology, probably a thousand apologies. But I can't change the past. I'm sorry we didn't work out but I'm also glad—now, you're free to find your true love like I did."

Ro bit the inside of her cheek. In the course of a few days she'd gone from a self-possessed woman who had decided to take control of her own life to feeling completely out of control about every aspect of it.

It had all gone wrong the minute Miles had spotted her on Deception Pass Bridge.

She shook her head.

"Do you know, Dick, I actually felt guilty when I tossed our engagement ring off Deception Pass Bridge?" She left out the part about when she'd done it—let him think it was as soon as she'd moved there.

"You shouldn't feel guilty. It was a cubic zircon. Fake. You knew that, Ro."

"Yeah, I did, but I forgot about that. It was all we could afford at the time, remember?" Another little fact she'd shoved down when she'd been willing to take less than she deserved.

"But you're right," she went on. "I shouldn't have been so melancholy." She looked at Krissy, then back at Dick. "You two really are happy, aren't you?" She shook her head again. "At least some good did come out of all of this. Who knows, if I'd woken up to my delusion of a life with Dick sooner, he could have ended up with someone else."

"No." Dick's immediate response shot across the kitchen. "Krissy is the one for me."

Ro smiled and started to laugh as the pure warmth of

good will flowed over her. It was going to be okay. All of this. Her family might always be crazy but she'd get through it—they all would.

"Yes, she is. I'm truly sorry I cut you off for so long, Krissy."

"Ro, you're too hard on yourself, as usual. We'll talk about this later."

Ro never thought she'd need Krissy's advice, especially when it came to emotions.

She felt a niggle of doubt. Hadn't she envied Krissy's ability to identify her emotions? Maybe being able to recognize feelings instead of bottling them up would have kept her from wasting so much time on Dick.

And the resulting fallout that kept her from being open to a new relationship.

If she started down the path of what she needed to change in her life, she might discover she'd wasted years on the wrong career, too. Her knitting and artistic yearnings had grown stronger since she'd moved to Whidbey. Gwen was right—she had an artist inside her, pounding on the door of her conscience, insisting on her time.

It scared her senseless.

"I'm crazy, aren't I? I always thought it was you, our family, that was nuts, but who was the one running all over the globe, chasing fulfillment that can't only come from a career?"

"Ro." Krissy's one-word admonishment took away the self-recrimination.

"You're right, Krissy. I need to lighten up and let some of this go. Enjoy your time here. Go on tours, see the Pacific Northwest. Then go home and get on with it—" Ro waved her hand between Krissy's stomach and Dick's chest "—your life together. All three of you."

She gave them her best smile but knew she had to get

out of there. Besides finding the emotional wrestling with Krissy and Dick exhausting, she couldn't shake the feeling that she was forgetting something. She was halfway out of the kitchen when she turned back around.

"Wait a minute." She looked at Krissy and Dick. They stared back at her, all wide-eyed innocence. "I knew it! You thought you had me on this one, didn't you?"

"What?" Krissy asked.

"When's Mom showing up?"

MILES PULLED OFF Highway 20 and let out a long breath as he coasted his truck to a stop in front of the animal shelter. He needed to get out and go for a long walk, then maybe a run later with Lucky. The tightness in his shoulders radiated down to his spine and pelvis. His glutes and hamstrings would be next and then he'd need a couple of weeks of physical therapy to work out the knots.

Relief from the physical manifestations of the Perez case wouldn't be immediate, but this was a great way to kick-start it.

He entered the main area and smiled at Sally, the volunteer on duty.

"Hi, Miles. What's your poison today?" The college student grinned at him as she referred to the myriad tasks he had to choose from.

"What needs doing? I'll muck out the dog kennels if you need me to."

"Myra's back there now, and she may just get the last of them done. Are you in the mood for walking some major leash-pullers?"

"Yes, ma'am." The bigger and stronger breeds that hadn't had any decent training were often nightmares on walks. They proved a challenge even to Max, and he worked out regularly. The seniors and smaller women who volunteered walked the dogs they could, but that didn't always include the big ones.

"You know where everything is. There's a new boy back there, a black Lab-shepherd mix who loves to play and jump."

"Got it."

Miles let himself into the kennel area and tried to stay positive about each pup in its kennel. He was grateful this was a no-kill shelter, so he didn't have to worry about saving all the dogs from being euthanized for lack of resources. Because he'd be bringing home every dog he saw if he didn't know they'd live comfortably here until they found their forever home.

He stopped in front of the last kennel and read the whiteboard that described its contents.

"Beauregard, eh?" The puppy leaped up, his head even with Miles's on the other side of the fence. "Why don't I just call you Beau?"

Huge black paws rested on the fencing as Beau tried to lick Miles through the gate.

Miles laughed.

"Okay, boy, let's get you out for a stretch." He took the leash down from the side of the kennel and made short work of attaching it to Beau's collar. Beau was a bundle of energy, all right, but even this young dude knew that in order to taste some freedom he had to wait for the leash to click.

Beau surprised Miles by walking like a perfect gentleman through the rest of the kennel, past the long line of doggie inmates who barked in acknowledgment of their buddy.

Miles kept his gaze straight ahead. He couldn't bear to look at all their faces, with their silent plea of "take me home, me, me!"

Once they left the shelter and were out on the main walking path, Beau shed his charm and made a lunge that threatened to dislocate Miles's shoulder.

Miles was ready for him.

"Beau, halt!" He yanked back on the leash and waited for Beau to stop freaking out.

Of course Beau didn't.

Miles switched to plan B—he kept walking in the opposite direction of where Beau wanted to go. Beau was a typical crazy young Lab but he wasn't stupid. He wanted to be in his small pack with Miles, and within a few minutes he automatically fell into step next to him no matter which way Miles turned.

Miles stopped and gently but firmly nudged Beau's rump with his hand.

"Sit." Beau sat.

"Good boy!" Miles patted Beau's head, pleased with the immediate job satisfaction. He slipped Beau a treat from his pocket.

As soon as he gulped down the biscuit, Beau jumped up, planting his paws on Miles's chest. Glancing down, Miles saw rich, wet spring mud glistening on his new microfiber workout jacket. There were telltale snags from Beau's nails.

So much for his training skills.

"Off." His knee pushed on Beau's chest and Beau sat, tail wagging, tongue hanging, his starstruck gaze on Miles.

Miles sighed. He wanted to be a tough-love trainer, but the boy needed affection, too. Miles crouched down.

"You're a good boy, aren't you? It's hard being in the klink." Beau sat in place as long as Miles rubbed his ears, the sides of his head.

Miles thought about Lucky and how she loved other dogs. It had nothing to do with Lucky, though—he wasn't ready to adopt a dog. Not quite yet.

"Forget about it, buddy. I don't have room for you. But

maybe we'll find someone at the base who needs a puppy. Come on, let's go."

He walked Beau for the better part of the hour he'd allocated to be there. When he first volunteered, right after he'd arrived at the base and Riva's death was still so painfully fresh, he'd tried to walk every dog possible in the shortest amount of time. He soon figured out that the dogs didn't benefit from a rushed excursion and he found nothing relaxing about running with dog after dog, sometimes two or three together, only to return them to their kennels too quickly and have them yelp in frustration for the rest of the hour he was there.

It was so much more relaxing for both dog and volunteer to take their time and go for a decent walk.

At first Miles's thoughts kept returning to the Perez case. What had he missed? Was there something obvious he and Ro were missing?

Ro.

That was what really had him jacked up. His protective leanings were on overdrive whenever he was near her. Worse when he didn't have a handle on where she was.

This was new to him.

He wasn't the controlling type—he knew that about himself from the other relationships he'd had with women. The constant fear for her welfare was coming from this blasted case. He wanted the coroner to wrap it up neatly and say it was definitely suicide, the result of wartime post-traumatic stress.

But the coroner said he couldn't rule out foul play. Beau stopped to sniff a mushroom.

"No, Beau." He gave a snap on the leash to make sure Beau understood to leave mushrooms alone and they kept walking.

"You're a great dog, Beau."

Beau responded with an upright wag of his tail and a beseeching glance over his shoulder.

Miles would've felt better if Ro kept a weapon in her home, but she'd made it clear that away from the navy, she had nothing to do with guns. She said her baseball bat next to her bed was enough.

Miles wasn't so sure.

RO MADE GOOD on her promise to herself to get a six-miler in. While she was running, her cell phone vibrated. She always took her phone with her for security purposes, but didn't answer calls when she was in the middle of a run.

She had to break her own rule since the investigation was ongoing. Slowing to a brisk walk, she answered.

"Roanna Brandywine."

"Commander Brandywine? It's Master Chief Reis."

Ro paused on the running trail, her breath slowing as her mind raced. What if the accusation Anita Perez had made was true? What if Master Chief Reis had an affair with Perez?

"Is everything okay, Master Chief?"

"Yes, ma'am. I'm very sorry to bother you on a Sunday, but we need to talk. About Perez."

"Okay. When and where—you name it, Master Chief."

"I think it's better if it's not in Oak Harbor. Can you meet me in Coupeville for dinner at one of the more crowded restaurants?"

"Sure."

"I know you're working on this with Warrant Officer Mikowski. It'd be fine if he came, as well."

Ro looked at the bark of a fir tree next to the path. She scraped the ground with her running shoe. Of course Master Chief Reis knew she and Miles were on the case. She was the command master chief. It was her job to know everything.

"We'll see you at the Dock, then, or in front of it, say around five?"

"See you then. And, um, Commander?"

"Yes?"

"Please, I beg you, don't tell anyone else about this meeting. It's important or I wouldn't be taking up your time."

"Got it. No problem, Master Chief. See you later."

Ro disconnected and immediately punched in Miles's number.

"Mikowski." Besides his garbled voice she heard barking in the background.

"Miles, it's Ro. Can you hear me?"

"Loud and clear." No explanation for all the ambient noise.

"Master Chief Reis just called me. She wants to meet us for dinner in Coupeville later."

She heard him whistle. "Is that so?"

"Yeah, I thought the same thing." She could read his mind—the truth of this case was going to come to them if they were lucky.

"Okay, thanks, Ro. I'll call you later to confirm the time."

"Bye." She checked her phone, then glanced up at the sky that glimmered through the canopy of trees.

"What next?" she asked the forest.

RO PADDED INTO the kitchen to get a cup of tea to drink while she knitted. As she went to get the milk, she saw her sister's writing at eye level.

> We went to enjoy the day in Victoria. We plan to stay overnight. Don't worry about us—we'll be back sometime during the day tomorrow. Love, Krissy and Dick

"As if I'd worry about either of you." She stared at the

dry-erase board on her refrigerator where Krissy had scrawled her note.

Worrying is your main occupation, she told herself.

Her phone rang.

"Ro, it's me. We still on for the dinner with Reis?"

She put down her knitting and stretched as she answered. After her long run she'd come back to an empty house. A long hot shower and nap, followed by knitting, had made this a perfect day.

"Yes, at five o'clock, down in Coupeville. At the Dock restaurant. Reis was very clear that she wanted both of us there, and asked that we not tell anyone else."

"Like we would. She knew we were both on the investigation, huh?"

"Of course she did. She sits right next to the commodore's office. I'll bet she knows things that would make our toes curl."

"I know ways to make your toes curl."

Before she figured out what to do about her body's instant reaction, he laughed.

"Teasing, Ro. I'm just teasing."

"Are you going to meet me there, or do you want me to drive?" Ignoring Miles was her best tactic.

"No, I can drive. It's okay to let someone else take the wheel, you know."

"Maybe, but you always drive." She took a deep breath. "Hey, if you want, why don't you drive to my place and park here? I'll drive us from here." Her voice shook a bit, whether from the chill of the cool spring air or the anticipation of seeing Miles again, "off duty," she didn't want to determine.

"Fine. But give me some leeway on the arrival—I've got to get Lucky out for a quick run. I'll need a shower after."

"I'll see you when you get here. Be careful on the roads

when you're running." She said it just to keep him on the line. She loved his voice.

"Are you worried about me, Ro?"

"No, I just want to make sure my partner in crime isn't going to get injured and not be able to finish the investigation."

"Huh." She heard his laughter, his teasing grin in her mind's eye.

"Miles, you promised to behave."

"I don't remember doing that. Maybe I did yesterday afternoon, but that was then. It's twenty-four hours later."

His banter made her feel like snuggling under her favorite merino wool blanket and listen to him for hours.

"The problem is, Miles, that I can't get involved. Not now, and not with you."

"Ro, Ro, you are too serious for your own good. I've got to get a move on, but I'll be over soon, and when I show up I want you to be more relaxed. Otherwise, you might miss something important that Master Chief Reis tells us. I'll see you later."

His voice was so much smoother than hers. Damn his EOD training!

"Later." She hung up. She wanted to pound her forehead on her desk calendar. She'd sounded like a schoolgirl.

She shook her head.

Krissy wasn't her problem anymore. Ro had quit her role of the family savior when she'd made her move out here. Underscored by when she'd tossed that ring last week.

Last week? It had only been three days ago. But it felt like so much longer, especially since she'd been working this case with Miles. Since she'd anticipated his touch.

It always came back to the Miles issue. She laughed out loud in her kitchen. The Miles "issue"? She really had to get away from her rigid navy life. Maybe a romantic fling was in order.

The dinner with Lydia Reis was work-related, but there was no need to look like a tired officer tonight. Besides, it would be better if she, Miles and Lydia blended in with the local crowd, just in case anyone from the wing was around or saw them.

Ro put on dark, tight jeans paired with her high-heeled leather boots that made her feel like the kick-ass woman she'd thought the navy would make her. She opted for a light sleeveless lilac tank under the black leather jacket she'd treated herself to when her ship had pulled into port in Naples, Italy.

Once she was dressed and ready, there was still a half hour before their meeting with Reis. She finished up another chemo cap while she waited for Miles to show up. This one was patriotic in red, white and blue. There were a lot of sailors with traumatic brain injuries who'd had their heads shaved for surgery and treatment. The female vets, especially, appreciated a nice hat to help their transition from baldness to a healthy head of hair.

She'd just tied off the last of the hat when the doorbell rang.

She opened the door and stared at Miles as he did the same—at her.

"Wow. The intel officer has become a woman." He grinned.

"I clean up well." Her insides quivered with anticipation—it seemed to be her go-to reaction whenever she was within shooting distance of Miles.

"Where's your sis and her hubby?"

"Gone to Victoria." She met his curious expression. The twinkling in his eyes grew steadier and his gaze dropped to her mouth.

"Good."

She met him halfway as he took her waist in his hands and pulled her to him. His lips landed on hers in a perfectly executed mission and his tongue wasted no time in making target.

Pure sensory delight flowed over her scalp, down her torso and pooled in her pelvis, which she brought as close to Miles as possible. His hands went from her waist to her ass to her face. She felt cherished, desired and irresistible. No man had ever made her feel simultaneously sexy and… precious.

Eager to demonstrate her gratitude and equally appreciative of Miles's desirability, she allowed her hands to linger over his pecs before her fingers made a slow but deliberate journey down his abs to his belt, then into the front of his jeans.

"Baby, I want to eat you up." He grasped her hands and pulled them out of his pants, holding them in between their heaving chests. "Let's blow off the meeting with Reis."

They both laughed if only to relieve the tension that was affecting them to the point of craziness.

"We can't." She took a step back and took a deep breath. "I can't. We have to keep this aboveboard."

"Oh, we're aboveboard, sweetheart." He looked at her with an intensity that made her toes curl. "Let's go to dinner. How long did you say your family will be gone?"

CHAPTER FOURTEEN

THEY SAT WITH buckets of mussels and empty bowls for the shells in front of them at a table that was removed from the main dining area. It overlooked the mussel-harvesting beds in Penn Cove and gave them a respite from the noise of the restaurant.

Lydia Reis looked positively human in a pretty cardigan set and linen pants. Ro had never really spent a lot of time with her—their jobs only overlapped if one of Ro's sailors got into trouble, which, thankfully, wasn't a typical occurrence with the caliber of sailor needed for a high security clearance.

Miles reminded Ro of the Cheshire cat as he sat between her and Reis. She had to concentrate on not being distracted by the heat she swore she could feel coming off his body.

"So, are we ready to talk?" Miles picked up a mussel and started to eat.

"Yes. I'm sorry if this was a bit of a drive for you, but I feel better talking about these things away from work." Lydia's face was calm but her eyes relayed a level of sorrow that Ro hadn't noticed before.

"You wanted to avoid other ears, too. We get it." Ro sipped from her glass of Washington State sauvignon blanc.

Lydia Reis sighed.

"I'm not sure how to begin, except to tell you that this is completely off the record. I'll deny telling you any of this if you take it to a higher level."

Miles put his fork down.

"You know we can't guarantee that, Master Chief. You play by the same rules as we do."

"And you know that this is off the record, so the rules don't apply here. Besides, it would be my word against yours."

Miles raised his eyebrows. "Okay, shoot."

"Petty Officer Perez came up to my office the first day he reported aboard. He had to—we'd known each other before."

"Before?"

She bit her lip.

"I was downrange, living in a base camp for almost a year. I had one R and R to Rota, Spain. I went to the mixed bar in civvies." She referred to a club where enlisted of all ranks could grab a drink and relax.

She gazed out at the water, as if that memory was so much happier than the present.

"We hit it off right away. He said he was also a senior chief, from an east coast command. I had no reason to question him. A lot of wine and a great meal later, I ended up in bed with him. It was the most spectacular night of my life."

Lydia's candor mesmerized Ro. This wasn't the command master chief she was used to working with at the wing.

"You can blame it on all those months in a war zone, having to live with guys and act like one. You can blame it on the wine, my poor judgment. But to me, it was real—not just a one-night stand. I actually believed—" a tear slid down her cheek "—that it was, *we* were, special."

Miles kept his expression open, his hands in his lap.

"The next morning we had breakfast on an oceanview hotel balcony. It was so Hemingway. A fluffy omelet, mimosas, another..." She broke off and clutched at her napkin. Compassion squeezed Ro's lungs.

"I had the hotel for two more nights, but he had to leave,

said he was due to go back downrange and then return to his unit in Norfolk. He told me his name was Juan Garcia—can you believe I fell for that? He took down all my information and promised to contact me via email and Facebook as soon as he could. Then he left."

She sighed heavily and flashed them a smile full of chagrin.

"I never heard from him again. No surprise, right?" She fingered her cloth napkin. "I'd almost convinced myself that it was for the best—that he hadn't been who I thought he was. I'd made a huge mistake. At least I'd done it in private, away from the prying eyes of my command."

She took a swig of her ice water.

"I reported to the wing and settled in. It seemed like I was going to be able to make a clean slate of it for myself. Until Juan Garcia walked into my office and told me he was really Petty Officer José Perez."

Both Miles and Ro leaned forward.

"What did you say to him?" Ro wanted to hear that Reis had read him the riot act, threatened to blow his farce.

"Nothing. He'd come up to see me so I wouldn't be publicly shocked when I saw him. Said that he was sorry he'd behaved so badly—that he never thought scoring a one-night stand would find him in love with a woman he could never have."

"Did he tell you he was married?" Ro asked.

"No, I knew that from his service record. I'd read it over before he came into the office, like I do for every meeting with one of my sailors. I saw that he had two children. Believe me, it took me a while to process the fact that the mystery lover I'd given my heart to in Spain was the aviation structures mechanic and family man who stood in front of me, under my command, on Whidbey Island."

"You started to see him again?" Miles asked the question quietly. They all knew the weight her decision would have carried.

"No, not romantically. I found I was still in love with him, however, against all odds. He claimed he loved me, too, wanted to be with me. I told him that unless he was divorced and willing to get out of the navy when I retired we had nothing to talk about."

She wiped her mouth with her napkin. Ro noticed that Lydia's hands were shaking.

"I didn't hear from him for a few months, until earlier this spring. He told me he'd moved out of his house. I realize now that he'd never moved back into it—his wife had started divorce proceedings before he came back from his latest deployment. He hadn't told me he was living alone because he was busy scoring every junior enlisted ass he could get his hands on."

There was no scorn in Lydia's tone, only resignation.

"Seems he's been a ladies' man for a very long time. But there are his kids—I would have thought he'd make more of an effort to save his marriage for their sake. Anyway, I agreed to talk to him, be his friend.

"I asked him where he was getting the funds to be able to afford an apartment and also child support and he said I should know—I worked for him." She paused. "Have you ever wondered how our maintenance records remain the best in the Pacific fleet, yet our maintenance department is always working, around the clock, on airplanes that can't ever get completely fixed?"

"The P-3C is an old frame. There's no such thing as a 'perfect' aircraft." Miles said what Ro had been thinking.

"Oh, but if you check our stats, on paper, we have airframes that don't seem to have aged one bit!"

"What are you saying, Lydia?" By using her first name, Miles made it clear that they were speaking person-to-person, in private. Off the record, as Lydia had requested. Ro gave him points for his savvy.

Lydia looked each of them in the eye before she replied.

"Perez had taken a total of twenty-two thousand dollars from Commodore Sanders to falsify maintenance and repair documents. So that Sanders's wing, *our* wing, had the best record in the fleet."

Ro swallowed. Hard.

"Do you have proof?" Miles stayed on task.

"Of course not. Nor do I have proof that he gave Sanders back the money, but I know he did. I gave Perez ten thousand dollars of my own funds so he could replace all the cash he'd taken from the commodore. He asked me to help him get clean of Sanders's dirt. He regretted ever entering into the agreement with the commodore."

"Why ten thousand dollars?"

"He'd spent ten thousand dollars on a down payment for the townhome he planned to live in after his divorce, so he'd be close to his kids but also be able to provide a place for us to live. He had half the original twenty thousand left. With my money he was able to repay Sanders. Completely."

"Were these transactions all in cash?" Ro knew from her work with LEAs that criminals kept to cash whenever possible.

"Yes, all cash. The last one was two mornings before Perez died. José went into the commodore's office at 0430 and waited for him to arrive at 0600—Sanders always comes in early. Perez handed him the funds and said their agreement was null and void."

"How do you know this?" Miles sounded incredulous.

"I was on the other side of the commodore's door, listening. I knew Perez would need backup if the commodore decided to go ugly on him."

"Go ugly?"

Lydia sighed. "Get physically violent. It's no secret that the commodore has a temper. You've seen him lose it in the AOMs. Imagine if he's being told by a junior that his gig is up. Then he doesn't have his shoe-in for his admiral's star."

Ro drank some ice water. She needed a clear head to process what she was hearing. A week ago she would have discounted all of this as crazy talk. It was frightening to accept that Lydia might very well be telling the truth.

"What did Sanders say?"

"Not much—just that Perez would regret it, when he needed the money later." Lydia put down her napkin. "You think I'm nuts, don't you?"

"No." Ro's response came out sounding too harsh. She saw the shrewd glance Lydia threw her. Lydia clearly knew she sounded like the proverbial other woman.

"This is interesting, Lydia." Miles leaned back in his chair. "Sanders gets put in his place by someone he considers a lowly staffer and he didn't pitch a fit? It doesn't sound like him."

"Agreed, but remember, he didn't want to draw attention any kind of special relationship with Perez. As the CMC I'm the one who deals with the enlisted folks and all their problems. The commodore is there to be either the benevolent dad or the bastard who has to kick them out of the navy."

Lydia had lines of exhaustion on her face and her shoulders slumped. Ro couldn't imagine the personal burden she must have carried these past months.

"Still, this is a strong accusation, Lydia." Miles pressed on. "You're saying Sanders was paying off a sailor to make his numbers look good. Now that sailor is dead. Why don't you come out and say that Sanders killed Perez?"

"Because I'm not sure he did. He had motive, but I think there's another woman involved in this."

"Another woman?" Ro gasped. "I thought he was getting things set up for you and him?"

"I did, too. At least, I wanted to believe it." She squirmed in her seat. "I wouldn't have sex with him, wouldn't see him until he was free and clear of his marriage, and out of his predicament with Sanders. I know, I was love-blind. I'm as ashamed and horrified as either of you will ever be."

Lydia bit her lip before she continued. "Perez was a hound dog. He screwed anything in a skirt. He really got off on seducing women he thought would ordinarily be 'out of his class.'" She sighed.

"We met after work a couple of times, by accident. Or so I supposed at the time. On the jogging path, at the gym or even in the mixed club. One evening a few weeks ago, he came in with that just-got-laid look. He even told me he'd 'scored.' When I asked who it was, he told me he'd bagged the highest ranking lady yet."

She looked at Ro. "I thought it was you."

Ro slid a glance at Miles. Lydia's story lined up with Anita Perez's too closely. Shivers ran down Ro's back.

Miles gave her a discreet, slight shake of his head.

Be quiet. Don't let on that we've heard any of this before.

"No, it wasn't me. My only relationship with Perez was talking to him on the hangar deck a couple of times. He said he was interested in switching to intel but it was too late in his career to do it."

"I don't believe for one minute that he wanted to change to intel, Commander Brandywine. He wanted to get in your pants, or he wanted to make sure you didn't know about his deal with Sanders, or both." She offered them a shaky smile. "I loved him despite his faults, but I did know him, through and through. He was the kind of man who'd never settle down."

"He did at one point—he got married and had two kids."

Miles's voice was low but Ro didn't miss the disgust in his tone.

"True, but let's face it, those kids and his wife were way better off without him, no question." Lydia shuddered. "So was I once I realized what kind of man I'd slept with in Spain."

Miles's expression remained steady. Ro felt she could read his mind. Perez still had a responsibility, a debt, to his children, not to mention the wife he'd led on for years.

But Ro had a hard time mustering any sympathy for Anita Perez. Her face was still too sore from the punch.

"What do you expect us to do with this information, Master Chief?" Ro held her breath after she asked.

"I want you to use it however you have to. The most important thing is that Perez doesn't get pegged with suicide—there's no way he killed himself. He doesn't—" she paused "—he *didn't* have an altruistic bone in his body. He wouldn't have killed himself to provide the life insurance to his wife and kids, especially since his wife was soon to be an ex."

"And the information on Sanders? If what you've said is true, it's enough to put him in Leavenworth for the rest of his life." Miles paused. "And you, too, Lydia, for failing to report a crime you witnessed."

Lydia shook her head. "Use it however you have to. It'll be impossible to prove, I'm sure. Unless Sanders was sloppy in how he got his money, and Perez was equally careless depositing it in his own accounts, I don't see how there'll be any way to trace it at all. Even if you did, it'd be hard to prove that Sanders was bribing Perez. It'd be my word against the commodore's. Without Perez here, Sanders will come out clean."

Unfortunately, what Lydia said was all too true. While senior officers didn't normally bribe their subordinates to mess with operational readiness statistics, there was always an element of political maneuvering when it came to numbers. Once officers were at this rank of operational command, they were on track to be flag rank and wouldn't allow anything to get in their way.

Sanders had simply cleared his path with some cash.

Extortion, bribery, fraudulent reporting—offenses that were felonies in the civilian world became court martial–worthy in the navy. But just as in the civilian courts, the evidence had to be there.

Lydia reached for her purse.

"I'm sorry, I've got a massive migraine coming on. Can I leave my portion of the bill with you?" She pulled out her wallet.

Miles put his hand on hers.

"No, Lydia, this one's on us." He glanced at Ro and she nodded her agreement. "It sounds like you could use a break."

"I can't." She raised her head and saw the expression on Miles's, then Ro's, face. "Okay. I'll accept the dinner as a favor from one sailor to another."

"Deal." Ro gave her a smile. "This wasn't easy for you, Lydia. Thanks for having the courage to tell us what you know."

"Courage?" Lydia snorted. "This has nothing to do with courage. It has everything to do with making sure Perez doesn't get blamed for his own death. He's done enough other things that were completely wrong. He didn't kill himself, though. Of that I'm certain."

CHAPTER FIFTEEN

"How truthful do you think her story is?" Miles posed the question as if he were asking her about the weather.

Ro shifted on her couch. They'd come back to her place after dinner, and she'd invited Miles in for a drink.

He was drinking decaf coffee and she had a cup of rooibos tea. Long workdays and early mornings didn't lend themselves to a cocktail every night.

"She doesn't have anything to lose. Unless she's hiding something else from us." Ro held the mug with both hands. The air still had a definite chill to it, and it was damp in her living room. Maybe she should light her woodstove.

"I'm on the same page as you. I think she really cared for him, against all odds and despite the facts. She's got no love for Sanders, but then again, most of us don't." Miles stretched out his legs on her ottoman.

"She accused him of some heavy stuff, Miles. Let's say it's all true. Then the onus is on us to find the evidence before Sanders figures out we've discovered his game."

"And if we're wrong, and Reis is playing us, we're in trouble for not defending him—and not reporting what she's told us right away." He gazed past her to the French doors and green garden outside. "But it sure makes sense that Sanders is involved in something ugly. Why else was he so eager to get us doing an 'unofficial' investigation?"

"I don't want to toot my own horn, or yours." She blushed as soon as she realized the connotation her last words could have. "You've lost a leg. Your operational career is over. In his eyes, you'd have nothing to lose by coming forward with any suspicions you have."

"Right. But what about you? Intel types are known for playing their hands close to their chest." His gaze wandered down to her breasts and her slight embarrassment transformed into all-out lust.

"Stop looking at me like that." She sipped her tea. "A lot of operational types, if not most, have a basic disrespect for intel. Tell me you don't, Miles. Tell me you'd take my tactical interpretation of a weapons situation over what your team dug up on its own when you're downrange."

He let out a long breath.

"Yes, you're right. It's not just the information dominance deal with intel." He referred to the umbrella classification that intel, cryptology and other information-based careers fell under. "It's all types of support staff and traditionally shore-based units that operators take issue with. But it comes down to personal connections. If you were out in the field with me I'd trust you."

"You always have a choice and you know it, Miles."

"I've worked with you for the better part of a year now. I've seen you in action. You know your stuff, Ro, and you don't bullshit when you don't have the answer. You go find it."

"Why, thank you, Warrant. I do believe I've made you eat crow."

"Careful. We have to rehash all of this before you start distracting me with your womanly wiles, Commander."

She turned away from him and hoped he couldn't see the color of her cheeks.

"We've established that Sanders doesn't trust either of us. Great. So much for my ego, thinking he put us on the case because he thought we were the most able officers to get the job done."

"So we both agree that Lydia's telling the truth?" Miles asked the most important question.

"Yes. As completely crazy as it sounds, I believe every word of her story. I'm not sure, though, that she's told us everything."

"Right—just enough to keep it clear that Perez didn't commit suicide as far as she's concerned."

"Hmm." Ro finished the last of her tea.

Miles set his mug down on the hand-carved wooden chest Ro had brought back from a brief detachment in the Azores. She'd had a glass pane cut and beveled to place on top of it, making it a coffee table.

"When did you say your sister and brother-in-law are coming back, Ro?"

His eyes glittered and she realized he wasn't focused on their work anymore. Not navy work, anyhow.

She blinked.

"Um, Krissy left a note saying they've decided to spend the night in Victoria. She confirmed it with a text while we were at dinner."

Miles took the empty mug from her hands. She watched his lean fingers as they set it down on the glass, so gentle and particular. His caresses would be like that—deliberate, careful, focused.

"So we have tonight."

"Yes, but, Miles, I'm not sure we're ready for this. Are you, really?"

"Yes." He closed the gap between them by slipping his hand around her neck and pulling her face to his. "You are, too, Ro. You're just scared. Let me keep you safe."

When his lips met hers she already had her mouth open.

She couldn't fight it anymore—she was willing to take whatever he'd give her.

In the end it didn't matter how many times she told herself it was a bad idea. No matter how many times she went over her reasons to stay out of complicated relationships. No matter how evident it was that once she'd been with Miles, she might never be satisfied with another lover.

Their chemistry was unavoidable.

It started sweetly enough. Miles sat up straight on the couch and leaned in toward her. She leaned toward him and their lips met. After that, all bets were off.

His fingers traced her cheek so softly.

"I don't want to hurt you." His shaky voice sent a bolt of awareness through her. He wanted her as badly as she wanted him.

"You can't hurt me, Miles. You're kissing my mouth, not my eye."

"Oh, sweetheart, I'm kissing more than your mouth tonight." He followed up his declaration with action. Ro loved a man of action.

His lips trailed down her neck and he nipped at it, sending ripples of gooseflesh down her spine. She reached for his chest, his hips. His belt was easily removed, but while they were both sitting, she wasn't going to get far with his jeans.

"Let me help you."

He stood and dragged her up with him, his mouth still on hers in possession and bare need. Pops of lavender and green light seemed to explode behind her closed lids as she accepted his tongue fully into her mouth and answered with her own.

"How do we, um," she gasped as she reluctantly pulled her lips from his.

"Make love with my fake leg? We don't." He kissed her

deeply, pressing her hips into his. He lifted her fully off the ground, and she had no choice but to wrap her legs around his.

"Miles!"

"Relax, sweetheart." He pressed her up against the wall and pushed into her. "I'm going to make you crazy. We're going to go to your room, and take off my jeans and my leg. Then we're in bed for the rest of the night." He sucked on her earlobe.

"You seem to have done this before." She licked both of his lips before sucking on the lower one.

"Only practice, Ro. I've never had the real thing until tonight." Again, the raspy need in his voice made her hot all over.

He was good. Very good.

After what seemed like endless kisses and urgent fondling, they went upstairs to her room. Ro lit two small votive candles she kept on her dresser, in front of a small angel statue she'd found in Ephesus, Turkey. The flames flared up and she turned back to Miles.

He lay naked and apparently ready for action across her knitted coverlet.

"You do have fast moves, Warrant." She smiled.

He held out his hand. "Come join me."

"In a minute."

For the first time in her life, Roanna was completely aware of every emotion she felt, every sensual move her body made. She shrugged out of her cardigan and pulled her tank top off over her head.

Her gaze stayed on Miles's. The flickers of candlelight kept his eyes a mystery to her, but she saw the desire and blatant lust in his expression. She knew they were mirrored in hers, too.

Her jeans fell on the floor.

"You're killing me here, Ro." But his hands were behind his head and Miles clearly enjoyed her interpretive foreplay.

"I thought you'd appreciate my underwear." She turned around and heard him hiss as she showed off the black lace bra and panty set she'd pushed aside her sexual timidity to purchase. She'd imagined the lingerie would be for a clandestine rendezvous with an unnamed future lover. A man with whom she'd have uncomplicated sex…

Fate had the last laugh as Miles was the first one to see her in the black thong panties with the pink bow that nestled perfectly at the base of her spine.

She unhooked her bra while she had her back to him and let it drop. As she turned around she sought his reaction.

"Come here, Ro. Now." The shaky need had been replaced by a predatory growl.

Ro walked over to the bed and before she could tease him any more by taking off her thong he had her on her back, his erection pressed into her.

"Whoa, where'd you learn that move?"

"Shut up, Ro." This time he teased her. He moved back a fraction of an inch and hovered over her, his eyes blazing with lust in the candlelight.

"Do you want me, Ro?" He leaned on his side and held his head up on his hand. With the other he made his way over her breasts, pausing at each nipple to swirl around its taut peak.

"Miles, please." Her heart pounded in her ears and she felt the blush of her orgasm waiting in the wings. And he hadn't even touched her everywhere.

"Shhh. Just enjoy this. Answer my question, Ro." His hand pushed aside her panties and his fingers plunged into her. "Do you want me?"

She screamed as her heat clamped down on his fingers. Her breath felt far away, her vision blurred.

"Miles, how on earth," she panted, needing more. Needing all of him.

"Answer the question, Ro."

"Yes, yes, Miles!"

"Yes what?"

"I want you. Now!" She pushed down her panties and kicked them off as though they were on fire.

She was on fire—for Miles.

Their eyes met and she knew it would never be like this with anyone else. He'd put on a condom when she'd taken her thong off and wasted no more time.

"Oh, Ro." He thrust into her and she gasped. He was large, strong, hot. She raised her pelvis to meet him stroke for stroke.

It was a marvel to watch his chest above her as he took her again and again. She allowed herself to fully feel him against her, inside her. He tensed and she waited for his release.

He only came after she screamed and he'd clamped his mouth back on hers.

"YOU DON'T TALK a lot about yourself, Ro."

She curled her toes under her bedcovers, needing the down-filled quilt against her skin. Her head was on Miles's chest as they lay in the predawn dark. They'd made love again, just hours after they'd fallen into a deep slumber in each other's arms.

"There isn't a lot to talk about." She played with the springy hair on his chest. "I work. I come home. I knit. I work out. Sometimes I fool around in my garden. What else do you want to know?"

"Why you kept refusing to go out with me, when it's pretty clear we'd be great together. Why you're hosting your sister and her new husband when the guy jilted you."

He turned to face her more squarely. "Those are the things I'm interested in, to start with."

She fiddled with the duvet cover she'd knitted out of a brilliant blue merino—the same color as Miles's eyes. She ran her fingers through her hair. For some reason she wished, at this moment, that she had long lustrous hair, the kind men loved.

"I've told you twenty times that I didn't want to go out with you because I didn't know you well enough to risk dating someone I worked with, no matter how peripherally."

Did he notice she'd used the past tense?

She wrapped her legs around him and put her chin on her hands, folded on his abdomen. The scent of their lovemaking lingered and she closed her eyes to savor it.

"As for Krissy and Dick..." She wasn't sure where to begin.

"Dick and I ended long before we, well, ended. I was hanging on to a dream, the hope that someday I'd stop needing to travel, to go after the next hard assignment, to conquer the world. It was also the way I kept my mother off my back."

"How so?"

"My mother is...difficult. To her, having a man is the mark of success. It's all about landing the right guy, marrying the best husband possible."

"Did she?"

"Did she what?" At his stare, Ro laughed. "God, no. She's only ever been married to my father and to Krissy's. She's hosted a string of nutso boyfriends, if you could call them that. In retrospect I'm grateful my sister and I weren't ever abused or molested—certainly that was a risk with all those different men. But most of them didn't last past a weekend of fun for Mother."

She heard the words, knew they were part of her story, but felt so dissociated from it all.

"So you and Dick?" Miles was relaxed. He looked like he'd be willing to listen to her all night.

"Dick and I were an arrangement of convenience. We met the summer after high school. You know, teenage hormones and all that. He had college and then med school, I had the academy and owed five years to the navy afterward. So those first ten years together flew by, with romantic meet-ups all over the world. But…it got old. We'd spent too much time apart, and more importantly, we weren't the same kids we'd been when we met at eighteen. He was too nice and I was too much in denial to break it off properly."

"So he did it by getting engaged to your sister?"

"In a nutshell, yes." She smiled at him and tried to suppress a giggle. "I can't believe I'm laughing over this when just last week I threw the engagement ring off the bridge." She stopped. Had she said that aloud? Really?

"So that's what you were doing, all batshit-crazy that morning."

She sighed. "Yes, that's what I was doing. It was long overdue. And I shouldn't have done it—I should have at least donated the ring to charity."

"Was it a big ring?"

"No. It was tiny, all we could afford as college kids. But I was sentimental about it, I didn't want anything bigger." Maybe she'd known all along that they weren't going to last. They weren't going to ever take the next step.

"You know what, Miles? Krissy did both Dick and me a favor. And the kicker of it is, I think they really love each other. Krissy's immature as hell, and Dick is a slave to his work, but there's a spark there that he and I never had."

"Like you and I do?"

She sucked in her breath. "Physical attraction isn't reason enough to start a relationship, Miles."

"Sure it is." He gave her that blinding white smile that lit up his face and made her even more aware of his masculine features. He wasn't the most handsome man she'd ever seen but he was definitely the sexiest.

"So we find out we're compatible in bed. Then what? We enjoy it until we're bored? Avoid each other at work once it becomes awkward?" She shook her head. "I don't want to ever feel uncomfortable at work." She'd invested too much of herself in her career.

"Do you really care about what everyone else says, Ro? We're not breaking any laws or regulations. We have every right to be together. Unless you were thinking about getting it on in the hangar?" His eyes sparkled with his teasing.

"No, no. It's hard for me, Miles. I've poured everything into my work up until now. I don't know how to flip the off switch." She closed her eyes for a moment.

"Before, I had Dick to cling to, to keep other men away. Now that he's gone, I'm faced with not only starting a new relationship but wondering if I should start a new career. It's been a long time since I considered any other option for my life but the navy."

His chest rose and fell and when her eyes met his she saw the embers she'd stoked with her confession.

"You've got 'work' down, Ro. The way I see it, you need to put more effort in your personal life. You have, what, nine years in the navy?"

"Almost ten, yes."

"So guess what? If you stay in until twenty—" the earliest she could retire with a pension "—you're going to have to find a life. But by then some of the opportunities you have available now may be gone."

"Like you? Are you threatening me, saying you won't be here forever?"

It was his turn to laugh, and he did—lustily.

"Ro, you really are a sweetheart. No, I'm not talking

about me—necessarily. I mean your chance to have kids. Do you want your own babies, Ro?"

Of course she wanted kids. She didn't think about it too much and she'd always been able to push any maternal yearnings aside. She'd had time. But now, not so much. He was right.

And the way he said babies… "Um, yes, eventually, I'd like a baby or two."

"In order to have babies, wouldn't you want a father who'd stand by you and the kids?"

"Yes." She so didn't want to talk about this with him, not after she'd had the best sex of her life.

"It's fair to say that a basic dating relationship would be the start of anything more lasting, deeper, don't you think?"

He sat up against her headboard, her pillows supporting him.

"Miles, I get it. Remember you're not a psychiatrist, okay?"

He chuckled. "I'm just Miles, and you're Ro, a woman I'm interested in. It's just us here. No uniforms, no investigations, no jobs."

"No kidding." She couldn't help the zinger—they were lying there naked.

Their eyes met again and laughter switched to desire in a blink. As Ro practiced her newfound sexual liberation on Miles, her heartbeat echoed in her ears. She was a goner.

CHAPTER SIXTEEN

KAREN SANDERS LISTENED to the hum of Leo's engine until he reversed out of the driveway Monday morning. Not until then did she go to the pantry, where she pulled out her huge plastic container labeled Bread Flour. She opened it and reached under the soft bags of rye, whole wheat and barley. Her fingers wrapped around the familiar glass neck of the bottle of cognac she dug out of the bin. She had her coffee cup perched on the shelf below so it was an easy move to deliver a generous splash of booze into her morning brew.

She replaced the bottle and heaved the container back on the top shelf of the pantry, shoving it back into its spot between the sugar and the oatmeal. In no hurry to leave the safe-feeling confines of the small walk-in cupboard, she drank her heavenly concoction.

It wasn't as if she was an alcoholic or anything. Stefanie was at school and Leo was at work; this was often her only time alone during the day and why not have a warming nip?

The drink soothed her nerves. But it did nothing to ease the ache in her heart. Of all the people to have a stupid, pointless fling with, she'd picked a doozy. The subsequent pain and confusion from the brief affair had served to make her life even more of a mess than it already was.

You have to tell Leo.

Tell him what? That she didn't like having sex with him anymore?

He'd figured *that* out. Their weekly Saturday morning

in-bed gymnastics routine didn't rate the difficulty level it had as newlyweds, but they both knew themselves and each other well enough to attain physical release. They'd settled for vanilla instead of rocky-give-it-to-me-road.

She stepped out of the pantry and into the morning light that flooded the sunroom, just off the kitchen. A lone bald eagle circled over the sound, a few yards from the edge of the cliff that her lawn backed up to. His high-pitched screech pierced the stillness and was sharp enough for her to hear through the glass-paned sliding door.

A mating cry.

A tear trickled down her cheek and she let it fall. Not only had she settled for vanilla, she'd settled for the wrong dessert entirely. Since she'd worked next to and spent hours with Daisy at the Navy-Marine Corps Relief Society, she'd known the most intimate emotional relationship she'd ever experienced. And when Daisy's casual touches became something she looked forward to like a teenager, she still fought the inner demons that told her something was wrong with her. Years of denial were hard to break through.

She sighed. Her family was all Louisiana born and bred, and unlike some of her distant cousins who enjoyed the relative open-mindedness of New Orleans, she'd grown up in the more conservative part of the state—the small-town, everyone-goes-to-church part. Being a lesbian wasn't an option in her mama's eyes. You lived and died by whatever the new preacher said in the regular fire-and-brimstone sermons.

But in those sermons Karen had also learned that God loved her. That she should always be truthful.

She'd been truthful when she married Leo. She'd loved him and couldn't wait to start a life away from her hometown. It was fate that she'd met him at that Mardi Gras during her senior year at Tulane. Otherwise, she would've had to go back home and become a schoolteacher as her mama had planned since she was born.

Instead, she'd seen the world. Had a baby—the most precious gift ever. Stefanie wasn't the easiest teenager to raise but what girl was at sixteen?

Those early years with Leo and the navy she'd had to learn that her needs came second to Leo's career. The needs of the navy had top priority. That was fine. For a while.

But during this extended time ashore, she'd put down some roots. She'd found a volunteer position that turned into a paying position. She was making a difference.

Her role as the consummate officer's wife had shifted and she was able to focus more on herself.

And she'd finally discovered what she'd known was missing all along—the piece of herself she'd never been able to put a name to. She was in love with Daisy.

Daisy suggested Karen see a counselor to wade through the years of pain that not living what she called her "authentic life" had bestowed on her. Karen fought the counseling at first, but then realized it was time to get real. Doing so, she was blessed with finding freedom and the ability to love herself, appreciate who she was.

But, in oh-so-typical Karen fashion, she'd screwed up, big-time. She'd had to prove to herself that it wasn't just because Leo was the only man she'd ever had sex with. That she needed a little time with a different partner.

She'd needed a different partner, all right. A woman.

Her coffee burned in her stomach. Her selfish self-sabotaging behavior had cost her the beautiful relationship she'd built with Daisy.

If only she hadn't pulled her stupid stunt while Leo was TDY last week. Now she could be a murder suspect. Worse, she could have implicated him if anyone found out about her and Daisy. They'd think Leo acted on jealousy.

But she knew he was innocent of any wrongdoing with Perez. He had no clue about her extramarital affair. He'd tuned her out long ago.

"I NEED TO SEE the last of the work Petty Officer Perez signed off on." Ro stood in front of the high counter that served as the nerve center for the maintenance department. She was surprised at how alert and focused she felt, after having less than a few hours of sleep in Miles's arms.

"He worked on aircraft from all the squadrons, ma'am. Is there one date or aircraft in particular you're interested in?"

The maintenance limited duty officer, Lieutenant Junior Grade Patsy Jordan, gave Ro a wary once-over. It was clearly none of Ro's business what Perez had been working on, since she was intel and had nothing to do with aircraft maintenance. But she needed to see those records to confirm or deny what Master Chief Reis had told her and Miles at dinner.

That Commodore Sanders was a liar, fraud and cheat.

"No, just whatever he worked on over the past three to six months. The wing keeps copies of all the squadron records, too, right?"

"Not necessarily. We do encourage the mechs to keep copies of whatever they do, and we try to hang on to copies of anything the wing gets involved in. But each squadron keeps its own records."

Ro gritted her teeth. There was no reason for Patsy to be so obtuse, except that she disliked anyone who worked "upstairs." It was inevitable—when you worked in the bowels of the hangar through all seasons and kinds of weather, it was easy to resent the office types who were always in air-conditioned spaces and never got their hands dirty except from their dry-erase markers.

Ro wanted to tell her to "bite me" but that wouldn't get her or the investigation anywhere.

"Okay, Patsy. Can you get me copies of what you have, please? Per order of the commodore." Ro held her breath.

"Whatever you need." Patsy turned back to her files.

Technically she was here on the commodore's orders, of course. Just doing her part for the case. But if Patsy decided to check it out and have her boss ask the commodore about it, that would get Sanders's early warning radar up and running.

If what Master Chief Reis said was true.

And if it *was* true, the commodore was murder suspect number one. If he'd killed Perez to save his career, he wouldn't be happy about anyone who was on to his crimes. She and Miles could be in the line of fire.

Stop it. Focus on the facts.

Her mind drifted to the memory of Miles's lips on hers. It was a brief flashback, yet it shook her. She wasn't used to being so easily distracted.

Patsy stood by a huge file cabinet behind the counter. Ro watched as she pulled out a total of eight large files.

She shivered. Patsy already knew which files out of hundreds were pertinent. As if she'd recently perused them. Or pulled them for someone else.

"I'll get what you need copied." Patsy's expression was neutral, her eyes downcast. What did she know?

"Thanks a lot, Patsy. I'll come back in a few." She didn't want the maintenance control officer to think she was trying to tell her how to do her job.

"It's going to take longer than a few minutes—this is our busiest time of day. I'll call you when it's ready."

"Roger."

Ro turned and headed out of the maintenance shop and ran squarely into Commodore Sanders.

"Whoa, Ro, where are you going in such a hurry?" He

smiled at her. She saw his eyes narrow as he glanced over her shoulder to see where she'd come from. The control desk.

Crap.

"I'm headed back to Miles's office. We've got a couple of appointments to line up for today."

He nodded. "Good. I trust you'd have been up to my office if you'd found anything new?" He looked interested as he stood in the same casual way he always had—one arm against the doorjamb, the ever-relaxed aviator. But Ro sensed his antagonism.

"Yes, sir, of course. We're still just gathering whatever info we can."

Damn it, that wasn't the right thing to say. She meant to throw him off her trail, politely blow him off with a brief blanket statement. Instead she'd blurted out far too much. Great.

"What kind of info are you getting down here, Ro?" He clasped her elbow and maneuvered her out of the entryway as sailors were coming in and out of maintenance control.

Was he threatening her?

Chill out. It's not Hollywood. Take your own advice.

"Nothing major, sir. I'm just validating the day and time I had that last conversation with Perez. Boring stuff."

She swallowed. She wasn't technically lying as she would no doubt be able to verify the time she'd had that chat with Perez. At least the watch shift he'd been working.

Sanders let go of her elbow. He released a long sigh.

"I'm sorry I've put you in such a position, Ro. I know you'd rather be studying message traffic and preparing for the squadrons' training cycles." He shook his head. "And your shiner—" he gestured at her multicolored black eye "—is more than you should have to pay for being an intel officer."

"No problem, sir. We're a team—we all do what we have

to." She managed a smile. *God, please let him believe that I mean it.*

Sanders patted her shoulder. "I know I can count on you, Ro." He had his good-humored demeanor back as he turned toward the door. "See you later."

She let out her breath and wanted to weep with relief—even more so when she peered past the commodore and saw that LTJG Patsy Jordan was nowhere in sight.

She should have let Miles get the copies of the records, after all. He would've charmed cranky Patsy, and the commodore wouldn't have had any reason to think something was up when he saw Miles down here. Miles's main office was upstairs but he had a desk in the weapons shop on the hangar deck.

Hopefully he was in the weapons shop. She had to talk to him before the commodore did.

MILES SPENT AS MUCH time as possible on the hangar deck as he loved to be around the hum of constant work, the excitement of upcoming missions. He didn't do too much with the weapons systems themselves, but he understood the explosive nature of the live weapons in ways the flyers didn't.

This was the reason he'd been assigned to the wing—to give him a not-so-demanding shore tour during which to heal and rehabilitate, and to give the patrol squadrons a go-to guy for training. He gave briefs on IEDs, mines and explosives of all types and shapes. His job was to familiarize the sailors, officer and enlisted, with what they'd encounter downrange. So many of them were serving next to their marine corps, army and air force counterparts that they needed to be as aware of the risks of IEDs as any infantry soldier or airman.

He instinctively knew that if he holed up in his much

cleaner, more modern office upstairs he'd never gain the respect of the wing or squadron aircrews.

Not too long ago, the navy was considered the "safer" service. On board a ship was a far better proposition than being in the jungle fighting off Vietcong, or on the ground sweeping mines.

Times and weaponry had changed. He'd been needed to clear that field for a mission. They couldn't wait for backup from the army. He used his experience to impress the importance of weapons training on the aircrew, especially the young sailors who thought they were immortal.

An instruction manual on the new patrol platform was open on his computer screen. It was imperative that he get through it but memories of Ro calling out his name when she came diverted his attention.

The P-3s were transitioning to the P-7, a jet aircraft that would be able to conduct long-range surveillance and support missions for years to come. Hell, probably for the next two or three generations, judging by how long the P-3 had remained operational.

"Miles." Her voice made his neck tense at the same time it made him hard.

He turned his swivel chair around to face the door.

"Ro."

She slid into the chair in front of his desk. She was breathing heavily and her cheeks were flushed. He'd loved watching her blush last night when she'd climaxed.

"Don't look at me like that."

"What? I'm just sitting here."

"You know what I mean." She leaned forward. "I ran into Sanders a few minutes ago."

Damn.

"In maintenance control?"

"Yup."

"Do you think he's on to what we've found out from Master Chief Reis?"

"Can't tell. Not yet." She leaned back in the chair. "I don't want to talk about it while we're in here."

"Good thing." He looked past her shoulder.

"Why?"

"Because he's walking straight over here. What did you say to him?"

"I told him that we're getting together now to plan our next appointments."

"Okaaaaay. So where are we going next?" He couldn't help smiling at her, even with Sanders on his way over. It was so hot to see her blush.

"Stop it, Miles, I mean it." Her voice was hushed and her discomfort palpable. Sanders was a second from being within earshot.

"It's okay." He wished he could reach across the desk and squeeze her hand but his words and glance would have to do. He relaxed in his chair as if they were having a normal conversation.

"It sounds like we'll have to run some more 'errands.'"

Sanders walked into the office and closed the door behind him.

"Where are you two going today?"

"We're just figuring that out, sir," Miles responded.

Miles and Ro stood up.

"At ease, sit down." Sanders waved them both back into their chairs and took a seat on a workbench stool. He nodded at Ro.

"I just ran into Ro in maintenance control. Have you two found out anything new?"

Miles felt Ro's gaze on him. They both needed him to step very carefully. Sanders was treading too close. Miles's gut tightened.

"Nothing we haven't already briefed you on, sir, or that you hadn't already told us when we started this investigation."

"I'd hoped we'd have our ends wrapped up before the memorial service."

Ro swiveled her torso toward Sanders.

"The date's been set, sir?"

"Yes, this Wednesday. Service at eleven in the base chapel."

"We'll have the facts from the coroner by then, sir, and if we hear anything sooner we'll let you know."

Sanders kept tapping his toe against one of the stool's legs. He wore a pained expression on his face.

"I got a call from NCIS this morning." He folded his arms. "The sheriff's department is ruling it a probable suicide, and NCIS concurs."

Miles was grateful for his EOD training. It kept him from appearing surprised or angry. Why hadn't Detective Ramsey contacted them?

"I thought they couldn't do that until the toxicology report was complete." Ro controlled her expression. Only Miles could see the pulse that jumped under her skin, on the side of her neck.

Sanders sighed. "Apparently there wasn't enough evidence to prove someone was with him that night."

"Have they mentioned any suspects?" Miles was actually relieved that the commodore was laying this on them now. It distracted Sanders from what Miles and Ro were planning, or not planning, to do next.

"No, and even if they had they wouldn't tell me." Sanders couldn't keep the bitter note out of his voice. Miles let out a long breath. He'd be happy when Sanders left the office. The guy's energy was draining.

"Sir, we'll go out to the coroner and get a hard copy of

the report, and we'll stop in at the sheriff's offices while we're there. Maybe we'll be able to get something out of them in person."

"Please do." Sanders stood up. His brown leather oxfords shone in the fluorescent lighting, bright against the concrete floor of the hangar deck. He stretched. Miles wanted to kick Ro under the desk, to keep her from gaping at the commodore's apparent ease with the entire situation.

Miles wasn't sure why but he knew the commodore's nonchalance was feigned. Sanders was as nervous as a wet cat.

"WHAT'S SO IMPORTANT that it couldn't wait until I got home from work?"

Leo frowned at Karen across the small table. She'd called him after his morning meetings and told him she had to see him downtown ASAP. She'd picked one of the local coffee shops. He looked around. There weren't many patrons inside, and the ones who were there had probably been retired for decades.

She'd wanted privacy. Kind of.

"I have to tell you something that's going to be very upsetting for you." Her eyes were red-rimmed and her usual perfect poise had cracked, judging by the manner in which she picked at her cuticles. Karen never exhibited nervous habits, especially not in public.

"Do I smell booze?" He was so tired of her drinking.

"You may." She took a shaky breath. "My drinking is another issue I'm going to have to face, but first—" She stopped.

He waited.

"Do you remember the gal I work with at navy relief?"

"What the hell does she have to with anything, Karen?" Son of a bitch, Karen really had no clue how much he did for the family, for her. To keep her in the lifestyle she deserved, even with her drinking. He faulted himself for her drinking, actually. If he'd been home more and paid more attention to her, maybe she'd stop.

"I'm in love with her, Leo."

"You don't have that big a drinking problem, Karen."

"I'm in love with a woman."

"If you're really worried, there are private rehabs you can get into."

"I'm a lesbian, Leo."

"WHAT DID YOU say?" Leo's eyes narrowed and his face went from tan to tomato-red. Karen recognized the warning signs of his rage. She was so grateful her counselor had suggested she do this in a public place.

"I'm gay." It was starting to feel good, the more often she said it. Like a huge weight was lifting, as though she was growing another six inches.

"What do you mean 'I'm gay'?" He mimicked her in his usual sarcastic manner. Getting divorced was her only way out, even if she'd been straight. Why had it taken her all these years to see it?

"I've known since I was in high school, but I pushed it down. You know Mama and Daddy would've skinned me alive, then sent me to some kind of holy-roller gay rehab camp. It was easier to just play the role of the perfect daughter."

"We were in love once, Karen. Or were you dreaming of a woman when I was kissing your—"

She slammed her hand down on the Formica tabletop.

"No, Leo! We're not doing it like this. I realize you're in shock, but the days of you telling me how to live my life are over. This has nothing to do with why I'm gay. I was born this way. It's sad, tragic, really, that it's taken me so long to figure it out."

She swiped at her tears.

"Leo, please believe me when I tell you I genuinely loved you. We created our beautiful baby girl together. That will never change."

He was fighting so hard for control. She knew it was the worst time to tell him, what with the death of Perez and all. But he had to know—everything.

"So is this all you wanted to tell me?" He tensed, ready to stand up.

"No, there are two more things." She took in a deep breath. Funny how easy this was, now that she'd started.

"I want a divorce. That shouldn't be a surprise." She waited for him to respond. When he didn't, she continued.

"I did something really stupid, Leo. Just to make sure it wasn't because of us. In a stupid, drunk moment, I had a one-time affair."

"Great, Karen. Is this making you feel better, your final confession? Because don't think you'll get any more out of me. You want a divorce, go ahead. Leave. But you'll get nothing. I'm not going to support you one iota."

She figured it wasn't the best time to point out that by his retirement, she would have stayed in the marriage for more than half his maximum navy time, so she was entitled to 50 percent of his pension. Not that she wanted a penny from him; she only needed child support for Stefanie.

"I'm not asking for that, Leo. But you do need to know who I had the affair with."

"No, I don't think I do."

"It was Petty Officer Perez."

CHAPTER SEVENTEEN

"YOU'VE BEEN AWFULLY quiet this morning." Gwen spoke to Ro as they both applied their makeup in front of the locker room mirror. They'd finished a run on base before starting the day.

"There's a lot going on at work."

Gwen paused, her mascara wand midair. "Yes, there is. I saw the reports last Friday—the war has another casualty, doesn't it?"

"I can't talk about my involvement in the case but yes, one of the wing sailors died. Whether it was PTSD or not hasn't been determined." Ro wasn't playing coy, just being truthful.

"They'll release the name soon enough."

She spread cherry gloss on her lips out of habit, not because she cared what she looked like today.

"How are your change-of-command plans going?" Ro asked out of genuine curiosity but also to steer Gwen away from the hot topic of Petty Officer Perez.

Gwen sighed and picked out a clear gloss from her small makeup bag.

"Fine. But I can't get Drew on board." She shook her head. "He won't even commit to helping me plan a party for it. I'd love to have both of our families out for the event."

"He's still upset you took the orders?"

"'Upset' is putting it mildly. He really thought it was time for us to settle down, maybe start a family and stay put in one place." Gwen was visibly distraught and Ro didn't blame her. Being chosen for command of a squadron was a Very Big Deal in the navy.

"But you *will* be in one place, after you get this tour done. Can't he understand this is what you've worked for your entire career?"

"He does, but he also thinks that goals change as we go along in life." Gwen's face was wistful now, an expression Ro wasn't accustomed to seeing on her best friend of over fifteen years. Gwen was about to become the commanding officer of a patrol squadron, one of the first women ever to do so.

Gwen was a pilot and had made her mark landing P-3s as a junior officer during the wars in Afghanistan and Iraq. She'd outmaneuvered enemy missiles, not an easy feat for the slow-flying P-3. Her reputation as a naval aviator was flawless, and her intrinsic ability to lead had earned her the command position.

"This should be a happy time for you on all fronts, Gwen. I'm sorry Drew isn't more supportive."

"It's my fault. We agreed to have kids 'later,' and now, after ten years of marriage, I'm nowhere *near* ready to have a baby." She sighed and shot Ro a frank look. "He got out after seven years to go back to school and become a physical therapist, so he's reached his big goal. I'm still going after mine."

"I've heard he's great at what he does. Several of the wing staffers have been referred out to him." Ro wondered if Drew was Miles's physical therapist.

"He's the best. And I did agree that once he got on his feet financially with his new practice, I'd consider getting out. But then I was selected for command..." Gwen's voice trailed off. Gwen was the poster girl for female naval officers. Fit, young, strong and bursting with enthusiasm.

For her career. Not her personal life.

"I wonder if it's possible to have both a successful personal *and* professional life? Especially with what we do?" Ro murmured.

Gwen smiled. "It is if you're willing to sacrifice and compromise. Look at all the gals from the academy who are promoting *and* have husbands and kids. Unfortunately, I've found out the hard way that compromise isn't in my DNA."

Ro mulled over the fact that they were both academy grads, both female and always used to being watched, prodded and encouraged to do their very best. Work-wise. When had anyone ever suggested they pay just as much attention to their private lives?

"What about you, Ro? Did you say 'yes' to Miles?"

Ro hoped Gwen would think her red cheeks were from their run.

"Actually, we're working together on this case."

Gwen raised her brows. "Go on."

"We're certainly spending a lot of time together. That, combined with Krissy and Dick paying me a surprise visit, has turned this week upside down, fast."

Ro had already filled Gwen in on the drama that had ensued after her sister and former fiancé showed up at her door. Mom was due any minute, too.

"Ro, I've known you for a very long time. You look like you've spent a week on a honeymoon, even with that ghastly black eye."

Ro had promised herself that she wouldn't get together with Miles again. Not like Sunday night. They hadn't seen each other after work yesterday; she was grateful they hadn't been able to meet with Detective Ramsey yet. She didn't trust herself around Miles and it scared her.

"Gwen, I have too much to lose. How stupid would I be to throw away all these years of hard work on a guy?"

"Probably not as stupid as you were to throw away your

life on Dick for all that time, kiddo." Gwen could always be counted on for her frankness, which was why their friendship had survived school, the navy, deployments, boyfriends, fiancés, a husband.

"Thanks. I'm sure I deserve that." Ro gave herself a rueful smile in the mirror.

Gwen put her hand on Ro's arm.

"Promise me one thing. Enjoy yourself. Let go. For once, stop worrying about what anyone else thinks. Be a girl."

Ro smiled at her closest friend.

"You mean like you have with turning your back on a navy career and becoming Suzy Homemaker?"

Gwen's mouth twisted in exasperation.

"This isn't about me. You've still got time to weigh your options more carefully than I have."

Ro watched Gwen gather up the rest of her cosmetics and put them in her gym bag. She didn't think it was a coincidence that Gwen had put voice to the thoughts that had been bombarding her ever since she'd allowed Miles to get close.

If it was the right thing for her to be with Miles, to reevaluate what she wanted out of life, would it be so messy, so complicated? Wouldn't it be easier to discern?

Ro liked dealing with facts. They were cleaner than emotions.

But they don't keep you warm when your woodstove's cold.

AN HOUR LATER Ro walked across the hangar lot and over to the row Patsy had told her she was parked in. She spotted the blue economy sedan, with Patsy sitting in the front seat. Ro tapped on the passenger door window and Patsy unlocked the door.

Ro slid into the compact seat and shut the door.

"Thanks for getting back to me." Ro owed her this much. Patsy had certainly taken her time but she hadn't forgotten.

"I thought it was better to meet out here instead of in the hangar. I don't want the commodore to have any clue about this."

"No?" Ro clenched her fists against the tremors of intuitive awareness. Patsy had checked over the records herself, apparently.

"No." Patsy turned to Ro and shook her head. "Is there any superior officer worth following anymore? I thought the commodore, even though he can be arrogant and self-serving as far as his career goes, was one of the better ones. I didn't think he'd hurt others, but if you see what he did in these stats—" she handed a thick envelope to Ro "—he didn't care if planes were able to fly safely or not. As long as his stats were solid for the high-profile reporting zones."

Ro took the envelope and let it settle on her lap. The weight of the pages made her aware of the possible criminal charges Sanders faced. If he'd been capable of putting aircrews at risk for political gain, what else would he be willing to do to protect his miscreant behavior?

"Patsy, I know we haven't worked together at all before, but I really appreciate you putting your neck out. After I look at the stats, I'll forward them to a place where this situation will be dealt with."

Patsy stared at her. "I put in some comments of my own—they're on the yellow sticky notes. Just in case some of the maintenance lingo is foreign to you."

Ro smiled. "Thanks."

"Just promise me one thing, Roanna."

"Yes?"

"If there's any way we can get him, do it. Fry his ass."

"Trust me, I will. *We* will."

Ro got out of the car and briskly walked over to her own

vehicle. She needed to get these papers off the base so she could read them without the risk of anyone seeing her poring over pages of aircraft stats. Intel officers notoriously didn't bring work home; they couldn't, since it was mostly classified and had to stay on base, secured. All she needed was for the commodore or even the CSO to catch her looking at paperwork outside the office.

Her cell phone vibrated in her jacket pocket and she answered it as she got into the car's front seat.

"Hi, Miles."

"Ro, where are you?"

"In my car. I've got some information we've been waiting on from maintenance."

"Great. Let me know as soon as you figure out anything more. I just got the call from Ramsey—we're in to see him later this morning."

"Great! I'm going to disappear for a bit and read over these papers."

"Okay. I'll pick you up in time to go to Coupeville." He paused. "Ro?"

"Yes?"

"Miss me." It was an order, a request. Not a question.

As their call ended, Ro stared at the phone screen and felt a smile warming her face. He didn't have to tell her.

IN STARK CONTRAST to the quiet of their Saturday meeting with Detective Ramsey after the autopsy, the Island County sheriff's department was buzzing late Tuesday morning.

Ro didn't like being the center of attention just because she was in a uniform, so it was a relief to share the spotlight with Miles. Although they were treated with respect, there was an underlying current of mistrust as they got closer to seeing Ramsey.

Unlike on Saturday, they couldn't go straight up to his office with him as their escort. They had to be identified and signed in at two different desks before they were granted access to the second floor—and only then with an administrative assistant to escort them.

"I feel like we've committed a crime," she told Miles as they waited outside Ramsey's office.

"I hear you. It's not us, remember. It's their job to make sure they have a handle on every person who comes in here."

"I know that, Miles." She was ready to remind him that her job involved intricate layers of security, as well.

"Come right on in, folks." Ramsey's voice reached them from his inner sanctum.

Ro was relieved to see the detective and have their escort close the door behind them. They faced Ramsey alone, with no distractions.

"I'm surprised it took you two this long to get back down here." He gave them a rueful glance.

"We tried to see you all day yesterday, Detective, but we couldn't even get through to your executive assistant."

Ramsey nodded. "Sorry about that. I suppose you're here for more than just the preliminary lab reports?" They all knew that some of the toxicology screens could take weeks, even months, to come back, depending on what had been ordered by the coroner.

"Yes, sir." Ro figured she'd err on the side of respect, despite her anger at Ramsey's lack of communication. "We're both curious—" she looked at Miles, whose complete attention was on Ramsey "—about why you called the commodore with the determination of cause of death as probable suicide, but never mentioned it to us on Saturday."

"You made it pretty damn clear that you didn't think Perez had committed suicide," Miles interjected, and Ro wondered if Ramsey realized exactly how perturbed Miles was.

"I made it clear that it was highly unlikely that Perez committed suicide. Not impossible." Ramsey stared at them for a moment, waiting for one of them to speak up.

After a few minutes of silence, he sighed.

"Sit down." He motioned to the chairs they'd sat in before. It was the same office, the same furniture, but Ro noted that the apparent camaraderie they'd shared on Saturday was as absent as their mugs of tea and coffee.

"Look, in this office we deal in facts. I know that in the military you may have more leeway with circumstantial evidence. I'm pretty sure I could have convinced the district attorney to go after a suspect on the suspicion of homicide or, at the least, manslaughter." Ramsey placed his elbows on the desk.

"No one wants to see justice served more than me. That's why I'm in this godforsaken career. But I can't ask the D.A. to stick her neck out for a case that not only doesn't have enough evidence to call it a criminal event, but also doesn't have any witnesses."

"What if we told you we have reason to believe someone had cause?" Ro asked.

"As in?"

"Ro and I had dinner on Sunday night with someone who believes the commodore had a fraudulent deal with Perez to falsify aircraft maintenance documents."

Ramsey stared at Miles. "Did this person give you any way to prove it?"

Miles shook his head. "No. This person is of the belief that this crime is too hard to prove."

Ramsey's face started to flush and his eyes sparked.

"Out with it, you two. Tell me what you've heard."

Miles turned from Ramsey to her. "We told Reis that we couldn't promise her anything."

She nodded. "This is about Perez, bottom line."

They turned back to Ramsey and told him what they knew.

MILES STUDIED RO across the diner's table. It had taken almost a year to the day, but he'd finally gotten her to share a meal with him. It wasn't the way he'd envisioned wooing her when he'd started asking her out last year. Far from it. They were in a beat-up greasy spoon only because of the investigation.

They'd spent the morning talking with Detective Ramsey and the coroner. The verdict remained that while the death looked suspicious, the sheriff's department couldn't call it a homicide. Miles was glad they'd been able to lay all their cards on the table with Ramsey. If there was even a sliver of hope that they'd crack this case, it would have been worth telling Reis's story.

Ro had been remarkably calm throughout the event. A far cry from the shaking gal she'd been at the beach on Friday, or in the autopsy room on Saturday.

Miles liked seeing her in such close proximity, without the noise of their offices and all the other staffers running around.

Face it, what you really like is that you have her all to yourself.

His laugh grumbled, along with his stomach.

"What?"

Ro's eyes narrowed in wary observation and he wanted to reach over and rub the creases off her forehead. Her short wispy hair framed her delicate features and it was all he could do to keep his mind in the present and not wander off to visions of her naked in bed.

"Is it really this tough to be alone with me?" he asked.

"I never said it was tough being with you." She played with the cheap plastic salt and pepper shakers on the rickety table. "It's not my fault that you took it personally when I wouldn't go out with you."

They sat at one of five tables in the joint and every inch

of the place was coated with grease and grime. They'd each ordered a slider, as it appeared to be the safest choice on the chalkboard menu.

"So why wouldn't you go out with me for so long? And don't give me your B.S. about us working together. It had something to do with that ex-fiancé of yours, didn't it? That Dick?" He tried to make her laugh to no avail.

She pursed her lips, her quandary playing out on her face.

"Yes, no, partly." She offered him a brief flash of a smile. "I wasn't B.S.-ing when I told you I don't date work colleagues. I never have. Have I dated since I broke up with Dick? Yes, of course. It's been well over a year. I'm not a nun."

"I've never pictured you as a nun, Roanna."

He relished the flush that bloomed on her cheeks. Not because he'd made her uncomfortable, but because he knew she was as attracted to him as he was to her. He'd felt it when he'd kissed her the night they'd started the case, and he knew she'd felt it as strongly as he had when they'd made love Sunday night.

"I'm not totally opposed to dating someone like you—I mean, someone I work with but am not in the same chain of command with." She was flustered. Satisfaction warmed his belly—she was no less affected by him than he was by her. They hadn't spent all of their passion in one night.

"Ro." He covered her fidgety hand with his.

She stopped fiddling with the salt and pepper and looked at him.

He wanted to lose himself in the depths of her luminous baby blues.

"It's okay. We're two adults, and we like each other. What we want to do in our private time is our business."

"I get that, Miles. But the things we've seen together these past few days—they'd bond any two officers, don't you think? It's possible we're caught up in the heat of the moment."

"No, I don't think that at all, Roanna. We could just as easily have made life a living hell for each other, refused to cooperate or go after the same goal. Our kind of chemistry isn't common, and it's not due to the intensity of this investigation."

He watched her digest the idea. Her defenses were down to nil but she still wouldn't admit it.

"I'm not saying we don't have great chemistry, Miles. My point is that just because we made love on Sunday doesn't mean we're automatically going to do it again."

He laughed. "There's nothing automatic about making love to you, Ro."

"Number three!" The waiter-chef-owner shouted out the number on their receipt. Miles stood up.

"I've got it." He walked the few steps over to the counter and picked up a tray with two baskets of hamburgers and glistening French fries.

"Ketchup's on your table."

"Thanks." Miles took the tray back to the table where Ro had already moved their drinks to the side.

"Good thing I don't have bad cholesterol. This is a heart attack in a basket." Ro squirted ketchup over her fries, and added more salt to the entire meal.

"Well, my cholesterol isn't so hot. They've already put me on statins." At her raised brow he nodded. "Yeah, I know, I don't look like I'd have a cholesterol problem, but it's genetic. My grandfather had a heart attack and died at age thirty-seven. My father had his at fifty, but he's still here, thank God. He works out nearly every day at the gym."

He thought about forcing the conversation back to her idea that their lovemaking had been a mistake, but they were both beat. It had been a long six days, and they had the memorial service to get through tomorrow.

He decided not to wait any longer. He bit into his burger and enjoyed the whole fatty thing. It was delicious.

But not as delicious as watching Ro devour hers.

"You were hungry, too," he said around bites.

"Famished." She took a sip of soda through her straw. "I don't eat like this all the time so it tastes even better when I do, if that makes sense."

"Absolutely."

They enjoyed a companionable silence except for the sound of their appreciative groans.

Ro wiped her mouth when she'd finished her burger.

"Now I know why you're at the gym all the time. I thought you were keeping in shape because you had to, to be able to function fully with your prosthetic."

"That's true to a point, but I've been a gym rat for years. I used to eat really clean to the point of being nuts about it. I've chilled out. I'm older, and after living through the blast that I did, I value moderation more than ever. I enjoy everything I want to, without overdoing it."

The smile she gave him made her eyes light up and he felt he could go run a marathon from the sheer pleasure it conveyed.

"What?" he asked warily.

"There's a lot more to you than meets the eye, Warrant. I thought you were an overmuscular, geeky, bomb-defusing dude. Now you're talking like some kind of tree hugger."

He laughed.

"Tree hugger. That's not one I've been accused of before." He threw her a wink and she giggled.

"Careful. If you have too much fun the Lieutenant Commander Brandywine we know may disappear."

Their eyes met and Miles sucked in a breath.

He'd loved a few women in his life, made love to several more. He knew what pure chemistry and lust were. He enjoyed them both immensely. But this thing between him and Ro was life-altering. Had been since the day he'd dumped the cat in her arms.

And he was going to jump her right here in this burger place if she kept looking at him like that.

"We need to address how to stay in constant contact with each other in the event anything unexpected happens with this case." Personal security was a safer topic with Ro since getting her naked in this diner was a nonstarter.

"We have our cell phones. Isn't that enough?" She toyed with her straw.

"Only if we're on a call with each other." He hated to think of her in trouble and unable to reach him. "I want you to promise me that if you find yourself in any kind of trouble you'll dial my number, and leave your phone on. That way I can listen to whatever's going on if can't talk."

"Sure, no problem. And you do the same." She glanced out the door of the diner, toward the street. In profile she was as beautiful as ever, her fine features accentuated by her long neck and short, pixie haircut.

She turned back to him as if she felt the weight of his stare. Her eyes were bright, her cheeks flushed.

"Ro."

"Yes?" Her voice was low and soft. She felt it, too.

"We're good together."

Ro collected their trash and carried the baskets to the counter since she didn't see a trash can in the dining area.

Breathe, girl, breathe.

It wasn't fair that Miles could break through her "B.S.," as he called it. Not only had he broken through her defenses, he'd turned her on in a wicked way.

You need to get back to the office.

Miles was quiet as he held the door open for her and let her exit the café first. She slipped her sunglasses out of her black uniform purse and perched them on her nose. The glare of the sunlight off the water was blinding without shades. Only after she had them on did she brave a glance at Miles.

His eyes were also covered by his sunglasses but his expression seemed neutral. Casual.

"I meant what I said, Ro." He leaned toward her as they walked side by side. "I happen to think we make a great couple."

She stopped and faced him.

"It's not that simple, Miles. What I started to say back there, before we were distracted by our food, is that I'm not willing to stick my neck out for a casual relationship with someone I'd have to see at work after we stop dating."

She watched his expression go from patient to incredulous to grim.

"Let me get this straight, Ro." Miles had his hands on his hips and she didn't miss how purely masculine his stance was. "You think that what we had Sunday night was *casual?*"

She'd pissed him off.

"Let me explain, Miles."

"No, you've said enough. It's my turn to do some talking. You agree, or at least don't disagree, that we make a good couple. But you're also certain we wouldn't amount to more than a casual fling. Do I have that right?"

"Maybe." Stubborn pride kept her from completely relenting.

He gave a low whistle. "You really have it all figured out, don't you, Commander?"

She ignored his dig at her self-righteous demeanor.

"No, I don't, but this isn't an intel brief, Miles. This is the truth. I'm a realist—it's my job to be factual. How many active-duty couples do you know who've made a go of it? How many do you know who hooked up once or twice, only to have to face each other in the office or on the hangar deck every day until one of them transferred? How awkward is that?"

Miles wasn't even looking at her anymore. He was looking past her, his expression resolute.

He shook his head as he rubbed the back of his neck. "Hell, Ro, you just assume that we'd have a few rolls in the hay, and that'd be it? Who do you think I am?"

She didn't say anything. Inexplicably, she found herself on the verge of tears.

Do not cry.

She felt a tear escape and slide down her cheek. She would have ignored it if she thought Miles wouldn't notice. But Miles noticed everything.

Damn EOD.

"Ro, what's this really about?" His voice was gentle, too gentle.

She wiped away more tears.

"I cry when I get really angry. It doesn't mean I'm sad or anything." Her explanation sounded feeble even to her.

Miles sighed and put his hand on her elbow to start them both walking again.

"Can I get one thing straight?"

"What?" She sniffled.

"How long does a casual fling last?" His smile made light of what had been a heavy conversation.

Miles had more to him than she'd ever given him credit for.

MILES AND LUCKY finished up their run early Tuesday evening with a walk to cool down. As his breathing slowed and Lucky relaxed her gait, Miles took in the forest scenery that met the edge of the road. Low-growing ferns kissed the sides of the larger trees, creating a bright green carpet in an otherwise sunless area. Except for a few shafts of light that pierced the canopy, the road was in perpetual shade.

Miles loved how Lucky sniffed only when something seemed different to her. She was a great dog who remained buoyant throughout their runs and just paused to check out the unfamiliar. She knew these roads better than he did, he mused.

They were a half mile from home, and Miles was starving. He'd grabbed a banana before they left but it was long gone after a seven-mile run. They reached his driveway and Miles bent to pick up the newspaper. As much as he relied on his iPad and laptop, he liked to read the *Whidbey Times* and know what was going on in the civilian community as well as the naval air station.

Lucky growled and the short brown hair on the back of her shoulders stood up in warning.

Miles froze and looked around. Sure enough, there was a stranger on his front porch.

"Can I help you?"

The stranger turned around and smiled.

"Miles, how are you? I see I've caught you at just the right time."

Commodore Sanders.

"Lucky, it's okay." He and Lucky walked up to the commodore.

"What can I do for you, sir? Would you like to come in and have a coffee?" Miles wasn't about to invite the commodore for a meal. He didn't have a lot of food in the house, and besides, this was unprecedented, to have his boss show up unexpectedly at his private home.

"No, no, I just wanted to thank you for what you've been doing." Sanders smiled benevolently at Lucky.

"Ro and I are doing our best."

"Yes, of course you are." Sanders stood there as though he couldn't wait to get off Miles's porch. Yet he stayed.

"Sir?"

"I'm sorry. This whole tragedy has me in a tailspin. Any chance you and Ro learned something new yesterday?"

"No, sir. We called it an early night. There wasn't anything actionable. We didn't get much out of the sheriff's department today, either." He wasn't going to tell the commodore that they'd implicated him by retelling Reis's story.

"What about the coroner's report?"

"Nothing other than what I gave you this afternoon, sir."

Sanders rubbed his chin. "Without it we can't have full closure. The longer we wait, the longer his family suffers."

"Understood, sir. We can't rush the lab results, though."

"Lab results?" Sanders had an odd expression on his face. This was the same officer who'd heard their report—the coroner took all kinds of blood and bodily fluid samples while Perez's body had still been on the beach.

"Blood, et cetera."

"Of course." The commodore slapped Miles on the shoulder. Lucky stiffened next to his good leg but, to her credit and thanks to his training, she didn't growl.

"Well, let me know the first news you get." Sanders took the five steps down to the pavement as quickly as Miles had seen anyone do it.

"Yes, sir."

Miles waited until the commodore had turned left at the end of his driveway and he knew Sanders couldn't see his porch. Then he unlocked his front door and let Lucky inside. He unhooked her collar. "Good girl. Watch the house."

He clicked the door shut behind him and ran down the

stairs and back up his driveway, looking down his road. He had a clear view for about a quarter of a mile, where he saw the commodore's trademark BMW. The commodore was just reaching his car.

Miles turned back and made his way inside. He didn't want Sanders to catch him spying.

But what the hell had Sanders been doing at his house?

Lucky wasn't in the foyer.

"Lucky?" He whistled. Lucky bounded up from the basement and barked at him. A short, sharp bark that he recognized as a tell, Lucky's way of letting him know something was wrong.

"What, girl?"

She barked again and wagged her tail before she bounded back down the basement steps. He followed her to the sliding glass door.

He hadn't put the bat in the door, in case he and Lucky got locked out. He'd lost his house key more than once on a run. But the bat was in the door as if he'd put it there, to lock it from the inside.

He went back over when he'd unlocked the dead bolt on the front door. He'd been in a hurry—had he heard the bolt click?

No.

Sanders had been in his house.

But why?

He went back upstairs and glanced around his living room. The television was on, a precaution he automatically followed to give the impression that someone was home.

"A lot of good that did, Luck," he said to the dog who followed him from place to place.

His laptop was still open on the kitchen counter.

"Son of a bitch." He could kick himself. He'd left the screen saver off because he'd been following a recipe for slow-cooker stew and didn't want the screen blacking out when he was in the middle of adding spices.

Sanders could have seen everything Miles had perused on the internet for the past several sessions. He scanned his open browser windows. Nothing incriminating—but he didn't like it that he'd left himself so vulnerable.

Of course, he never would have expected his boss on Whidbey Island to become the enemy.

CHAPTER EIGHTEEN

RO RELISHED THE QUIET of her home. It had only been less than a week since her life had turned upside down. She wished she could blame the Perez investigation for all of it but she knew that was futile.

It would be even easier to blame Krissy and Dick for showing up, acting as though they were fighting—just to help her save face—in an effort to find out how she was really doing. And the impending visit by her mother wasn't something she looked forward to, either.

Her family was convinced she was crazy. They'd never understood her need to get out of Trenton, to see the world. Of course it was natural for them to think she'd never make it without them...and without her fantasy of a life to return to.

She could never go back to Trenton. It wasn't the location. It was her family. And it was who she'd been before she'd discovered what she was capable of.

She *had* thought she'd found herself, her dreams, in the navy. Now, she wondered if this 'getting to know oneself' was actually a lifelong occupation.

She held up her knitting to the light. The deep red hue of the lamb's wool turned fuchsia when backlit by the sun's rays. This hat would be great for a woman with a deeper skin tone. As she moved the needles through the stitches, her mind wandered. She'd like to make herself a sweater for next fall and this was a good time to get yarn on sale.

Thoughts of baby items popped into her consciousness as she remembered Krissy was pregnant.

She was going to be an aunt.

No matter how much Krissy had hurt her and annoyed her over the years, this was about blood. Her baby niece or nephew deserved a nice hand-knitted outfit from their auntie.

Krissy had left one of her ubiquitous notes on the refrigerator indicating that she and Dick had gone for a long day-trip into Seattle and not to expect them back for dinner. Ro planned on eating something light and easy and simply enjoying a quiet night to herself. Tomorrow was going to be hell with the memorial service to get through.

A glass of wine might help. She stood up to stretch and see if she had an open bottle in the refrigerator. The harsh knock followed by her doorbell startled her. She dropped her knitting on the sofa and ignored her rapidly beating heart. It wasn't like Miles to come over without calling.

She squinted through the peephole.

It wasn't Miles.

She unfastened her chain lock and opened the front door.

"Karen, what a surprise!"

Karen Sanders stood on the front porch. Her hair was askew and her eyes darted back and forth.

Was that booze she smelled?

"Oh, uh, hi. Glad to see you." Karen stepped over the threshold and into her front entryway.

Ro accepted Karen's superficial hug. To do anything else would have been too awkward in the small foyer and with just the two of them there.

"So this is how you live. Really nice, Roanna. Cuter than I'd imagined for you."

What the hell?

Ro remained silent. She didn't want to appear rude, nor

did she want to encourage Karen to stay any longer than necessary.

"I'm sorry to crash in on you like this, but there's something I have to talk to you about." Karen looked up from a knickknack Ro had purchased in Bahrain.

"Okay, well, why don't you come on in? I was just about to, um, have a cup of tea." She ditched her plan for her own glass of wine. She really didn't want to be drinking with the commodore's wife. Especially since Karen smelled as if she'd already had her afternoon cocktails.

"Oh, I don't need anything. I'm just here to talk to you."

"Let's sit at the kitchen table, then."

They entered the kitchen area and Karen sat down at the round table that was covered with a purple linen cloth.

"Oh, this is so cozy!" Ro recognized her comment as Karen-speak for "too small for me." Karen was her boss's wife, so it was important for Ro to be professional and gracious with her. During duty hours or at official functions. Not off duty in the privacy of her own home.

There is no off duty for a naval officer. Some of the first words she'd learned as a plebe at the naval academy.

"I like it. Are you sure you don't want anything? I can make up a cup of coffee if you'd rather have that than tea?"

"Coffee? Okay, I'll take it. As long as you're having one."

"I'll have tea. I have a machine that makes both, lickety split."

Five minutes and two steaming mugs later, Ro broached the unspoken tension.

"So what brought you out here tonight, Karen?"

Karen gulped down some of her coffee before she answered.

"I understand that you and Miles are working on the Perez case. That's why I saw you two at his house the other night."

Tread carefully. You work for her husband, not her.

"Miles and I are helping things move along, yes. But neither of us are CACOs, of course."

"Nor are you NCIS or the sheriff's department." Karen's eyes, although bloodshot, sparked with a keen intelligence.

"No, we're not." Ro sipped her tea and wished in vain it was her leftover chardonnay.

"But you're working with them, right?"

"No, not really. We're cooperating with all of the LEAs, just like anyone else who knew Perez." Ro wasn't going to reveal the assignment she and Miles had been given by the commodore.

"I need to tell you something that I can't count on Leo to admit, and I want to make sure he doesn't get into trouble for anything he's not responsible for."

This was getting dangerously deep, fast. Her fingers itched for her mobile phone. If only she could text Miles and have him here to listen with her.

"Okay. But maybe you want to tell both Miles and me?"

"No." Karen's answer was unequivocal. She'd come to see Roanna.

"All right." Ro tried not to squirm in her seat. Karen's pained expression made her own muscles tighten with anxiety.

"Leo and I aren't doing well, as a couple." Karen sent her a blank stare and then brought her gaze back to her coffee mug. "I don't suppose that's earth-shattering news. A lot of navy marriages don't make it."

"I'm sorry, Karen."

"I've decided to leave him." Ouch. This was getting too personal. Karen didn't even like her, so why was she sharing this?

"Does the commodore know?"

"Yes, but he's in denial." Karen guzzled her coffee as

though it were cold water. No doubt it was a lot weaker than whatever she'd ingested earlier in the day.

"I see." Ro didn't know what else to say.

"No, you don't 'see,' Roanna. There's more to me than meets the eye." Karen squared her shoulders. "I'm gay."

Karen stared at Ro as if she expected her to explode or faint. When she did neither, Karen continued.

"For your generation it's not a big deal, is it? But for us, for me—it wasn't something that was ever talked about. I didn't understand I had choices in life other than what my mother had chosen for herself. The only difference between us is that I got a degree and had a decent career for a few years, before Leo and I had Stefanie."

Karen brushed her hair out of her eyes. Ro noted how odd it was to see Karen like this—not at all her usual polished self.

"Once Stefanie came along, she was the center of my world. As Leo and I grew further apart, I fought to keep Stefanie's needs first."

"I don't mean to be obtuse, Karen, but I think you need to be talking to the commodore about this. And I don't see what this has to do with Petty Officer Perez."

"Let me finish." The glint in her eyes was an indication of a steely strength Ro had never given her credit for.

"It was hard for me to accept, at first. That I'd fallen in love with a woman. It's been lonely in my marriage for several tours. It's always about Leo and what he needs done at specific times in his career—none of this is news to you, I know. I worried what my discovery would cost Stefanie. Kids are so mean to other kids."

Ro was relieved to hear that at least Karen had been looking out for her daughter. As for the commodore's career needs, Ro silently sent up a prayer of gratitude that she didn't have to kowtow to any man or his navy career; the only career she needed to worry about was her own, thank you very much.

"I needed to make sure it wasn't just the person I'd fallen for, to prove that I couldn't have as intimate a physical experience with a man as I'd had with a woman."

Ro fought to stay put in her chair. This was way out of her expertise. She was happy that Karen had come to terms with who she was, but still didn't see why she had to be dragged into the most personal details of her boss's life.

"To make it short, I had a brief, one-night affair with a man. It was horrible and a total waste of time. I was drunk and, of course, that made it worse."

The self-recrimination on Karen's face left Ro cold.

Karen smirked at Ro and revealed the name Ro had already guessed.

"I had the affair with José Perez."

"When was this?"

"A month ago."

"So why does this have to be such a big secret—I mean, as far as you and the commodore are concerned? You're not on active duty. You didn't do anything illegal. But…what if the commodore sought reprisal from Petty Officer Perez?"

"Leo didn't kill Perez. Leo's stubborn, has a terrible temper and can be single-minded, but he's not a murderer."

Ro marveled at how a woman who'd been so unhappy in her marriage could still defend the partner who'd no doubt added to her angst.

"Look, Roanna, I'm not a saint—far from it. The entire island knows I drink too much. Some might say I'm an alcoholic. I've got enough reason to drink for all of us. I've spent years in a loveless marriage to a spouse who's the wrong sex for me and I haven't been able to pursue my career. If not for being a mother, what else would I have?" Karen addressed the empty space between them.

Ro chewed on the inside of her lip. She really needed to talk this one over with Miles.

"I need you, and Miles, to let the sheriff's department or NCIS, whoever, know that Leo isn't a suspect. Once word gets out that our marriage is over, or if anyone finds out I had an affair with José Perez, the cops are going to pin Leo for a crime of passion." Karen laughed, a harsh, sneering sound. "Pretty funny, isn't it? That they'd call it a crime of passion when we haven't had any passion in so long?"

Ro didn't find anything remotely funny about Karen's declarations, but the way Karen was behaving, she didn't want to comment. She wanted Karen to finish telling her whatever she needed to, and then get out of her house.

"I suppose you're wondering why I told you. It'd be easy for no one to find out about my indiscretion, right?" Tears pooled in Karen's eyes. Ro tasted blood as her teeth grasped the inside of her mouth once too often. "Well, I had to tell the woman I love what I'd done. She was entitled to know. I've probably lost her forever. But while I was telling her, we weren't alone. I didn't realize until it was too late that other people were in the office who might have heard us. So if anyone did, anyone who's aware of what's going on with the Perez case, they could put two and two together and think Leo found out."

"Are you sure someone overheard you? Did you tell Leo any of this?"

"I saw the way people looked at me when I ran out of the office. Trust me, they heard." She fingered her mug. "Of course I told Leo—but only after Perez was dead. That's how I know he didn't do it."

Ro listened for another fifteen minutes as Karen got the rest of her transgressions off her chest. It was the longest quarter hour of Ro's life. When Karen asked to use the bathroom, Ro jumped on it and encouraged her to use the one upstairs. As soon as she was alone, she sank to the kitchen floor, her back against the wall, listening as Karen went upstairs and closed the bathroom door.

It seemed to her that Karen was getting more sober but Ro couldn't be sure. It was possible that she was sober enough to drive, but Ro didn't want to take the chance. Karen didn't need a DUI to add to her personal woes, and Ro wasn't going to allow a drunk to get behind the wheel.

She'd either have to put Karen in a taxi or drive her home. It was another miserable complication and definitely took the pleasure out of Ro's quiet night, but allowing Karen to drive drunk wasn't an option.

Ro waited until she heard Karen running water in the bathroom. Then she leaped off the floor and got her phone from the living room end table. Her hands shook as she hit the speed dial for Miles's number. She saw belatedly that he'd left her several text messages. She'd had her notification alerts turned off.

"Where are you?"

"Here, at my house. You have to come over. Or, no, wait, I can come there."

"Slow down, Ro. Are you safe?"

"Safe? Yes, I mean—" The front door shook as several loud knocks reverberated through her front hall.

"Ro, what is that?"

"I don't know. The commodore's wife, Karen, is upstairs—I don't know who's at the door."

"Go check your peephole. Be quiet about it."

She didn't reply but crept over to the front door. She was grateful she'd left the lights off and the only lights that filtered into the living room were from the kitchen.

"Ro, who is it?"

She looked through the peephole and gasped.

"It's the commodore."

"Ro, don't answer the door. Does he see you?"

She looked through the peephole again. The commodore's eye was huge in the lens. She jumped back.

"Ro, I know you're in there. Open up!"

"He's pretty pissed off. I think he's going to break in!" She breathed deeply, trying to fend off her panic.

Miles was silent.

"Miles? Miles!" She hissed into the phone. He didn't answer.

The doorbell rang and the commodore pounded on the door again.

She stood in the darkness of the foyer, shaking and wondering how long it would take Miles to get there.

She had complete faith that he would.

KAREN CAME DOWNSTAIRS as soon as Ro placed the phone on the hall table.

"Are you expecting your husband?"

Karen flipped her hair out of her eyes and frowned.

"Leo's here?" She darted past Ro and put her hand on the front doorknob.

"Wait!" Ro grabbed her shoulder and spun her around.

Karen yanked her bony shoulder out of Ro's hand and snarled, "Don't touch me! I can handle my husband." Karen turned back to the door and Ro let her go.

She knew Miles had to be nearby; he only lived a few blocks away.

The door opened and Commodore Sanders's arm was in midair, aiming to pound on the door again.

"What the hell are you doing, Leo?"

The commodore's stare went from Karen to Ro and back.

"I've been searching for you." He let his arm drop to his side. "Are you okay?"

"Am I okay?" Karen mimicked the commodore so well that Ro bit back a smile.

"You've been gone since dinner." He lowered his voice. "Can we please go home now?"

"I'll come home when I'm ready."

"Are you sure you should be driving, Karen?"

"Go to hell, Leo."

"Okay, let's all chill," Ro interjected. "Commodore, why don't you come in? Would you like a coffee or something?"

"No, thanks, Ro. I'm sorry if there's been a problem here." He gave Ro one of his "we'll talk later, I've got this" looks. It was a nonverbal message mastered by all commanding officers. The confident nod that was sometimes even accompanied by a wink.

Ro contemplated breathing a sigh of relief. If she could get rid of both Sanderses before Miles got here, she'd be able to relax and assure him that she'd handled it, after all.

"Leo, I've told Ro about the divorce, and that I'm gay."

Ro winced.

"Let's keep our personal issues just that, okay, Karen?"

Karen let out a string of expletives that rivaled the worst blue streak Ro had ever heard on the carrier deck.

The commodore's expression remained neutral, considering that his wife was dressing him down in front of one of his subordinates.

Ro shivered. With the door open, the evening air swirled around them and the temperature couldn't be more than fifty degrees Fahrenheit.

Maybe she was a *sweat*—navy-speak for worrywart—a nervous wreck who couldn't handle a real-world mission to save her life.

Bullcrap.

"I think it's an excellent idea that you two go and work

out whatever you need to. Karen and I have had enough time together tonight."

Karen turned to face her.

"I wasn't done."

"Perhaps not, but I am." She wasn't going to state the obvious—that they were all going to Perez's funeral tomorrow.

"Whatever." Karen looked around the foyer. "Where did I leave my—"

"Here." Ro thrust Karen's designer bag into her midsection. Karen had no choice but to clutch the bag to her.

"Come on, Karen." In the glare of the porch light the commodore looked tired. Not for the first time since she'd been assigned the investigation, Ro wondered how she'd handle what he asked her to do.

But there was a good chance Sanders had committed bribery and defrauded the United States government.

He might have committed murder.

She fought the shivers that continued to race up her spine. Where the hell was Miles?

"Good night." She waited until they were off her porch and down the driveway. Before she could close her front door, as if he materialized from her thoughts, Miles came out from around the side of her house and bounded silently onto her steps.

"Hey! Quick, let me in."

She stepped aside as he slipped in through the door. She gave one last glance over her shoulder to ensure that the Sanderses hadn't turned around and seen Miles.

They were gone.

"IT'S A DAMN good thing Karen Sanders wasn't carrying a weapon. I could have been dead ten times over with the length of time it took you to get here!"

"I was here. You left your phone on, just like we talked

about at the diner." Miles appeared completely unperturbed by the fact that she could have been killed.

She had left it on as they'd discussed. Just in case something like this happened. But she'd forgotten that she'd done so in the heat of her conversation with Karen.

"You're right." She shook her head. "I left it on for you."

"I heard it all, Ro, except for the few things the commodore said. Did I miss anything important?"

"From the commodore? No." She looked at him closely.

Now that the Sanderses were gone and she was regaining her sense of security, she was able to take in Miles's appearance. Clad in a black hoodie and equally dark jeans, he filled the description of a man she'd never want to meet alone in a dark alley. He had a Bluetooth earpiece that verified his claim that he'd listened to everything.

"Wait—why did you put the fear of God into me about the commodore being here?"

"You mean, why did I bother telling you not to open the door when you were going to do it, anyway?" His exasperation with her was evident.

"Karen opened the door. She was very convincing about her ability to snap him into shape."

"Don't get cute, Ro. You could have been hurt, or worse. You don't have a weapon, do you? Your baseball bat doesn't count."

"Karen's three sheets to the wind. Or least she was, when she first showed up. The commodore went all shades of crazy when he saw her. I think he's had a rough week." She heard her own voice and knew her underlying anxiety was perfectly clear to Miles.

"Funny, Ro." The muscle leaping below the surface of his jaw implied his belief to the contrary.

"Go ahead. Call me a sweat."

"Tell me you weren't sweating it a little bit, Ro. Tell me

you had complete confidence that neither of the Sanderses were going to do something violent."

She met his gaze and swore.

"Which brings us back to why you were camped out next to my house instead of coming to the door to help diffuse a potentially violent situation?"

"I didn't want to tip our hand. I was here, ready to jump in if I had to. But Sanders showed up at my house first, and after he left, I figured out that he'd broken in. I think he wanted to see if Karen had been there, but then he took some extra liberties with my laptop and the papers on my desk."

Ro blanched. "That's awful! He must be suspicious of us and what we're figuring out. But why would Karen go to your place?"

"Same reason she came here. To tell one of us whatever she thinks we need to know about her involvement, and Sanders's culpability—or lack of it—in the case. All from her perspective, of course. She probably doesn't have a clue that he might have been doctoring maintenance records."

"Probably not. So you think the commodore followed her to your place, had a look at your computer and then followed her here?" She shuddered to think of Sanders lurking on her property while she and Karen were inside, vulnerable.

Miles raised his brows in exasperation. "Ro, come on. You're intel. He doesn't know what the hell she's going to say from one minute to the next—she's obviously an alcoholic who is off her rocker about what her navy wife duties are. He's been covering for her drinking binges for years from what our colleagues at the wing say. Now he's trying to keep her under control while he's busy putting out fires."

"Fine. You win. I need some kind of protection. But I'm not keeping a loaded gun in my house. Do you?"

"No, but I have a dog, remember?"

"You're *babysitting* Lucky. What will you do when she goes back to her owner?"

"Ro, this isn't pertinent. I do think it'd be smart for you to consider getting a dog."

She shook her head.

"Too hard. What would I do when I PCS?" She'd seen friends with pets go through hell when they received their permanent change of station orders to far-flung corners of the globe. They'd had to jump through numerous hoops to bring their pets with them.

"Ro, at some point you have to realize that your safety and your home life is worth whatever extra effort it takes. No, moving wouldn't be as easy, but what's so great about being able to pick up and leave a place as though you never lived there at all?"

"I don't think this is pertinent, Warrant." She used his own tactic against him. "Let's keep our focus on what's important."

"So the commodore's wife is gay." Miles cracked his knuckles. "I didn't see that one coming. It's kind of obvious that they've been on the rocks for a while, with her drinking adding to the problem."

Ro sighed. "It's a tough life, holding a marriage together while raising a kid and moving all over the country for the navy."

"True, but none of us are forced into this, Ro. We're all volunteers."

"*We're* volunteers, Miles, but our families aren't. No one knows how difficult being married to a sailor's going to be until they've gone through a few tours."

"To get back to what Karen Sanders told you—" he stretched and sat up straighter on the couch "—I don't think Sanders knew about her and Perez, not until she told him. If it's even true. Her story could be a figment of her drunken imagination."

"I thought about that, too, but I do believe her. She had a quickie with Perez—why would she make something like that up?" Ro shuddered. "That guy couldn't keep it in his pants, could he?"

"Maybe not, but he still didn't deserve to die, Ro."

"I'm not saying he did. I don't see the commodore giving two shits what his wife does, frankly. I think it's wishful thinking on her part that anyone would even suspect he'd killed Perez out of jealousy. She said herself that their marriage fizzled out a long time ago."

"Other than too much information on the commodore's marriage, we don't have anything new, anything we could tell Ramsey, do we?"

"No, I don't think so. How about you?"

"I agree. Nothing new to report." He glanced down at his watch. "Let's go around to all of your windows and doors, make sure they're locked. Then I'm leaving." She couldn't interpret his expression.

"I can lock up by myself, Miles." The sooner he left, the better. Her best resolutions turned to ashes when he was near.

"I'll feel better if I do it."

Miles took ten minutes to check her locks, and he tried the dead bolt on the front door from the outside. When he was confident her house was secure, he stood in the foyer. Taller, tougher and sexier than ever.

"Ro, come here."

She looked at him but stayed a few steps away.

"I'm not going to do anything you don't want, Ro." Oh, but that was the problem. She wanted him to do everything he'd done Sunday night and more. Again and again.

She walked toward him and he grasped her hands and held them to his chest.

"Are you ready for tomorrow?"

"Ready? No way. How can you ever be ready for a colleague's memorial service?" She paused. "Stop worrying about me, Miles. I'm a big girl."

"I know you are, Ro." He leaned in and softly kissed her lips. She ached for him to make the chaste kiss more but he didn't.

"Good night, Ro. Turn the dead bolt as soon as I leave."

She watched him turn and walk out her door.

CHAPTER NINETEEN

"I'M SORRY TO HAVE to call you both in here. I know you're up to your asses in alligators with the case." Commodore Sanders was dressed in a white formal shirt and black tie; his uniform jacket hung on the back of his office door, ready for the memorial service.

Ro and Miles stood by his desk in their service dress blues. There was no doubt what the commodore had called them into his office to discuss just hours before Petty Officer Perez was laid to rest.

"I deeply regret any distress my wife caused you last night, Ro. She's unpredictable at best, and when she's been drinking all bets are off." He tried to cover his discomfort with a chuckle but it failed miserably.

"It's not an issue, sir. I've already forgotten about it."

"Even the part where she told you she was gay?"

Roanna didn't respond.

Commodore Sanders put his face in his hands for a long moment, then dragged his palms over his cheeks and looked up at both of them.

"It's one thing when a marriage ends. We see it all the time in here." He motioned to his desk and the piles of papers in neat stacks around its periphery. "It's part of everyday life and the navy isn't immune to it.

"But she thinks we fell apart because she's gay." He shook his head. "It sure explains the arctic temperatures in our bedroom these past several years."

Ro's stomach tensed at Sanders's terrible attempt to make light of his personal troubles. Of Karen's obvious suffering. The fact that he was so worried about his damned self on the day his sailor was being buried only highlighted his narcissism.

"Sir, we need to get ready to head over to the base chapel." Miles had been silent until now.

"Did you tell him—" Sanders motioned his head toward Miles "—what my wife said?"

Ro stiffened. Was this the commodore's attempt to figure out just how close she and Miles were?

"Only the pertinent details, sir." In truth, Ro believed that none of what Karen had told her last night pertained to the Perez case. Not even the alleged affair. What difference did it make if it happened? Perez had been close to getting a divorce and having affairs with all kinds of women if they were to believe what Lydia had told them.

"It's okay if you said something to Miles, Ro. I put you two together on this, so I can't expect you to keep information from each other." He stared at Miles, and Ro wondered what Miles had done that got under the commodore's skin.

Maybe you're getting under his skin, too. You're too close to the truth—that he's a fraudulent bastard who's had his command's records forged.

Ro had had enough.

"Is that all, sir?"

"Yes, that's all, Roanna." Sanders nodded for them to depart.

CONTRARY TO THE somberness of the occasion, the sky was cerulean blue without a cloud in sight as Ro walked up the sidewalk to the base chapel. She'd come over from the wing spaces on her own, as had many of the staff. It wasn't a time for socializing.

They waited to enter the church as hundreds of mourners funneled into the A-framed building. Ro noted the intense quiet not commonly associated with such a large group of sailors.

She'd been to far too many of these services over the past decade; they all had. It was the price of war, and every single person in uniform knew that.

Ro was only beginning to see the deeper costs. Going to the Perez home had opened her heart to the suffering the surviving family members endured. Anita Perez was unique in that her marriage was already ending, or had ended, from what she'd told them. Yet it didn't appear to diminish her pain. Ro wore the physical proof of Anita's pain on her face, in the form of stitches.

As they filed into the chapel they diverged into two lines and filled the pews accordingly. Ro felt a tug on her sleeve as she was about to slide into the next available pew.

"We've saved you a seat closer to the front." Miles had walked around the back of the chapel and across a still-empty pew to reach her. She followed him through the pew and up the side aisle to a row only four or five from the altar.

She took her seat and inhaled deeply before she looked around. Most of the wing staff and dozens of enlisted sailors from other squadrons within the wing had crowded into the chapel. The chapel's roof reached heavenward with its exposed wooden beams that glowed in the soft sunlight, but even the majesty of the quintessentially Northwest architecture lent little consolation to the funeral attendees.

It was never easy to lose a shipmate, but it was worse when it was assumed to be a PTSD-related suicide. They'd all been touched by the war, and a majority of them had wrestled with their own post-traumatic stress demons. Suicide was rampant in the military, to the point that each service had regular suicide awareness briefings for all its members—mandatory workshops that lasted anywhere from an hour to a full day. Suicide prevention among returning war veterans garnered attention from the highest levels of government, and for good reason.

The nation was losing too many of its most promising young citizens. Citizens who'd stepped up and put country before self.

All the prevention in the world hadn't stopped Perez from taking the plunge off the West Beach cliff. Ro had heard the commodore say the same thing repeatedly over the past few days. She'd felt compassion for Sanders in those moments, even knowing that he most likely committed fraud over the aircraft-frame maintenance stats. It was hard on a leader when one of his own was in pain or suffering. Perez was dead and nothing the commodore did could bring him back.

Of course, if Sanders *had* committed murder, her compassion was moot. She forced the harsh thought away. There'd be time to figure out the truth surrounding Perez's death later. This was the time to focus on his passing.

Ro sat next to Miles in the midst of their colleagues. They wore their service dress blues as the navy hadn't yet switched over to summer whites. Not until Memorial Day.

They stood as the starting music swelled on the classic organ. The pipes resonated with the grief that echoed in each one of them, but especially the Perez family. They were brought in from the side altar door and seated in the front row. Ro made out Anita, her two children and her parents. There were other people with them who she assumed were extended family and close friends.

Anita had mourned the death of her marriage a while ago, but it didn't make the situation any less tragic. Especially for two innocent children whose father was taken from them too early.

The casket came up the center aisle in a classic military

procession with all the honors due a fallen hero. Ro bowed her head as the casket moved past their pew and she welcomed the sure, warm grasp of Miles's hand, uniform or not.

The chaplain was at the front of the center aisle, and raised her hand to begin the service. Then she blessed the casket.

The chaplain was a navy captain and of a nondenominational Christian faith. Ro tried to focus on the chaplain's soothing words. She had obviously found her calling as she managed to create tiny rays of hope even in these dark circumstances.

It occurred to Ro that she'd found her own calling as an intelligence officer—she could never have come up with the words to comfort family and friends of the deceased the way Captain Brunello did. But the flag-draped casket made her question whether her calling was the same as it had been a decade and a half ago. She was free to leave the navy at any point; she didn't owe time for graduate school and had long ago completed her obligatory service.

Had Perez ever found his calling? She didn't imagine that he had, he'd died so young.

Several of Petty Officer Perez's colleagues stood up to make their own statements after Perez's brother gave the eulogy. Ro listened for anything that was contrary to what she and Miles had already learned over the past few days but didn't hear anything out of the ordinary.

What she did find interesting was that each speaker spoke of what a great guy Perez had been and how he'd helped his fellow sailors whenever possible. A few of the sailors mentioned that they'd met him in a support group that Ro assumed was AA. They said that Perez had taken them under his wing and walked with them on their journey to sobriety.

"It doesn't add up. How could he be this great guy and do what he probably did?" she whispered to Miles.

"We all have several sides to us, Ro," Miles whispered back, and she fought to not close her eyes and simply absorb the warmth of his breath on her face, the minty scent he always seemed to have. That was due to the ginger mints he was fond of. She'd seen the tin of candies in his truck.

"Either I'm tired, crazy or these people knew a different guy than we've been finding out about."

"We'll work it out later." Miles was squeezed next to her on the uncomfortable wooden pew, so it was easy enough for him to hold her hand without anyone noticing. He squeezed tightly for several seconds and met her gaze.

Trust me.

His silent plea was as loud as if he'd used the microphone on the altar's podium.

Ro wasn't ready to accept his request, or figure out if he was trying to express something more profound than his shared sorrow. She turned her attention back to the front of the church.

The commodore stood up from his seat next to Karen and walked to the podium. He looked up from his prepared statement and his stare seemed fixated on her. Steely gray and none too pleased, judging by his disapproving expression. She gulped. Could he really see her and Miles from several rows away?

"Petty Officer José Perez served his country with the utmost dignity and respect." Sanders turned to Anita and her kids. "You can be proud of your husband's service until the end of your days, Mrs. Perez." He went on to address the children and ended with, "Your father loved you both very much."

Ro sighed. Of course the commodore had to make those remarks. He'd been Perez's last boss, after all. But maybe he should have asked around before he tried to paint Perez as the perfect family guy. It wasn't necessary and it was downright shameful to put Anita through this. The kids were one thing; they needed to know their father loved them and that he'd died doing an honorable job for his country.

It wasn't so honorable if what CMC Reis told you is true.

She tried to ignore the thought.

"What?" Miles whispered.

She shook her head.

"Nothing."

How could she begin to explain that she was thinking horrible things about the deceased? And that in this moment of grieving she was gaining clarity on her own life—if only she had the courage to take advantage of it?

The commodore stood in front of the altar, ready to present Anita Perez with the flag from Perez's casket. They'd opted not to do the usual graveside ceremony at the funeral service, as Perez's will stipulated he be cremated and his ashes scattered at sea. Anita had requested that the casket stay in place in the chapel as everyone left, giving the mourners each a chance to file by Perez's remains and pay their final respects.

When it was her turn to stand in front of the casket for a few seconds, Ro did what she always did at military funerals. She placed her gloved hand on the casket and said a silent prayer that José Perez had found lasting peace.

Ro looked up as she turned to walk out of the church and for the second time caught Sanders eyeing her.

He knows.

She had no idea how or when, but somehow Sanders knew that she and Miles suspected him. Maybe he'd found out they'd been with the command master chief. Lydia's statements had been damning, and if he knew she'd told them about her affair—and knew, therefore, that they hadn't told him—he'd have every right to be angry with her and Miles.

Unless he was guilty of bribery and falsifying government documents. Then his anger would be based on fear.

And dangerous.

RO LEFT THE CHAPEL and walked out to the side parking lot. There wouldn't be a flyover with the missing man formation since Perez hadn't been aircrew. All she wanted was to get back to the office and change into her civilian clothes. The commodore was giving the entire wing the afternoon off.

"Ro, wait up." Miles fell into step next to her. "Can I bum a ride? I walked here."

"Of course." She pushed the unlock button on her key fob twice and motioned to the passenger's side. "It's open."

Once inside her small fuel-friendly sedan she turned to Miles. With his size, he looked like a walking stick insect squeezed into a baby-food jar.

He gave her a bemused smile.

"This is why I prefer to drive, by the way. I fit in my truck without breaking my neck."

Ro thought he looked adorable—and completely silly. Her laughter caught her off guard, and when her chuckles turned into all-out mirth she clasped her hand over her mouth.

"I'm sorry, Miles, you just seem so uncomfortable," she gasped between howls.

"Hey, if it can make you laugh on a day like today, it's worth my spine, believe me."

As if he'd flicked an invisible switch, her laughter turned to soft sobs.

"Aww, come here, babe." He pulled her into what had to be the most awkward position for a hug. But it was the best hug she'd ever had. He held her while she quietly cried into his shoulder, never telling her to be careful of his jacket while her eye makeup ran all over it.

"You're very kind, Miles." She sniffed.

"I'll blame that on the sadness of the day. You'll remember why you hate me in the morning."

"Don't make jokes at a time like this. It's… uncouth."

"That's my girl. See, your fight's coming back." He pulled back as much as the cramped passenger seat allowed and raised her chin with his finger. His long, lean finger. She sighed.

"Ro, I can't kiss you. Not here, not in uniform. So don't give me that look."

"How am I—?"

He shook his head, a slight but definite move.

"It doesn't matter. I'd love nothing more than to kiss the sadness away until all you think about is me, us. But I'm not going to take 'us' anywhere you don't want it to go."

She drew back and flipped down her visor mirror.

"I look like hell."

"Your eye was much worse a few days ago."

She stuck out her tongue at him.

"Thanks a lot, comrade."

He laughed and the low, warm sound of it soothed her aching muscles and the weight that had sat on her chest since she'd woken Monday morning and realized she'd gotten in too deep, too fast—with the worst possible match for her.

It's not that he's the worst match for you. It's because he just may be the best.

She studied him as she pressed on the clutch and turned the key in the ignition.

"Let's get back to the wing, shall we?"

Ro backed her car out of its space and switched to first gear, ready to leave the parking lot.

"Ro, stop!" Miles had his arm in front of her.

She stepped on the brake and clutch.

"Why?"

He didn't reply; he didn't have to. She followed his line of sight to where a base police car and an Island County sheriff's cruiser had parked sideways, lights rotating, in front of the main sidewalk to the chapel.

"What the heck?" She craned around Miles's head to see what the big deal was.

Two sheriff's deputies were escorting a handcuffed woman to the cruiser.

"Is that Master Chief Reis?" She barely breathed the words.

"Yes." Miles's mouth was a grim straight line and the vein on the side of his temple stood out.

"Why on earth would they do this here, now, when the family can see it?"

"The family's not out here, Ro. They're in the chapel with Perez's remains." Miles turned to her, his eyes a stormy blue. "They did it in front of the wing, hell, most of the base."

"Sending a message? And what would they arrest her on?"

"What we told Ramsey must've had some truth to it—maybe it's about the airframe issue."

"No, it can't be. That's navy business and she'd be court martialed—the civilian LEAs wouldn't want to touch it with a ten-meter pole."

Miles nodded. "You're absolutely right. That leaves us with one conclusion," he said.

Ro gasped. "You don't think she killed him, do you?"

RO PRACTICALLY CRAWLED into her house after she drove home from work. The grief of Perez's funeral had been topped by seeing a woman she'd thought of as the best command master chief in the fleet arrested in front of all her subordinates.

The vision haunting her the most was that of the commodore as she and Miles had pulled away from the chapel. The sheer relief on his face was palpable. As if he could go on now, as if maybe the entire wing could put this behind them.

As if the death of a sailor was nothing more than an aircraft mishap to be studied, filed and forgotten.

The house smelled of apples and cinnamon.

Oh, no. Not now.

"Roanna! Honey child, I've missed you so much!" She was enveloped in one of Delores's immense hugs, a huge smack of a kiss bestowed upon her cheek. Her injured cheek.

"Oh, my, honey—Krissy said you had a shiner but I had no idea you had stitches, too! Come over here and let me see you."

"Mom, I'm not in the mood for this."

"You're never in the mood for your family, Roanna. What else is new? Now turn around so I can see how you really are. Are you eating enough? You're still running, aren't you?"

Ro stared at Delores, her mother and the source of many hours of therapy that she'd paid for out of pocket so it wouldn't show up on her navy medical records. Even though it was perfectly acceptable to receive counseling while on active duty, Ro had preferred to keep her anonymity.

She bit back a grin. Miles would be shocked to know the rigid officer he pegged her for had broken some rules of her own.

Delores looked good. At least her hair was no longer that awful "silver-fox" gray her mother had called it. Delores was wearing it short, like Ro's, but instead of her natural brunette, she sported a particular shade of red that reminded Ro of the eggplant-hued dyes that were common in many parts of Europe.

"You look good, Mom."

"Thank you, honey. You've been better, but you look

okay, too." Always a twist, always a thorn with any compliment.

"When did you get in?" Ro kicked off her boots and shrugged out of her fleece hoodie. She left both in the hallway. She'd pick them up later.

"This morning. Krissy and Dick came to get me in Seattle. You know I hate those pesky commuter puddle-jumpers."

"They're safer than driving two hours on I-5, Mom." Ro headed to the kitchen for a glass of sparkling water and Delores followed on her heels.

"What smells so delicious?" Of course she knew the answer. Mom always made her an apple crumb pie wherever she'd visited her, be it in the States or overseas. It had been Ro's favorite as a kid, while Krissy preferred a fluffy lemon meringue pie. Ro liked to think she was more practical than anyone in the family, even when it came to dessert choices.

"You know what it is, honey. Your favorite! Dick and Krissy are out at the grocery store getting the best vanilla ice cream they can find to go with it. I said to be sure it's made from real cream, because I don't want to put a chemical cocktail on top of a homemade treat!"

"I'm sure you did." Ro held up her bottle of water. "Can I get you something, Mom?"

"Oh, no, honey, you know me. I make myself right at home wherever I go."

That she did.

"Mom, please don't take this the wrong way, but I really need to lie down. I have a splitting headache and this past week has been awful."

"Oh, no, you're not fighting with your new boyfriend, are you?"

"I don't have a boyfriend, Mom."

"Krissy said you do, and that he's perfect for you. All big and strong and very navylike."

Holy sockeye salmon, was nothing sacred in this family?

Apparently not.

"Mom, sorry to disappoint, but I don't have a boyfriend. I'm a career girl, remember?"

"It's just that after the whole misunderstanding with Dick and Krissy, I thought you'd moved on."

"I'm going upstairs for a nap. We'll do some more catching up at dinner." Ro paused before she left Delores in the kitchen. "Where are you sleeping, Mom?"

"Oh, I've already made up the sofa in the front room. I'll be so nice and cozy there, with all the blankets you've made. I don't know how you find the time to knit when you have such a big job in the navy, Roanna."

"See you later, Mom."

Ro took the stairs two at a time despite her exhaustion.

CHAPTER TWENTY

AT LUNCHTIME ON Thursday, Ro parked her car at the end of Coupeville's Main Street. The tiny downtown clung to the banks of Puget Sound, its clapboard buildings reminiscent of a New England seaside village.

She picked up the plastic bag of caps she'd knitted and headed for a large brown building. The downtown had been painted all white years ago for a Hollywood movie, but most of the shops and homes were back to their owners' preferred hues.

Ro admired the Whidbey Fibers sign that stuck out over the sidewalk at the yarn shop and fiber cooperative/clearing center. It was hand-scrolled cedar and had balls of yarn on one side and profiles of fiber-producing farm animals on the other. Ro recognized a llama, sheep, goat and rabbit.

A bell jingled as she entered. Bins of spun wool in every imaginable color dotted the old wood-planked floor. Shelves as high as the ceilings spilled with skeins and hanks of yarn.

Ro breathed in deeply. The combined scents of wool, lavender, cedar, pine and ocean water was like a balm to her soul. The hurt and shock from yesterday's memorial service and Master Chief Reis's arrest faded.

She wished she could smell this in the hangar every day.

She bit back a giggle.

Yeah, right.

"Can I help you—oh, Ro! Nice to see you again!"

A lovely woman with fine features and wavy, shoulder-length blond hair, Winnie Ford, greeted her from behind the merchant counter. She'd entered from the door in the back wall of the shop.

"I don't have long to shop, but I wanted to drop off these chemo caps. I noticed your sign a few months ago and I meant to bring some of them in sooner, once I completed them, but I lost track of time."

"Easy to do when you're on active duty. Have you had any more emergency landings?" Winnie referred to the emergency landing her husband, Max, had made with a B-17 bomber during Whidbey Island's air show last year. Ro had been on board and had almost lost her life, too.

Ro was unexpectedly pleased that Winnie asked.

"No, I've stayed on solid ground for the most part."

"We talked about the knitting you did on the carrier the last time you were in here, didn't we? Besides the chemo caps, are you still knitting regularly?"

Ro laughed. "You have a great memory. Yes, I'm always knitting. I don't know how *not* to knit. I'm sorry I haven't been back more often." She lovingly squeezed a hank of mulberry wine alpaca that was in a basket on the counter.

"I get it, believe me. I'm married to a navy man. Retired now, but just as busy." She smiled at Ro, who smiled back.

"I heard via the island winds that you and Miles are an item."

Ro knew her flushing cheeks gave away the truth.

"Yes, we've been spending time together, but we're both so involved in our careers...." Winnie was nice but Ro wasn't about to tell her the intimate details of her love life.

Love life?

"How long have you been in the navy, Ro?"

"Just about ten years. I have another year or so here."

"And then where to?"

"I'm not sure."

"Have you ever thought about getting out, starting something different?" Ro didn't miss the speculative sparkle in Winnie's eyes.

"Not really. But I suppose I should at least weigh all my options."

What? Were these words coming out of her mouth?

"You're really talented, Ro. Just look at these caps!"

Winnie reverently removed each cap from the plastic grocery bag. "Cable, intarsia, Fair Isle, brioche. Your choice of colors and fiber weights is spot-on. And I remember you not so much because you told me about knitting while at sea, but because of the lacework cardigan you were wearing that day."

Heat flashed up Ro's neck. She was getting used to acknowledging her emotions while in uniform because of the upheaval Miles's presence and Perez's death had brought into her life. But this was different. This had nothing to do with her uniform, her military composure. It had everything to do with who she was as a person.

A woman.

The uniform wasn't her entire identity, and Winnie, a passing acquaintance, recognized it.

So had Gwen.

"Thanks. I do love to knit."

"I know you've got lots of other talents or you wouldn't have your position in the navy. What branch are you?" Winnie squinted at Ro's warfare insignia that was pinned over her ribbons. "I don't recognize that one."

Ro wore the Information Dominance insignia. It comprised a gold shield with the world, a sword and an anchor set on ocean waves. It was worn not just by intel but by other information and communications experts.

"I'm support staff." Ro was still reluctant to tell people she didn't know well that she was an intelligence officer. It wasn't classified or a secret by any means, but she preferred to err on the side of caution.

"Well, I'm looking for someone to take over the business side of the shop for me, on the off chance you ever thought about getting out and doing something completely different. I want to focus exclusively on fiber production and sales. The island needs a yarn shop, though. It's the heart of our crafting community, at least for knitters, crocheters and needlework folks. The quilters have their own thriving group."

Winnie ran her hands over her middle and, with a start, Ro realized that despite being skinny everywhere else, there was a bit of a tummy on her.

What the hell—first Krissy, now Winnie. She'd heard navy wives joke that there was something in the Whidbey Island water supply that made everyone so fertile.

Winnie didn't miss Ro's raised brow.

"My husband and I just found out we're going to have our third child. I'm not going to be able to give the yarn shop the attention it deserves."

"I'm sure you'll find someone." Ro started to drift away from the counter, distracted by all the luscious fibers and the visions of projects they evoked.

"It takes a special person to run a yarn shop, Ro, you know that. How many yarn shops have you been in that you really loved? Where there are classes, and customers drop in to knit and share stories on a regular basis?"

"Not many, but the ones I've found have been wonderful. You have a great shop."

"Thanks. I want it to stay great." Winnie walked over to Ro. "Have you ever instructed a class in the navy?"

Ro blinked.

"Yes, I give training to aircrews on a regular basis." She didn't describe what kind of training and Winnie didn't seem to care about it, anyhow.

"Then you'd be a natural to teach knitting classes."

"Oh. Oh!" Ro clutched a skein of Italian merino wool to her chest. "I can't possibly consider it—I mean, I'm really flattered that you think I'm a good knitter and all, I just, well, I can't do anything besides the navy while I'm on active duty."

Winnie sighed. "Of course you can't. I understand, believe me. And I'm really sorry if I've come on too strong—these damn pregnancy hormones have me reeling this time. You'd think after two babies I'd be fine with it the third time around." She gave Ro a bemused smile.

"It's no problem, really." Ro looked around the shop. "In another life, I'd jump at this. But I do have to provide for myself, my future."

At Winnie's stricken expression, hot fingers of humiliation crept up Ro's chest.

"Oh, gosh, I don't mean you wouldn't pay well!"

"But it's the truth. I'd pay you a salary, of course, with hope that as the future of the company improved so would your pay and benefits. But in this economy, with a luxury product, I can't promise anyone anything."

A stillness overcame Ro. "And you shouldn't have to. Whoever takes the job should love the work, be passionate about coming in here every day."

"You got it."

Ro looked at her watch. Thirty minutes before she had to be back on base. That left her ten more to play in the shop.

"I've got to go but I want to buy enough of this to make a sweater." Ro held out the skein of merino she'd crushed against her chest. Strands of it clung to her rows of ribbons and popped the magnetized decorations off her uniform.

"Oh, no! Here, let me take that from you while you get yourself together. You can use the back storeroom." Winnie gently removed the yarn from Ro's hands and ushered her to the door in the wall.

"Thanks, it'll only take me a minute." Ro smiled at Winnie and opened the door.

Ro closed the door behind her and glanced up.

She gasped.

This was no ordinary storeroom. The ceiling rose toward the sky, like an aircraft hangar. Fiber in all forms was stored neatly on shelves, in bins, on drying racks next to dye pots. The entire place had to be as big as a football field.

She walked into the center of the warehouse. Just for a minute.

The energy that hummed through the dust motes made Ro smile again.

She'd felt this sense of belonging only a handful of times in her life. One was when she was at the academy—as difficult as it was, she'd known it was part of her destiny. The other time was more recently.

With Miles.

"Come out when you're done. Feel free to look around." Winnie had opened the door a crack and spoke through it. Ro barely caught the words and started back toward the entry.

"Sure thing. I'll be just another minute." The door closed and Ro was left alone in the magical space again.

Her hands shook as she pulled her uniform blouse out from her slacks and unbuttoned it. She placed the ribbons and their magnetized backing in place and got dressed.

Before she went back into the store, she cast a slow look around the warehouse.

What was happening to her? She wanted to blame it on Perez's death and being so close to Miles these past two weeks. But it wasn't accurate or fair to do so. Miles had been getting to her since the day he'd climbed out of that tree with Henry the Eighth.

She was changing. The fact that she'd been able to live under the same roof as Dick, Krissy and her mother without gutting any of them was proof that she'd moved past her failed engagement.

The fact that she'd allowed Miles to make love to her and, more important, allowed *herself* to completely give in to their passion, demonstrated that she was finding herself. Finding the real core of who she was.

She wasn't the same young woman who'd cultivated a navy career by going to the academy, and she wasn't the person she'd been at the start of that career.

Could her newfound self continue as before, always going for the next hard tour, the next step toward promotion?

Or were her ideas of success changing? Was happiness more than any uniform or career?

She smoothed out her uniform and went back into the yarn shop.

"WELL, LOOK WHAT the cat dragged in." Miles greeted the man doing lat pull-downs in the far corner of the fitness center.

"Warrant!" Max Ford, a retired navy commander and Miles's longtime workout buddy, let the weighted bar ease up over his head before he stood up from the bench.

"How the hell are you?" Max held out his hand and Miles took it in a firm shake.

"I'm doing all right. What's retired life like?" Max had retired from the navy almost a year ago. Since then he'd gotten married.

"Well, it's been an adjustment, let me tell you." Max smiled and shook his head, hands on his hips. "I thought I'd seen it all in the navy but I have to tell you, being a full-time husband and dad has been the hardest thing I've ever done. The most rewarding, though, and I absolutely love it, but tough."

"How's Winnie?"

Max couldn't keep the warm light out of his eyes, even a hard-boiled sailor like Miles could see that.

"She's wonderful. Cracking the whip, of course. She's got me helping with her business, which I do in between getting the island hopper airline in order."

"Do you need more pilots?"

"No, but I could sure use an EOD-type in the security area." Max smiled but his tone was sober. "Seriously, there's more to it than I imagined when I dreamed up pulling together a small fleet of commuter aircraft and a handful of pilots. The paperwork with the TSA is a job in and of itself."

"It's the times we live in, boss."

"Hey, you can't call me that anymore. I'm retired."

"So I can call you whatever I want, and it'll always be 'boss.'"

Max shrugged off the implied compliment.

"Did I tell you Winnie's pregnant?"

"No way. You sure move fast."

"Well, our oldest is in high school and little Maeve is getting ready for pre-K. Plus we're both older. We couldn't wait too much longer."

Max's voice rang with pride and happiness.

A tug at his solar plexus made Miles listen to his own heart. Was it possible for a man to have a ticking biological clock? Making babies with Roanna sounded like heaven to him.

"So, what's new with you? Anyone special in your life?"

"Nah. You know how it is—long days, short nights. No time for that right now."

"Bullshit. Remember who you're talking to, Warrant."

Miles laughed and Max joined him.

"Touché." Miles knew he couldn't put a claim on Ro, which made him want her all the more. He hadn't seen her much since the memorial service yesterday and he was experiencing withdrawal.

"There is that gal I met when you made me climb that tree last year."

"The intel type?"

"How did you—?"

"She was in the B-17 last year, remember? And I saw her a couple of times at the wing AOMs before I retired."

"Oh, yeah?"

"Yeah. Tell me what the deal is there—if you're so inclined."

"You may recall she never agreed to go out with me."

Max nodded.

"We've been assigned to a sensitive case together, and it's allowed us to spend more time with each other."

"I trust you're taking full advantage of this time?" Laughter glittered in Max's eyes.

Miles rubbed his chin.

"Yes and no. Of course I'm not stupid, boss, I use every chance to show her I'm not that much of a nerd, and to try to find out more about her. But our case has been a little hairy, to say the least. It hasn't made my efforts to convince her I'm not such a bad guy any easier."

Max didn't ask any questions about the case. He'd been a career officer and knew that if the information wasn't volunteered it was for a good reason. Miles had missed their comfortable way with each other.

"I'm finding myself in a position I haven't faced before. The rules are different downrange—if something needs to get done, you do it. As long as you're on the right side of the mission, it's all good. But here, I find I can't trust everyone like I did my colleagues in the war."

"Don't forget you worked with the top experts in their fields, Miles. You're EOD. You're used to working with only the highest caliber of operational service members. I'm not saying the guys and gals here aren't excellent at what they do, but if they haven't been downrange, and if they're not used to high-risk operations, it's tough for you to identify with them."

Miles regarded Max with new eyes. Max was the man who'd suffered major trauma, including PTSD, after saving his unit from a terrorist bomber. Max and Miles had met while still in their initial phases of recovery and physical therapy at the Walter Reed National Military Medical Center in Washington, D.C.

Max knew better than most what Miles had gone through. And he'd been the best workout buddy a man could hope for during those early months on Whidbey.

In all their time together, though, he and Max had never really discussed their different career paths. They were two sailors who needed to recover so they could continue to serve their country.

"Thanks, boss. I appreciate it."

"There's nothing to thank me for, Miles. It's the truth." Max paused. "Are you safe? Do you feel like someone's undermining you?"

"Whoa, are you Houdini or something?" Miles wanted to keep it light but they were already in very deep territory. "It's not being undermined—it's being used for the sake of a superior's career motives. I get it, I know the game. I don't play it except when I have to. And when my boss tells me to do something, as long as it's not an illegal order, I do it."

"Roger that. Listen, Miles, you don't have to say any more. I've been there. It's a different ball game on shore duty, at a command where everyone thinks his or her job is indispensable—yet you know damn well that there are people taking bullets for all of us in more important roles, right at this moment."

Miles shrugged. He wasn't used to this touchy-feely stuff. Marriage was never going to soften him as it obviously had Max Ford.

"Just do the job you need to do, Warrant. The rest will work itself out."

"It had better, boss."

"One more thing, Warrant?"

"Yeah, boss?"

"Let me know when you get that woman of yours."

Miles shook his head. "Ain't happening anytime soon."

"My wife knows her."

"What?" Max had his complete attention.

"Ask her what she does with her free time."

"She's a knitter. She probably buys yarn from your wife's shop, right?" Miles wasn't too familiar with the work Winnie did. He knew she was a navy widow and Max had been her CACO many years ago. She'd stayed on the island after her first husband died since her family lived up in nearby Anacortes. She ran some kind of craft business was all Miles knew.

"Her corporation is taking off and she needs talented, knowledgeable people to come on board and join the team."

Had Ro decided to resign her commission?

"And?"

"Like I said, ask your lady friend about it." Max smiled.

Miles shook his head again and held out his hand.

"It's been great seeing you, boss. Don't be such a stranger here."

Max clasped his hand.

"You, either. I'll talk to Winnie and we'll have you over for a barbecue when it gets a little warmer."

"That'd be great."

"It'd be nice if you brought your lady friend, Warrant. Sounds like she and Winnie have a lot in common."

Miles said goodbye and walked toward the showers. He didn't want to disappoint Max, but Ro was the furthest thing from a domestic wife.

But she does knit. A lot. And she's been questioning her career. You've seen her at her best and worst this past week.

He understood that Ro didn't want anything from him other than a roll in the hay. He blamed himself for not waiting, not courting her properly. But it wasn't in him; courting was for men who wanted to settle down.

Ro deserved more than he had to give her.

CHAPTER TWENTY-ONE

RO LAUGHED AT the sixth stupid joke Bill Brannigan had made in three minutes. He'd cozied up to her at the bar of the N.A.S. Whidbey Officer's Club shortly after she'd arrived a half hour ago. It wasn't her usual Friday after-work routine but she'd decided she needed to step out of her usual routine.

She drank some of her diet soda.

"When do you deploy again, Ro?" He beamed a grin at her that she knew he'd used to get other gals in the sack. Bill was an EA-6B jet pilot who never failed to let others know he was a naval aviator.

"I don't, Bill. Not on this tour. Unless I push to go on detachment downrange, which I don't plan on doing."

She blinked and tried to focus on Bill's words.

"Ah, that's right. You were already over there a couple times, weren't you?" He patted her shoulder. His hand lingered on her shoulder a little too long and a shudder ran up her back.

Bill had always made it clear that if she ever wanted more than a friendship, he was open to it.

This is creepy. He's like a brother to you.

"Um, yeah." She surveyed the bar, which was filling up quickly—Friday happy hour was always a hit. Active duty personnel as well as their spouses, significant others and significant-other-hopefuls contributed to the cacophony.

A couple of officers had just been promoted and were paying for their squadrons' drinks at the bar. A young female pilot had completed her final check ride in a P-3C Orion, which her shipmates were celebrating with her.

Face it. You can't get Miles out of your head.

Bill leaned in and his breath smelled like greasy French fries and beer.

"Do you have a cut on your eye, there, Ro?"

She put her hand to her cheek. "It's just a few stitches from the black eye I got last week."

Bill peered closer. Her instinct was to lean far away but she forced herself to sit still.

"I'll be back in a minute, Ro. Don't go away." Bill sauntered off toward the bar's restroom. She realized she'd probably be giving him a ride home if he kept throwing back his beers. Or calling him a taxi.

She looked over her shoulder through the O Club's large window and stared out at the water. A run along the base path would have been a smarter option than coming in here and trying to pretend she hadn't just finished the most tumultuous week of her life.

A familiar hand slapped down on the bar next to her and made her jump.

"Commander Brandywine, imagine seeing you here."

She turned to glare at Miles. He had that damn smug expression on his face, not unlike the one he'd worn after he'd made her come so hard she'd screamed.

"What do you *think* I'm doing here?" She turned to face the bar head-on. Hopefully he'd get the hint.

"You look like you're here to pick someone up. But I know that can't be true." At his tone, she wanted to dump her diet drink over his blond head. Her fingers itched at the memory of running her hands through his hair when they made love.

"What I'm doing here is none of your concern, Warrant. We're off duty."

He slid onto the stool next to hers and she bit her lip. For the umpteenth time in a week, Miles was screwing up her carefully composed itinerary to freedom. She should have known from the very first kiss—no matter how effective it had been at hiding their presence from the wing staff—that she was in deep waters with this man.

"Ah, that's not quite accurate, is it, Commander?" His voice held a timbre that was its own caress. She fought to keep her hands on the bar in front of her and not reach up and rub her neck and cheek where she felt every vibration of his presence.

"Spare me, Miles. There's nothing going on now, nothing we can do about it until we get more information. If we ever do. Besides, everything's shut down for the weekend."

"Not true, Ro. We can be called to a new situation at any time. You know that." Miles waved down the bartender. "I'll have whatever you have on tap today."

He turned to her.

"What are you having? Rum and Coke?"

"Coke. Diet." She spit the words out. How was it that Miles, who'd been through the same things she had this week, appeared so much more the pulled-together officer than she did?

"Why aren't you drinking?" His question was open, nonjudgmental.

"I never drink when I'm out unless someone else is driving. I'd rather wait to get home and have my glass of red. Single malt Scotch is good, too, if the weather is cold enough."

She fiddled with her straw. "I don't drink when I have to drive, ever. I know 'one drink, one hour' is legal but I'd never forgive myself if I messed up."

"You really are a sweat, Ro." He grinned at the navy reference to someone who is responsible to the point of obsessive-compulsive. "But I respect you for it."

"I'm not a sweat. I make my own choices, is all."

"You're in my seat, buddy." Bill clasped a hand on Miles's shoulder.

Miles stood. "We haven't met. I'm Miles."

"Miles, eh?" Bill's gaze zeroed in on Miles's warfare insignia.

"I'm EOD. That's what the little bomb means, friend." Miles took a gulp of the beer the bartender put in front of him. Ro stifled a giggle. Bill was too obtuse to get that Miles was poking fun at him.

"What's an EOD dude doing on Whidbey?" Bill reached over for his own beer. Ro found it annoying but not surprising that she was completely out of the equation at this point. Miles and Bill were doing the "whose penis is larger" routine, only it involved their navy career paths and wartime exploits.

"I'm here to conduct training, and to recover from my war injury."

"Okay." Bill took a slug of his beer. Ro was impressed that Bill didn't ask what the injury was. In uniform, Miles's lost leg was undetectable. A wartime injury could be anything.

"So how do you know Ro?"

"We work together at the wing." Miles kept his gaze on Bill; his unspoken claim on Ro was unmistakable.

Bill wrinkled his forehead. "Hey, Ro. You never mentioned that, uh—" he read Miles's name tag "—Miles."

"What's to mention, Bill? I see you here once or twice a week at lunchtime. We don't usually talk about who we work with." No, they always talked about Bill and what a great pilot he was.

As she watched Miles and Bill play their testosterone game, she was struck by how tuned in her body was to Miles. His every gesture, the nuance in how he modulated his voice.

No one compared to him.

MILES CONVERSED WITH Bill as though he gave a crap about Bill's EA-6B exploits. The entire time he watched Ro. She sat at the bar with a neutral expression on her face and nursed her soda. Too cool for school.

His gut had twisted when he saw her sitting at the bar. He hadn't gone there looking for her, but he'd seen her car in the lot. He stopped in at happy hour on the rare instance someone he knew was promoted or the commodore invited the staff out to drinks after a long week.

He didn't have Ro pegged as a happy hour frequent flyer, either. Maybe once or twice over the past twelve months their paths had crossed here. Since they hadn't had the investigation to bring them together, there'd been no reason to talk.

He'd tried. Every damn time they were in any kind of social situation he'd tried to win her over, show her he was fun, didn't need a commitment. That he was trustworthy, someone to have a good time with. That he'd never kiss and tell.

Her face, her lips, taunted him with what they'd shared Sunday night. He didn't come in here only because he saw her car in the lot.

He wanted, needed, to be with her again.

He told himself it would do him good to have a beer and hang out with some friends. Unfortunately, his best friend, Max Ford, had gone and retired and was a newlywed. Yesterday at the gym he should have asked Max to meet him here, but he didn't realize he'd be stalking Roanna like this. No matter, as Max would have been a no-show, anyway. Most retirees didn't hang out at the O Club happy hour.

Face it. You're here for Ro.

"I'm sorry, what did you say?" He held his hand to his ear to indicate that the ambient noise and not his own thoughts had distracted him from Bill's banter.

"How much time did you see downrange?" Bill's voice

was loud in Miles's ear. Miles knew Bill's type. Good guy, trustworthy in battle. He didn't like him, though, simply because Bill had the hots for Roanna.

"Enough." Miles nodded toward Ro and motioned with the glass of beer in his hand. "How do you two know each other?"

Bill put a possessive arm around Ro's shoulders. From her expression, she'd have preferred he didn't. Miles bit back the urge to let out a loud *"whoop!"* He kept it to a slight smile.

"Ro and I have known each other since we were kids, haven't we?" Bill sent Ro the briefest glance before he leaned back toward Miles and shoved the neck of his beer bottle at him.

"We met when we were plebes at the boat school. Ro was all of ninety-nine pounds soaking wet, but she sure had spunk!" Bill grabbed Ro's shoulder and squeezed her against his body. Miles had to take a swig of his beer to keep from laughing at the look of pure torture on Ro's face. He hadn't had this much fun in way too long.

"Did you guys date back at the boat school?" Miles used Bill's nickname for the naval academy.

"No." Ro spoke up as she eased herself out from under Bill's arm. Miles suspected that the smell from Bill's flight suit wasn't so pleasant up close. The fire-resistant material was similar to battle fatigues and had a penchant for harboring the pungent aromas of jet fuel and body odor.

"We never dated."

"Not that I didn't try, right, Ro? We had a couple of close calls here and there—" Bill grinned at Miles "—if you know what I'm talking about."

"Oh, I know, man, I know." Miles laughed and hoped Bill thought it was with him. He couldn't ignore the ominous sparks in Ro's eyes.

"Hey, B.B.!" A group of male voices yelled from across

the club for their leader. Bill held up his bottle of beer to acknowledge his minions.

"Gotta go. Be right back." Bill didn't even glance at Miles again. He was in his element with his squadron buddies as he lunged across the bar toward them.

Miles stood closer to Ro as she remained seated on the bar stool. He couldn't attempt to kiss her here. It would probably earn him a smack if he did.

"It must be tough for you to share Bill's attention."

"Shut up, Warrant." She didn't appreciate his humor.

"Wait a minute." He put his glass on the bar. "Are you glowering at me, Ro?"

"As if." She rolled her eyes and sipped from her nearly empty glass.

"Let me get you another one." He motioned at the bartender.

"No, I've had enough." He watched her spare one last glance at Bill, in the far corner yukking it up with his cohorts.

"Wait, Ro, I'm sorry. I'm just yanking your chain." He put a hand on her forearm. "Your eye looks better."

"Yeah—for a Gila monster. Stop kidding yourself, Miles. What you're doing isn't 'yanking my chain.' It's being the same pain in the ass you've been since you saved my mother's damn fur ball."

Uh-oh. Her eyes were glassy, just like they'd been on Tuesday. His heart sank. The last thing he wanted to do was make Ro cry.

"And here I thought you were an animal lover, Commander."

She sat up straight and narrowed her eyes.

"I happen to love animals—the four-legged kind." She turned away. "I'm allergic to cats. Not that *that* has anything to do with anything." He noted how her whole face seemed to droop. Her pretty eyes were sad with thoughts unspoken and the slope of her shoulders conveyed exhaustion.

"You're beat, Commander. We could get a call at any time, even this late in the game. You should get some shut-eye."

She shot him a sheepish smile.

"We call it 'rack time' at the academy."

He groaned. "Please tell me you're not a ring-knocker like your buddy Bill?" He detested academy grads who flashed their class ring around like a sword. He knew Ro wasn't in that group but had to call her on it.

"Hardly. Do you even see my ring on these hands?" She held up her fingers and wiggled them at him.

"I've noticed your ring before."

She smiled, and he wanted to slap himself for such an obvious giveaway. He was going to scare the hell out of Ro if he reminded her that he'd been aware of her since the day they'd met.

"I didn't realize you cared so much, Miles."

He'd scared *himself* with how much he cared.

"Ro, any chance you'd let me take you out on Sunday?"

"Out where?"

"A day trip. A getaway."

"Don't ask me now, Miles. I'm not in the mood." She walked off without further comment.

He fought every instinct to go after her as he watched her leave the club.

It was a new thing for him, to fight his instincts.

RO WALKED AS swiftly as she could to her car and let out a sigh of relief once she was safely locked inside. It was the first moment of solitude she'd had since she drove to work this morning.

The car warmed up and chased away the late-afternoon

chill brought on by the fog bank that had rolled in while she'd been at the club. She eased it into gear and made her way out of the lot, dreaming of her bed.

Except she wasn't guaranteed peace and quiet at home, either. Krissy, Dick and Mom were still in town, and would most likely be at home. She wanted to scream. Instead, she turned on the radio.

Before she could find a radio station playing the kind of music she needed to blast her head clear, her eyes caught a tall figure leaving the O Club.

She immediately recognized Miles. Even in the fog and dimming daylight. Guilt at how viciously she'd shut him down tugged at her.

It was going to take all her energy to get through the rest of her tour with him so close. Energy she didn't have.

She'd let him too far into her life.

How the hell had the week in which she'd planned to start her new life turned into a week of being bombarded by every emotion known to woman?

CHAPTER TWENTY-TWO

"I THOUGHT YOU'D have gone to dinner." Ro took in her dining room table, rarely used, which Delores had set with a combination of Italian and Polish ceramics. It was a beautiful table, Ro admitted. She should do this for herself, have a few friends over, more often.

"No way, honey! I decided it'd be the perfect night to sit down together over a home-cooked meal. Your hours are crazy, Roanna. I'll bet you eat out most of the week, don't you?"

"No, I actually eat at home most nights, Mom." Because her life was so damned boring. Until this past week.

"Well, I went ahead and made us a nice pot roast with all the trimmings. There're still a few pieces of pie left, and I baked cookies while you were gone today."

"Where're Krissy and Dick?"

"Upstairs. They needed a nap after running all over the island today. Krissy says it's the most beautiful place she's ever seen!"

"Mom, you should have gone with them." It was just like her mom to stay in and play the martyr cook and housekeeper.

"I wasn't going to impose on their time. Besides, it's you I'm here for, Roanna. It was important to me to have a nice meal ready for you. Maybe you'd like to invite your friend?"

Ro's heart broke. Delores was overinvolved and smothering whenever she put her mind to taking care of either of her girls, but she was only doing the best she knew how. And Ro wished she did have that special "friend" to invite over.

You would if you hadn't been such a bitch to him.

"Mom, can I get back to you on that? Let me go for a run and I'll be home in time to eat. Are you thinking an hour from now?"

"Yes, that should give Krissy long enough."

RO MADE IT OUT of her uniform and into her running gear in five minutes flat. Before she could talk herself out of it, she ran out the door—and over to Miles's house. It was less than two kilometers to his door and she gained more courage with each step she ran.

This was the right thing to do. Apologize. Make sure Miles knew it wasn't him; she was the one who had the problems.

Her bravado melted away at the sight of his truck in the driveway. He was home, and this wasn't just an idea any longer, it was a reality. She had to take action.

After she knocked on his front door, she waited for Lucky to bark in alert.

At the ensuing silence, she figured Miles had gone for a run with the dog. Disappointment washed over her as she turned to go back down the steps.

"Ro."

His voice stopped her and she turned back. He'd opened the door without a sound and stood in a pair of boxers and an old T-shirt. He'd needed to get out of his work clothes as quickly as she had.

"Where's Lucky?"

"My buddy came back early. She's back with him, happy as can be." He shrugged but she saw the defeat in his eyes. He was thinking about Riva again.

"Oh."

"What can I do for you?"

"I, um, want to apologize for being such a bitch back at the O Club. You aren't the reason for my issues, Miles. I am. The problem with us isn't you, it's me."

"I see. Well, don't worry about it. It's been a long week."

She bowed her head and scuffed the wood porch. This was crazy but what *hadn't* been since she'd kissed Miles last week?

"Look, my mother's in town and is in the midst of fixing a dinner that rivals Thanksgiving in the chow hall. I'd love it if you'd join us. You'll need to ignore their stupid chatter, and understand that they'll try to marry us off. But don't worry, we're friends, we have to be friends. I know you understand—"

"Ro." His finger was on her lips. "Yes, I'll join you for dinner. No more explanations needed. What time?"

RO WANTED TO KICK herself for bringing Miles into her family drama. What the heck had she been thinking?

They sat around the kitchen table, drinking coffee and tea. The dining room table had been resplendent with Delores's best recipes. For that, Ro had been grateful. She hadn't cooked Miles a homemade meal yet. It smacked too much of long-term to her. Besides, they'd been too busy with the Perez case.

"Ro tells me you're a war hero, Miles." Delores batted her eyelashes at him.

"I did no such thing, Mom." She turned to Miles, who was squeezed between her and Delores. "Not that you aren't. Of course you're a war hero."

"Having a lifelong disability from a war injury doesn't qualify me as a hero." His comment, his attention, was all for her. In the midst of her psycho family, Miles made her calmer than any prescription tranquilizer ever could.

"You were injured?" Dick had his surgeon's face on.

"I lost my left leg, below the knee." Miles stirred his coffee as if he'd just spoken about the Whidbey Island weather.

Krissy gasped.

"Why didn't you tell us?" Her demand was aimed at Ro.

"It's not my business to tell you." Ro secretly hid her smile of satisfaction and quiet pride for Miles. Unless someone met him at the gym or when he was wearing shorts, there was no way to tell he was an amputee.

"It's not a secret, folks. I'm lucky to be able to have shared this great meal with you. A lot of my friends and our colleagues—" he nodded at Ro "—never made it back."

Delores was under Miles's spell. Men were the most important thing in her life. "Just think, you saved my dear cat by climbing up that big tree, all with one leg! No wonder you've been able to convince Ro to date you!"

"We're not dating, Mom." Ro hid her annoyance by shoving another peanut butter cookie in her mouth.

"Oh, that reminds me." Krissy's eyes were innocently wide. "I think I have your undershirt, Miles. I found it in Ro's room on Monday morning."

Miles shot Ro a rueful smile. His eyes conveyed compassion.

"What were you doing in my room?"

"I was cleaning and doing your sheets for you. I know you've been under a lot of stress at work and since we've all barged in on you I wanted to help."

Ro scowled at Krissy, too angry to speak.

"I know it's Miles's shirt because it has an emblem on it with the word EOD on it. You said he's EOD, didn't you, Dick?"

"Yes, honey."

"Ro, we're all adults here. No need to hide your relationship with Miles. Right, Miles?" Delores put her hand on his forearm.

"Whatever." Ro suddenly felt the weight of another foot on hers under the table. Miles winked and sheer lust bolted through her at his touch, the unexpected intimacy. As she continued to meet his searching stare, the lust turned into something deeper. Riskier.

She'd fallen in love with Miles.

"I've been trying to convince Ro to let me take her away on Sunday. Maybe you three can help me."

The revelation that she'd fallen for him turned to resistance.

"No help needed. My family's only here for a short time, right?" She nailed all three of them with her frostiest glare. "I need to spend Sunday with them."

"But we've already booked Mom and us back to New Jersey for Sunday night. We'll return the rental to the airport. There's no reason for you to stay here on Sunday, Ro." Dick's use of "Mom" for Delores should have bothered Ro since he'd never been so familiar with her while they'd dated, but it didn't.

Nothing seemed to bother her much lately, except Miles.

"What do you say, Ro? It'd do us both good to get off the island and away from it all. Don't make me go alone." Miles smiled and she had to give him points for his steel balls. The old Ro would have run from him, faster than ever now that she'd figured out she'd fallen for him.

They'd never work out.

It didn't mean they couldn't spend a day together, though.

She sighed.

"Where are we going?"

CHAPTER TWENTY-THREE

THE FERRY PULLED away from the pier and made a huge white froth in its wake. Ro stood next to Miles, her hands on the deck railing. It had sounded like a good idea, to go to Canada with him for the day, but now as the hours stretched before them she wondered what they were going to talk about.

"Smell that air? There's nothing like the smell of the Pacific Northwest." Miles put his arm around her shoulders. "We've got all day to enjoy it." He smiled and took in another deep breath before he turned to face her. His expression sobered when he saw she wasn't as enthusiastic about their trip to Victoria, British Columbia.

"Why so grim, Ro? This is going to be fun, I promise." He rubbed her right shoulder in an effort to soothe her. It only made her more aware of his nearness, his ability to captivate her with a single touch.

"Maybe I'm just tired from all the running around for the investigation." She gave him a smile. She couldn't see his eyes clearly as they both wore sunglasses but the crinkles around them told her he was smiling as he focused on her.

"It's out of our hands at this point, don't you think? With Reis's arrest I don't see what else we can do. Did you ever figure out anything more from the aircraft maintenance stats?"

"No, and even if I do, what good would come of it? As Reis told us, there's no hard proof. If the commodore did bribe Perez, there's no evidence. No charge, certainly not one that would stick. Besides, now that they arrested the master chief, how can we even be sure that what she told us was true?"

"I thought the same thing." Miles kissed the top of her head. "I do think it's strange that we haven't heard anything from or about Reis, though. We'd know if she was still in custody, but all I heard was that she's put in for an extended leave."

"That is odd, I have to admit."

It was so calm out here with Miles. She hated pushing her point, but had to, one last time.

"We still don't know whose footprints those were on the cliff, Miles. Whoever they belonged to could have pushed him. In any case, we'll never get the proof that the commodore paid Perez to falsify the safety inspections. You know all of this, too, but I have the feeling you think everyone will come to justice. I don't get it."

He dropped his arm from her shoulders and gripped the railing with both hands.

"If there's one thing I've learned while I was at war, and after, while I was sweating bullets to get through physical therapy, it's that life isn't fair. The bad guys don't always get caught, you're right. In this case, we might have more than one bad guy, or gal," he said, referring to Master Chief Reis.

"You don't really think Lydia did it, do you?"

"No, I don't. But we have to keep all possibilities on the table.

She nodded slowly.

"Come here, Ro, let's sit." He put his hand on the small of her back and gently nudged her toward the wooden bench that ran the length of the ferry's upper deck.

She sank her spine against the aged bench and marveled at how it was at once so comfortable and so unyielding. The curve of the seat was perfect to lean against and enjoy the view of sea, sun and mountains.

"Do you agree with me that we're close to finishing the case?" she asked.

"Yes, I do think we're close. But I can't sit idle if there's a chance that someone out there is a murderer. Especially if they think they've gotten away with it." She crossed her arms in front of her.

"My point exactly, Ro. They haven't gotten away with anything. Even if Perez went out to the cliff to walk and clear his mind, he ended up dying. Probably at the hands of another person, yes. Whether that person meant to kill him or just scare him doesn't matter—the result is the same."

Miles stretched his arm along the back of the bench, behind her neck. She rested her head on his arm and listened to his voice as she stared up at the sky.

"The result I can't stomach is that he's dead. Anita Perez is a widow and his kids will never know their father as more than a memory." Ro's voice cracked on her last word and she swallowed hard. She sat up straight and leaned over to hug her legs.

"Doesn't it bug you that someone could be out there, a killer? How do we know they won't hurt someone else?"

"We don't. But I believe the truth will turn up. Maybe not while we're on this case, maybe not even in the near future. We have to accept it however it plays out, Ro."

"This is why you're EOD and I'm support staff." She rubbed her arms. "My training makes me need to get to the bottom of everything. I have to find the answers. It's my job."

"It's your job when it comes to planning a flight mission. We're talking about people behaving badly, here, Ro. Worse, it's intelligent people behaving badly. They're smart enough to cover their tracks, for the most part."

"If only the sheriff's people had captured a clear set of footprints from the top of the cliff."

"They did their best, Ro. And so have we." She felt the cool tips of his fingers on her chin. He lifted her face to his.

"Let it go. Just for today. Let's forget about the wing, Perez, the whole thing. Can you do that?"

She blinked.

"I can try."

THEY DEBARKED AT Victoria port and Ro was struck by the quaintness of the lush greenery all over the city. Rosebushes climbed and tumbled and crept over every stone wall and fence. Planned arbors looked as though they'd been painted by a Dutch master. Even this early in the season, the roses were blooming and her mind's eye imagined the full vibrancy of the blooms in another month or so, when they'd be at their peak.

They walked at an even pace next to each other. Miles took her hand and she clasped his, reveling in the warmth they created together. When had a man last treated her like someone he cherished? Other than the odd dinner date that led to at most a few more dates, when was the last time a man had appeared to truly enjoy her company?

"What are you thinking? Your mind just drifted, didn't it?" Miles didn't miss a thing.

"I'm thinking I can't believe how much fun this is—just hanging out. Nothing to do with work."

"It'll get better and better if we're both willing to work at it, Ro." He stopped, tugging on her arm. She turned and faced him. They were in Victoria, on a beautiful walk, alone among the rhododendron bushes that towered over them, their blooms a brilliant splash of yellows, reds, whites and violets.

The foliage blocked the constant wind that buffeted the island and Ro heard birds chirping. Nothing was louder than her heart, which pounded like the ferry's motor.

"What are you afraid of, Ro?" He was so close, but didn't move in to stop their conversation with a kiss. She leaned toward him and he held up his hand, his fingers on her lips.

"No, not yet. Tell me. What's holding you back?"

"Um, our work schedules?" Even she knew that was weak. "Okay, do you really want me to tell you? I don't trust myself to know what I want." She tugged on his hands. "Do you remember the yarn shop I told you about? Winnie's, in Coupeville?"

"Um, yes." Clearly, yarn wasn't what Miles had been thinking about.

"She actually runs a huge export business for fibers of all kinds. She needs someone to manage the shop. And as stupid and financially irresponsible as I know it is, I've thought about getting out and being an artist—a fiber artist. Running a yarn shop, maybe even owning it someday, would be a dream come true."

"From what Max told me, it's more than a full-time job. Winnie works constantly."

"I'm not afraid of hard work, Miles."

Miles was silent.

"Crazy, right? I've worked so long and hard to get here. All I've ever wanted was to have my own career. The academy was my ticket out of my home life and gave me a way to serve my country. I never thought I'd stay more than the minimum five-year commitment." She bit her lip, then went on.

"You know how it goes—the navy draws you in. The sense that the job won't get done unless I do it." She raked her fingers through her hair.

"These past few weeks—no, longer..." She had to tell

him. Miles deserved to know. And *she* deserved to know that she was strong enough to tell him the truth.

"Since we met, I've been changing. I suppose I would have come to this metamorphosis soon enough, but the very fact that you asked me out, risked having the other guys think less of you for dating a woman in uniform, spoke to my heart. It made me start thinking about what I really want out of life."

They began walking, hand in hand.

"I was so sure that reaching twenty years and having a pension would be the be-all and end-all in terms of life goals and achievements." A sob caught in her throat.

"Seeing Perez lying there, his life gone, it shook me. Then when we got together, it made me sad that I'd waited so long to give in to my feelings for you." She stopped and turned toward him.

"I don't want what I used to, Miles. I want more."

"Just tell me I'm part of that 'more,' Ro." His voice was low, and she knew his eyes were bright behind his sunglasses.

"Yes, I mean, that would be nice. But the logistics of it, Miles. Do you want to stay here? How long will you stay in the navy?"

His hands were on either side of her face and his lips crushed to hers before she could say another word, ask another question. His lips were cold but they warmed as she wrapped her hands around his wrists, urging him to continue kissing her.

MILES WATCHED THE sunlight play across Ro's features as they enjoyed their second beer on an outside patio at a quaint café. They'd talked and talked some more as they went in and out of the city's many souvenir shops. He'd told her about his volunteer work at the animal shelter, about Beau, the lovable Lab-shepherd mix. She shared her passion for knitting chemo caps, and how in spite of all the angst they'd caused her, she still loved her family. As long as she didn't have to live too close to them.

"This has been the best day of my life, Miles."

"You need to up your ante, sweetheart." He clasped her hand and smiled. His chest was full of so much hope for them. Silently he prayed he didn't screw it up.

"Maybe you're right." She laughed.

"I should have done this from the get-go. You deserve to be treated like the lady you are."

"Knock it off, Warrant. I'm as much to blame as you—I didn't agree to go out with you, remember?"

"Hmm." He raised her hand to his lips and kissed her knuckles. A movement out of the corner of his eye caused him to pause and turn.

A man who looked a lot like Commodore Sanders was sitting at a table in a café across the street from them. Staring at them.

"What?" Ro sensed his alertness.

He turned back to her as though he hadn't noticed anything amiss.

"Don't look now, but I think Leo Sanders is across the street. Checking us out."

She kept her attention rapt on him, never showed a break in her demeanor.

"Why would he be here or care what we're doing?"

"Hard to say. It may have nothing to do with us. But my gut tells me otherwise."

"Let's do what you made me promise, Miles. Just for today, let's forget about it. He's probably here to get away from Karen."

"Maybe." Her lips distracted him and he claimed a kiss before he paid their bill. He wanted Ro to himself.

"THIS IS MAGNIFICENT, Miles." They paused on top of the rise, high above the Pacific Ocean. They'd hiked from downtown Victoria to an outer ridge. They passed several other hikers along the way but the wind and sheer beauty of the open space made them feel completely alone.

"It's incredible, isn't it?" He scanned the horizon and she watched the sunlight dance across his expression.

She wondered why it had taken her so long to admit her feelings for him, if only to herself. It was crystal clear to her that she'd fallen in love with Miles, probably before he'd ever kissed her.

She'd definitely broken most of her own rules in doing so.

"I'm so happy to share this with you." He smiled and met her eyes briefly before he put his arm around her and pulled her close. They stood, her back to his front, his arms around her waist and hers resting on top of his, for a long while.

Ro gained a sense of security from the simple rhythm of his breath, the sure warmth of their bodies, how they fit together.

It's okay to enjoy this. It doesn't mean you're committed for life or anything.

"Hmmph." Her response to her mind's rationalizations wasn't meant to be verbal.

"You okay, Ro?" Miles's voice was a soft murmur next to her ear.

"Absolutely." She had to keep this light. Their bond had deepened far beyond that of colleagues or even friends, but her ability to give in to it completely was questionable at best.

If she were different, if she were the type who could quit the navy and just go after her whims, she'd have nothing to worry about. She and Miles could stay together for as long as it worked for them, after the case was closed.

"Miles, you know I'm supposed to transfer before the end of my three-year tour, right?"

His arms stiffened.

"Only if you want to stay in, Ro. It's your choice."

She turned in his arms and faced him.

"They don't let us intel types stay on shore duty for longer than thirty-six months. I'm nearing the eighteen-month mark and I have to turn in my preferences for placement to the detailer."

The detailer was the officer at the naval personnel command in Memphis, Tennessee, who would write her orders. In a single stroke, her fate for the next two or three years would be written orders that she was obligated to fulfill.

"There's no chance of orders in the area for another tour, if you decided to stay in?" His question was loaded. It was in the weight of his voice, the way he held his chest just beyond her touch.

"Not if I want to keep my career headed in the right direction, no." Her options were overseas, overseas, overseas. She'd had all CONUS—Continental United States assignments applicable to her rank and time in service, other than her deployed ship time and tours downrange.

"I can't tell you what to do, Ro. Are you sure the navy's going to give you everything you want out of life?"

She'd been resolute about her career. It was what she knew, where she was comfortable. Everything else would fall into place.

When she raised her gaze to his, her throat squeezed tight. Whatever sure response she had simply fizzled.

"Ro." Miles lowered his face and she closed her eyes. Their lips met in a bittersweet acknowledgment of what they shared, what could be and what would absolutely never be if she stayed loyal to her career.

What about being loyal to yourself?

When he lifted his head, his breathing was labored and he drew her into a tight embrace.

"You haven't asked me what I'm doing for my next tour, Ro."

She pulled back.

"What are you doing?"

"I don't know yet. I can take a position at the Pentagon, running EOD programs. My injury won't keep me from anything like that." He looked over her head out to sea.

"The Pacific Northwest has grown on me. Max started the commuter airline for the islands and it's booming."

"Yes, Winnie mentioned they're as busy as ever." Again, the shared connection.

Miles rubbed her upper arms. "Max offered me a job doing security for the airline. It's a relatively small startup and he could be out of business in no time, but it could also be a great investment. I love it here, and if that didn't work out, I'm sure I could find a job on base. They might even have a place for me as a civilian, conducting basic EOD informational classes and instruction."

"Wow, you've given this a lot of thought." She pulled out of his arms and held his hands.

"I've thought about a lot of things since I watched my dog die on that godforsaken field."

She swallowed. Leave it to Miles to be such a damn hero about everything. He didn't even mention that he'd lost his leg and almost bled out on that same field. He put everything in the perspective of another's suffering—in this case, his dog's.

Ro knew that such noble instinct wasn't in her makeup.

"I think you should go for it, Miles. You're right—life's short and if being a desk jockey for the rest of your life isn't palatable, the airline is a perfect option. You'd be able to go around to airstrips on the other islands, wouldn't you?"

"Yes, with the occasional trip to Seattle for TSA training and such."

"That's great. You'd be crazy not to explore it." Her stomach tightened and tears threatened to spill down her cheeks.

"What about you, Ro?"

He asked her the question again, but this time she heard so much more in his words. He was asking about them, about the possibility of a shared life.

"I don't have the luxury to quit my job, Miles. I'm years from the minimal retirement. I won't have anything coming in once I leave the navy unless I wait until I hit twenty." Her twenty-year fulfillment wasn't for another six. Two, most likely three, tours more.

"I need to take care of myself. I have to count on needing to take care of my mother at some point, too."

"Bullshit, Roanna."

Miles's retort was as effective as if he'd waved a white flag in front of her face.

"Ex-squeeze me?" Her attempt at Will Ferrell humor was ill-timed.

"You've admitted that you've done too much for your family over the years. You've funded her cross-country adventures when she's perfectly able to work for herself. She's a trained nursing assistant—she can make a decent living and has since you stopped forking over a portion of your paycheck to her each month."

Ro opened her mouth to stop him but he held up his hands. He'd really been listening at the family dinner.

"Your sister doesn't need you—hell, Roanna, she sucked you dry, too. She took your fiancé, for God's sake! When will you learn that some people are going to take and take from you?"

"I hear you, Miles, but even if I don't provide for my family financially, I have to provide for myself. I don't have a guaranteed pension."

His eyes narrowed.

"There are other ways to earn a living and benefits, Ro."

So he did think she was as crazy as her family. Crazier.

"I'm sorry, Miles, I know this isn't what you want to hear."

"This isn't about me, Ro. What *you're* not hearing is that it's not about the pension or financial security. It's about living your life for you. Not your family, not the navy, not me." He put his hands on his hips.

Gwen had been telling her the same thing for years.

"Let's say you stay in for the full twenty. You retire with half of your basic pay as your pension, and of course you get the lifetime health-care option. But what will you do then? What do most of the folks who retire do? They go to a government job or civilian job that's very similar to what they were doing in the navy. They think they're too old to try something new. They lose out on the chance to find out what really makes them tick, what ignites their passion."

"I think you've been to too many transition program briefings." She referred to the classes and workshops the navy provided to sailors who were getting out or at least contemplating it, whether by resigning or retiring.

"You're going to do what you need to do, but make sure you're not just knee-jerking this. Make sure you're doing what's best for the Roanna you are *today*. That's all I'm saying."

MILES WATCHED HER expression go from stubborn to hurt to bewildered. He'd said too much. He knew better, which only pissed him off more.

Ro had literally blossomed over the past month. He'd seen

the rigid I'm-an-intel-officer-damn-it girl turn into a sensual woman who was an artist at heart. That didn't preclude her from being a great naval officer by any means, but he'd seen how happy she was among her yarns and in her house. Or when they were out in nature, be it for fun like today or working on the case.

Well, so much for fun. He'd bulldozed that option the minute he'd asked her what she was going to do for her orders.

"Thank you for being honest, Ro." He held her hand and started to walk back down the weather-beaten path.

No matter how much it's killing me.

"How could I not be, Miles? I don't want to be less than completely fair with you. I'm going to transfer and unless you are, too, to the same place, this isn't going to end up anywhere positive."

"Did he hurt you that much?"

"Actually, no. I hurt myself with the illusion of a family life that I never had, and never will while I'm serving my country. But I chose this path and I'm grateful to serve, I really am."

"You think you're being a quitter if you don't make it to retirement, don't you?"

She missed a step and he steadied her.

"I don't know."

"Sure you do. All of you boat-schoolers are the same. You had it pounded into your heads that only lifers are 'real' officers. But there's a war on, Ro. Do you think any of the reservists who've taken bullets for us are less-than? Do you think any less of your classmates who've gotten out?"

She was silent as they picked their way down the narrowest stretch of the twisting path.

They reached level ground and she looked up at him.

"I've never thought about it. I suppose I did have some of

that black-and-white thinking, in the beginning. But I don't feel that way anymore."

Sure you don't.

He kept it to himself. She'd made it clear; she was transferring and their relationship wasn't.

CHAPTER TWENTY-FOUR

WITH THE INVESTIGATION at a standstill since Lydia Reis's arrest, Miles took advantage of the extra time to court Ro. She tried to convince him that they were going to stay "casual" but he ignored her. Let her convince herself—he knew that what they had was once-in-a-lifetime.

Three weeks after their trip to Victoria, Miles managed to convince her to join him for a day that he promised her would be fun and all-outdoors. It still kicked him in the gut that she hadn't admitted they needed to take their relationship to the next level. He'd never been a quitter. If he hadn't learned anything else from his mishap downrange, he'd learned to appreciate what he did have, even if just for today.

And just for today, he had Roanna with him for what he hoped would be the outing of their lives. She'd been ready when he'd picked her up late in the afternoon. It was mid-June and the sun wouldn't set until after 10:00 p.m. or so. They had a gloriously bright, breezy day.

Perfect for his mission.

RO KNEW SHE was playing with fire, setting herself up for more pain once she inevitably transferred from Whidbey.

From Miles.

He'd seemed so earnest when he'd asked her out today that she couldn't see any reason to turn him down. They'd gotten together once or twice since the trip to Victoria. The last date had led to making love all night, this time at his place. Still, she'd done her best to convince herself that she'd be able to walk away.

She had to. After being pulled apart emotionally she'd accepted that she wouldn't feel right about quitting her navy career and taking up the life of an artist without a more solid plan. Her ability to plan for all outcomes was perhaps the only thing she could still rely on.

"So, are we going on a hike?" She had to admit—it felt awfully natural to be sitting in his truck again.

"We're not hiking. I've got something else in mind." Miles wore the smug expression she'd only seen on him when he made her climax in record time. This was going to be interesting.

"Okay. So, where to?"

"Trust me." How often had he said that to her in the past month?

He pulled into what appeared to be a private driveway. The road snaked through low-hanging branches and Ro caught glimpses of moss and lichen that covered the visible rocks and ground in a layer of carpet that rivaled any wall-to-wall she'd ever seen.

"This is the secret part of the Pacific Northwest that I love." She turned to Miles and smiled. "It's like a private fairy land."

He laughed. "Maybe it is."

The shelter of the firs and pines gave way to an open meadow that reached out to the ocean.

"Is this a private beach?" She prided herself on her familiarity with the island and its beaches. They were close to Deception Pass, she knew, but she'd never been to this particular stretch of the island.

"Hold on to your hat, Ro."

As they got closer to the water Ro made out a solid dock

and a good-size motorboat. Miles maneuvered the truck into a spot between an SUV and a BMW.

He turned off the engine.

“Ready?” His eyes sparkled but not from the reflection of the water. It was the way he looked whenever he was happy.

“Sure.”

She had unexplained butterflies in her stomach and she wanted to giggle—always a sign that she was on edge. Her premonitions never steered her wrong. What on earth was Miles up to?

MILES HAD TO BITE his cheek to keep from grinning. Ro wasn’t an easy woman to impress, much less surprise. Krissy, Dick and Delores had been all too eager to help him get Ro to go with him the day they went to Victoria. Today was harder; he didn’t have them there to convince her. He’d played on her sympathies, telling her how much he missed having a dog and how he found himself with more free time than usual. Even he wasn’t sure why she’d agreed to come along; he was simply glad that she had.

“Let me grab something out of the back.” He didn’t want her to catch on to his entire plan, not yet. He pulled out what he hoped looked like an oversize backpack, just a place to stash a couple of sandwiches and drinks for a little picnic.

Instead, he’d painstakingly packed a chilled bottle of champagne and several different gourmet finger foods he’d found recipes for online. He wasn’t a bad cook but after taking nearly half the morning to prep, cut, dice, slice and construct fancy snacks, he felt as if he could win one of those cooking show contests on cable television.

Ro didn’t say anything when she saw the backpack. Her eyebrows rose in query.

“Is what I’m wearing okay?” She gestured at her fleece-lined windbreaker and jeans.

"Perfect." He'd rolled up a space-age blanket in the backpack, too.

They walked up to a small shack that had a Closed and Be Back at Five sign hanging from a rusty chain. Miles glanced at his watch.

"They should be back in the next ten minutes or so. We'll enjoy the view until they get here."

"Who's 'they'?" She had that line between her eyebrows again. He knew he couldn't push her too far or his hope for a joyous day would be marred by her confusion. A laugh escaped him as the thought formed in his mind.

"What's so funny, Miles?" Now she had that tic under her left eye, the one that had reappeared after her black eye had completely healed.

"Nothing, nothing at all. We're waiting for the man who owns this place to come back with a group of tourists."

"On a boat, I take it?"

"Yes. Then we're going to get on the boat."

She peered at the shack. A weathered sign bore the words Deception Pass Tours—Three Seasons.

"Deception Pass?"

"Yes. I know you run over the bridge during your workouts, and that you hike down to the beach to collect sea glass. So I thought you might enjoy seeing the pass from the water."

She smiled and he lost his breath.

He'd lost his heart the moment he climbed out of the tree with Henry the Eighth and handed him to her waiting mother's arms. He'd never looked at Delores. He'd only had eyes for her.

"This is going to be a fun day." She bounced in girlish delight and he would have pulled her to him for a decisive kiss but the sound of a motorboat stopped him.

He turned toward the water and saw Chuck bringing his

last group of tourists into the pier. With the ease that came from years of practice, Chuck was out of the boat and had secured the lines to the cleats. He turned back to help the half dozen passengers out of the craft and onto dry land.

"Miles, isn't that the commodore?" Ro's voice was soft and urgent next to his.

His gut turned over when he recognized Sanders.

"Yes."

The memory of Sanders in Victoria when they were there flashed in his mind.

He should've known he couldn't do anything on this island without someone they worked with finding out. Not that it mattered; Sanders had already put two and two together.

He knew Miles and Ro were an item, he just didn't know how *much* of an item. Miles didn't plan to tell Sanders anything about his private life, and even less about Ro. His gut told him the less Sanders knew about their relationship, the better. He didn't trust the guy.

They'd both stayed away from talking about the Perez case, and the commodore's probable involvement in fraud, since that trip to Victoria. He'd only seen the commodore at the AOMs.

"Hey, Miles. Ro." The commodore nodded at them, and Miles gave a brief nod back.

The commodore's daughter stood next to her father. Her expression had the pasted-on smile that Miles was all too familiar with. So many of the navy brats were schooled from a young age to behave a certain way around anyone who worked with their parent, especially when that parent was of such a high rank. Miles felt sorry for the girl. With Sanders so career-bent and his wife, Karen, a mess, he hoped their daughter had another adult she could count on.

Miles didn't like the way the commodore looked at him

and Ro, as if he knew they were on some kind of intimate outing.

As if he knew Miles's secret.

"Is Chuck taking another group out today?" Sanders started in on small talk, which Miles loathed, and he knew Ro didn't want to prolong her contact with the commodore, either.

"No, they're taking themselves out." Chuck, the boat owner and operator, ambled up from the dock. "Miles here is a good sailor. I had him take me out last week to make sure he could handle the currents in the pass."

"It's not so tough with a motorboat." Miles needed this conversation to end quickly.

"You trust this guy with your life?" Sanders directed the question at Ro.

"Of course I do. But I don't expect this jaunt to become a life-or-death scenario." She laughed and Miles wanted to kiss her. She could charm the pants off a jet pilot pulling five Gs.

"Jaunt?" Sanders angled his head at Miles.

Miles said nothing.

"Yes, I collect sea glass and I often find some on the beaches in the pass. With the boat, Miles can point out some of the beaches I've missed, especially on the Fidalgo Island side."

Ro put her hand through Miles's arm. "Ready?"

He tore his gaze from Sanders and looked at her upturned face. The hell with it. He gave her a big kiss and smiled at her.

"Sure, sweetie."

Sanders coughed.

"Well, I'll leave you two to your adventure. See you in the office on Monday." Sanders walked off with his daughter, and Miles released his breath. He pulled Ro into the safety of his arms.

"You are amazing, Ro."

"No problem. Besides, what's the big deal if he thinks we're on a date?"

"He might think we're blowing off work to play."

She sent him a brilliant smile. "Aren't we?"

"Perhaps." He kept his own smile small. He didn't want her to figure too much out before they got to the pass.

It wasn't every day you asked a woman who barely admitted you were dating to marry you.

"YOU'VE BEEN QUIET." Ro sat next to him in the motorboat as he steered them around the point and into the depths of the pass. The water went from strong ocean surges to calm, but the currents underneath the glassy surface converged into whitecaps at the deepest part of the pass, under the bridge.

"Hmm." He reluctantly took his arm from around her shoulders and pointed out some huge eagles' nests. "Look, there's the couple that built the one over there."

The sight of two bald eagles perched in the green fir trees distracted Ro, which gave him a few heartbeats to think.

What was it about Sanders that had his hackles up?

He replayed the conversation in his mind.

"Is Chuck taking another group out today?"

Ro turned to him. "Miles, what is it? You look like you've seen a ghost."

"Sanders knew damn well that Chuck didn't have a tour later today. The sign on the shack posts it clearly—two tours on Saturdays, the last one at five."

"So?"

He couldn't allow the motor to idle as they had to get away from the ocean swells and into the relative calm of Deception Pass.

"So, what if Sanders did kill Perez? And what if Reis was telling the truth—that the aircraft status sheets were forged by Perez, who was paid by Sanders?"

"Patsy Jordan had the statistics on the airframe maintenance we'd asked for—plus the expenditure accounts from the past several months, remember?"

"Go on."

"It's clear from both that while the wing and its squadrons had near-perfect safety and maintenance records, the costs for repair and spare parts was off the charts."

"And the commodore signed off on it all."

"Yes." Ro chewed on her lip. "I wanted to come tell you what I did with the information, but I felt that if one of us was going to fall on our sword, it should be me. It's about damn time I stopped following all the rules, all the orders I've been given, when I know the right thing to do is report Sanders."

"You turned the paperwork in to the hotline?" He referred to the toll-free fraud, waste and abuse line that any service member could call to report suspected wrongdoing. Without repercussion, technically.

"Initially, yes, I was going to do that. But then I realized that if Sanders is lying, how do I know he doesn't have other people in his pocket up the chain of command, even on the GSO side?" She crossed her arms over her life vest. "I took the papers to Ramsey. He seemed surprised, but was very grateful that I did. He also mentioned that Reis was free and clear of any charges. I sensed that he wanted to say more, but then he didn't."

"Ro, come here." He had to keep his hands on the wheel. She moved closer to him.

"Let me kiss you."

It wasn't as long as he wanted it to be but he did his best to assure her that there was more where this came from.

When she pulled back, her eyes had that dreaminess that made him wish he could drop anchor and kiss her again. *More* than kiss her again.

"Ro, you're incredible. I'm so proud of you. If Ramsey's as sharp as we think, he's already figured out what I know—Sanders did kill Perez."

She shook her head. "There's no proof—no one saw Sanders or anyone else shove Perez off that cliff. And without Perez here we'll never know if the commodore gave him the money or not. It was a lot of money, but in the grander scheme of things, not *that* much. But at least we'll get him on fraud. Hopefully he'll get kicked out."

"Ro, you're the one who was so upset we weren't finding the killer. I'm telling you, I think we have. It's Sanders."

"Okay, I don't disagree with you. But again, what are we going to do without any proof?"

"It's not what *we're* going to do or not do. It's what Sanders is going to do. He knows *we* know about the airframe records. He may also know we spoke to Reis, or at least that we knew about her relationship with Perez. It's common sense that people would come and talk to us once they learned we were doing the unofficial investigation."

Miles shook his head as he maneuvered the boat into the center of the pass, where the currents were most turbulent but the view most spectacular.

"If the police didn't buy her stories, it's because she didn't tell them, Ro. Remember, she loved Perez. For better or worse. She didn't want his name sullied in front of his family. Even after she'd realized he was a pig."

"So she was willing to take the heat by admitting she'd had an inappropriate relationship with him—" Ro kept their story rolling "—but never spoke about the affair in Spain. She didn't need to. They'd never find out."

"Right, which brings me back to Sanders."

"Okay."

"He thinks, knows, that we're the only two people alive who may have been able to piece everything together. If you're a killer, if you're the type who's willing to put others at risk for the sake of your career, what would you do to us?"

Ro gulped. "But he…he was friendly on the dock."

They were well into the pass. The bridge loomed up ahead.

"Of course he was. But he wasn't surprised to see us, was he?"

"No, not from his reaction."

"Just like in Victoria. Ro, I think he's been following us." It all made sense now—the several times they'd "run into" Sanders over the past few weeks.

"So what if he has? He's not with us now."

"No, but he could have watched me come out here last week, and then casually asked Chuck what I was doing. Chuck didn't know he knew me, or care."

Ro's expression was pale and her lips tight.

"Oh, God, Miles, you're scaring me." She took in the jagged scenery. "You said he'd been in your house that night he and Karen showed up at my place. Do you think he found anything out then?" Tall cliffs shot out of the water's edge and rose over two hundred feet. "Do you think he's watching us now? Waiting with a weapon?"

Miles nodded. "That's how he figured out he could find us in Victoria. I had my internet open to the ferry schedule for the day we went." He wanted to kick himself for being so slow on the draw, but there wasn't time for that. "He could have a weapon, who knows?"

Miles turned the boat around.

"I'm not going to wait to find out." His gut told him the same thing his mind did.

They were in trouble.

Ro's cell phone rang in her front jeans pocket. She pulled it out with a shaky hand.

"Who is it?"

"I don't know. It says 'Private Caller.'" She answered. "Hello?"

Miles watched as Ro's face grew even paler. Her eyes widened and she had her mouth open in a silent cry for help. Without a sound, she cut off the connection.

"It was Sanders. He said it's been a pleasure working together and that he's left us a gift in the stern of the boat."

"Hold this." Miles didn't wait for her to take over the steering wheel before he went to the back of the boat. "Shut the engine off."

He saw the bright yellow cooler that was tucked underneath a back cabinet. His training kicked in and he leaned forward, gingerly pulling the square container up by its strap.

"What is it, Miles?" Ro shouted from the ship's wheel. She'd cut the engine and they were at the mercy of the currents.

"Call in an SOS." He saw her dial the numbers and he turned back to the cooler.

Sanders wasn't smart enough to know how to rig a bomb this small. If it was a bomb. But why wouldn't it be? Sanders wanted them both out of the picture. He didn't know that Ro had turned in the incriminating paperwork to Ramsey. He didn't know that his career was over no matter what he did to Miles or Ro.

Ro.

He couldn't risk that this wasn't a bomb. He'd seen enough of them, felt the weight of them. It wasn't safe to handle or throw over the edge.

He ran up to Ro and grabbed her by the shoulders. "Help me get my pants and prosthetic off, now."

Wordlessly, she did as he asked. She'd grown familiar with his artificial limb since she'd seen him remove it and put it back on before and after their lovemaking. God, he prayed they'd be alive to do that again.

"Did you make the call?"

"Yes."

"Do you trust me, Ro?"

"Absolutely."

"Then let's go. We're jumping."

ROANNA FOLLOWED MILES into the deep water without a second thought. Years of jumping from the ten-meter board at the naval academy during swim class, followed by helo dunker training that taught her how to exit an aircraft submerged underwater in pitch darkness, made her actions automatic.

Once the icy water soaked through her clothes and the violent tug of the currents started to make her feel like a useless jellyfish, she cracked.

"Miles!"

"I'm right here."

And there he was, a few yards from her, fighting the same rip currents that Deception Pass was infamous for.

"Catch this, Ro." He slung a nylon cord toward her. It took two tries, but she finally caught it and arm-walked herself over to him.

"We have to get to the beach, Ro." His teeth were chattering and she worried about his bare legs. *Bare leg.*

"Let's go, Miles, we can do it." She linked his life vest to hers as she'd been trained and determined where the closest point was.

"To your three o'clock, Ro." Miles helped her focus on their target landing spot. As the waves rocked them, she made out a beach with washed-up cedars on it. It was hard to tell from this vantage but judging from where they'd leaped off the boat they had two hundred meters to swim.

In water temperatures that could kill them from hypothermia within a very short time.

"Miles, let's go." She looked at him.

"Roanna, I love you with all my heart." His eyes burned with his love, and her stomach sank.

He thought they were going to die.

"Miles, we're getting out of this. I called Ramsey after I called in the SOS." Just in case the commodore had any other tricks to block their survival up his sleeve.

She started to swim with him to the shore.

Oh, hell. She had to tell him. Just in case.

"Miles, I—"

A deafening sound filled the air and the water felt as though a huge vacuum was underneath them, sucking them down. When they surfaced, it was to a fiery scene of burning planks and floating fuel fires.

Ro thanked God that their life jackets were still connected. She reached out to touch Miles's face and gasped in shock. He was unconscious, a huge gash across the top of his head. Blood streamed from his wound, down over his face.

"Miles, I love you! Don't you go now, no way." She gritted her teeth and started to swim them both to shore. He'd lost a limb in Afghanistan. She'd be damned if he'd lose his life in Deception Pass.

Ro was a strong swimmer and making the distance with both of them wouldn't have been impossible for her. But the water was so damned cold that she started to lose feeling in her extremities.

She pushed on, but even her love for Miles wasn't enough. She couldn't get them to shore.

A splash, then a burst of orange smoke surrounded her.

Dazed, she stared, her mental acuity slowing as her body temperature fell.

Flares.

Flares!

She looked up as she heard the *whop-whop-whop* of the rescue helicopter's blades.

Please let me get us to the hook.

It had been the hardest part of her survival swimming qualifications. Swimming through current and wind to reach the large hook that the helicopter would lower for her to attach to their vests.

But their vests weren't navy vests. Where was she going to put the hook?

A large splash sprayed salt water in her face and she was temporarily blinded.

No. They weren't going to die out here.

She blinked and when her vision cleared she saw the rescue diver.

"I'm going to get you into the basket. Just do what I tell you." The swimmer was clad in a wet suit Ro would have paid her life's savings for. It was her last conscious thought.

CHAPTER TWENTY-FIVE

MILES HAD A bitch of a headache when he came to. At first he tensed, petrified that he was back in the CSH in Afghanistan. But the combat support hospital hadn't had such clean, white ceilings and he'd felt a hell of a lot worse.

"How you feeling, Warrant?" A gloved medical person stood over him, needles and suturing thread in hand.

"How many stitches this time?"

The doc laughed. "I'm Dr. Dempsey. You'll have around twenty, all told. But you'll live."

Live.

Roanna.

He sat up.

"Whoa, big guy." The doc pushed on his shoulder and Miles felt another set of hands hold him back. He'd had his share of hospital corpsmen keeping him down on the rack while a surgeon patched him up.

"Where's Roanna?"

"I'm right here." She came into focus, looking like a wet rat wrapped in a big hospital blanket. Her hand found his and she leaned over. "It's okay. We're safe. We're going to be okay."

"Are we?"

Her eyes shimmered with tears and he knew his did, too.

"Folks, I've got to get this wound stitched up."

"Give us a minute, Doc." Ro's voice had never sounded so beautiful to him.

Her gaze didn't waver from his the entire time she ordered the doc around.

"I love you, Miles. If you still love me, we're good."

One week later

THE CHEERY COFFEE shop in Oak Harbor was crowded on a Saturday afternoon. Ro watched as Detective Ramsey spoke to her, Miles and Lydia Reis.

"I arrested Lydia with her full cooperation." Ramsey smiled as he drank his coffee. Black and strong, the same way he'd had it in his office.

"Believe me, if I didn't think it would help him catch Sanders I would never have allowed my sailors to go through that." Lydia was quiet and calm. "It's always upsetting when one of your leaders gets into trouble."

"Why did you pick the day of the memorial service?" Miles spoke up and Ro reached for his hand, under the table. She couldn't get enough of him since she'd finally admitted she couldn't live without him.

"It sent a clear message. It showed Sanders that we believed his lies about Lydia." Ramsey nodded at Ro. "Fortunately, you two shared what you knew with me before Sanders called me incriminating Lydia. He'd placed the cans of soda he'd used in the trunk of her car. It was a total setup."

"Cans of soda?" Ro was lost.

"The witness I told you about who saw Perez acting drunk had seen him leave the bar with Sanders the night of his death. The bartender served them each a can of soda." Ramsey cupped his hands around his coffee mug.

"Sanders wasn't stupid. He saved the cans, in one of which he'd dissolved a roofie."

"The date rape drug," Lydia clarified.

"Sanders didn't want to risk the cans showing up anywhere right after Perez's death, so he saved them. Maybe he intended to frame someone all along, who knows?"

"Did Sanders push Perez off the cliff?" Miles wanted his suspicions confirmed, Ro knew.

Ramsey shook his head. "We'll never be able to corroborate the evidence. He was seen helping Perez into his BMW outside of the club. That's it. But I suspect he walked Perez over to the cliff and pushed him off, yes."

"Will he be locked up for good?" Ro asked.

"With the superb D.A. Island County has, and the navy wanting to take him off our hands to get him to a court martial if the D.A. doesn't want the case? He doesn't stand a chance. At the very least he'll go to jail." Ramsey paused. "We have enough evidence on Sanders with the soda cans. The other thing he got sloppy about was that he never got rid of the rest of the roofies he had. They're an exact chemical match with what Perez ingested."

"None of this showed up in the toxicology reports?" Miles remembered everything, Ro thought.

"Traces, but not enough to call it clearly. Rohypnol doesn't stay in the system very long at all. By the time we found Perez and collected his bodily fluids, it was at least twelve hours from the time of death."

"Did Karen Sanders ever provide any evidence?" Ro had to ask.

"She was actually very cooperative with us and painted Sanders as a real narcissist."

"I hope she gets the help she needs."

"She is. She's in rehab. Her mother is staying with their daughter since Sanders was arrested," Lydia put in.

"I'm glad to hear it." Ro hadn't been able to shake the image of Karen Sanders, all strung out and bitter, when she'd paid her that surprise visit.

"What are you going to do, Lydia?" Miles asked the woman who'd been through hell and back.

"I'm retiring is what I'm doing. It's time for me to make a new start. I might even buy a houseboat and live on the water."

Ro shuddered.

"Not me."

They all laughed.

One month later

RO LOOKED AT HER reflection in the salon's mirror. Her hair was soft and the short style framed her face. Her eye was completely healed and the professional makeup the cosmetician had used covered the small scar on her cheek.

"Thanks so much, Rosy. You've done a wonderful job."

"It's my pleasure. Can I ask what the special occasion is?"

Ro beamed at her. "I'm getting married."

She paid her bill and exited the beauty spa. She'd wanted to have Gwen as her maid of honor in a quiet church ceremony, but Gwen got called away on deployment weeks before she was originally supposed to go.

Miles had convinced her to marry him, anyway, in an intimate ceremony. They'd have a big reception for her family in New Jersey, or one out here by the water later on. Neither of them wanted to wait any longer.

She pulled up to the base chapel, the same place where they'd paid their last respects to José Perez. Max Ford was waiting in a minivan with his wife, Winnie, just as Ro had asked him to.

"You look beautiful, Ro." Max smiled at her as he stepped out of the van.

"Oh, Ro, I'm so glad we can be here for you two." Winnie was much bigger than she'd been a month or so ago.

"It's going to be fabulous working with you, too. You're a natural artist!"

She referred to the fact that Roanna had turned in her resignation. In six months she'd be out of the navy and working for Winnie.

Ro wrapped her hand-knit white silk shawl around her bare shoulders. She'd chosen a simple A-line gown in a creamy ivory satin. It was strapless, so she'd knitted a lace shawl for the wedding. The project had kept her up for hours this past week.

"Do you have my boy?"

Max laughed.

"We do. Are you ready?"

"I sure am!"

MILES WAITED AT the chapel altar for what felt like an eternity. Out of superstition, Ro insisted on driving herself; she didn't want him seeing her beforehand in her dress.

All he could think about was seeing her afterward, undressed.

"I think I just saw them pull up. Are you ready to go, Miles?"

Chaplain Brunello smiled at him and he smiled back.

"I've been ready since I met her almost a year and a half ago, ma'am."

The doors opened and he held his breath. Then let it out when he saw Max and Winnie.

Max's laughter shot toward him.

"She didn't jilt you, did she?"

"Stop it." Winnie elbowed him as they made their way up the center aisle. They reached Miles, and while he was happy to see his friends, there was only one person he wanted, *needed,* to see.

All four of them stood, waiting.

The center doors opened and Roanna, a vision in white, walked in.

Pulling a big beast with her.

"Beau?" Miles blinked.

Ro walked up the aisle with Beauregard, who behaved remarkably well for the crazy pup he was. He even wore a tuxedo collar.

Ro smiled at Miles when they arrived at the altar.

"Do you mind? Taking both of us on?"

Miles couldn't speak for fear of blowing his tough-guy persona with a gush of tears.

He held out his hand to Roanna. She joined him on the altar, and as the chaplain read the opening prayer, Beau sat in between and slightly behind them.

A new navy family.

* * * * *

Navy Hug Hat

You need:
Size U.S. 8 circular knitting needles.
150 to 200 yards of worsted, or 4-weight yarn.

Abbreviations:
MH: make hug: (p1, k1, p1) all in one stitch
k3tog: knit 3 stitches together as one
k2tog: knit 2 stitches together as one

Cast on 88 stitches, place marker and join, taking care not to twist stitches.

Work brim: Knit all stitches for 10 rows

Pattern:
Row 1: purl all stitches
Row 2: *MH, k3tog*; repeat around
Row 3: purl all stitches
Row 4: *k3tog, MH*; repeat around

Work pattern for 18 rows.

Crown Decrease:
Knit all stitches for 8 rows

Row 1: *k6, k2tog*; repeat around
Row 2: *k5, k2tog*; repeat around

Row 3: *k4, k2tog*; repeat around
Row 4: *k3, k2tog*; repeat around
Row 5: *k2, k2tog*; repeat around
Row 6: *k1, k2tog*; repeat around

Finish: Cut working yarn, leaving a 6-inch tail. Draw the tail through the remaining stitches, cinch closed and secure. Weave in ends and enjoy.

To knit hat with 3 colors, use Color A for brim and crown decrease. Work pattern alternating 2 rows Color A, 2 rows Color B and 2 rows Color C for 18 rows.

To knit hat using 2 colors, use Color A for brim and crown decrease. Work pattern alternating 2 rows Color A and 2 rows Color B for 18 rows.

Visit Robin's blog for more patterns and info: www.knittingwithschnapps.blogspot.com.

Join her on Facebook for new patterns: http://www.facebook.com/pages/Delaware-Head-Huggers/250229674280.

Learn more about Delaware Head Huggers by visiting www.delawareheadhuggers.org.

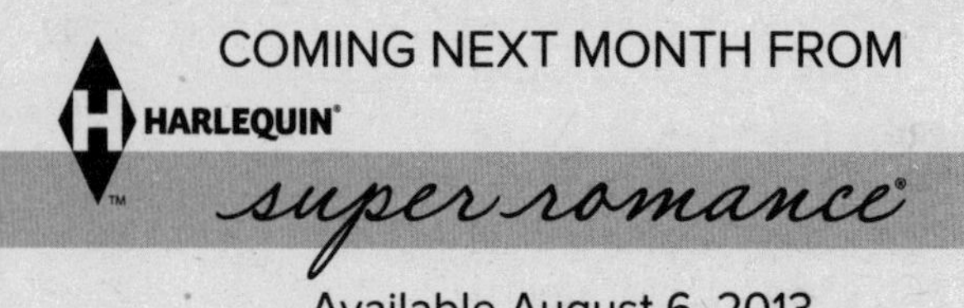

Available August 6, 2013

#1866 WHAT HAPPENS BETWEEN FRIENDS

In Shady Grove • by Beth Andrews

James Montesano has always been Sadie Nixon's soft place to land. Isn't that what friends are for? But something has changed. Instead of helping her pick up the pieces of her life, James is complicating things by confessing his feelings...for her! Suddenly she sees him in a whole *new* way.

#1867 FROM THIS DAY ON

by Janice Kay Johnson

The opening of a college time capsule is supposed to be fun. But for Amy Nilsson, the contents upend her world. In the midst of that chaos, Amy finds comfort in the most unexpected place—Jakob. Once the kid who tormented her, now he's the only one she can trust!

#1868 STAYING AT JOE'S

by Kathy Altman

Joe Gallahan ruined Allison Kincaid's career—and she broke his heart. Now reconnecting a year later, they're each looking for their own form of payback. But revenge would be so much easier if love didn't keep getting in the way!

#1869 A MAN LIKE HIM

by Rachel Brimble

Angela Taylor came to Templeton Cove to start over. But when the press photographs her in Chris Forrester's arms during a flood rescue, it's only a matter of time before her peaceful new life takes a frightening turn....

#1870 HER ROAD HOME

by Laura Drake

Samantha Crozier prefers the temporary. Her life is on the road, stopping long enough to renovate a house, then moving on. But her latest place in California is different. And that might have something to do with Nick Pinelli. As tempting as he is, though, she's not sure she can stay....

#1871 SECOND TIME'S THE CHARM

Shelter Valley Stories • by Tara Taylor Quinn

A single father, Jon Swartz does everything he can to make a good life for his son. That's why he's here in Shelter Valley attending college. When he meets Lillie Henderson, Jon begins to hope that this could be his second chance to have the family he's always wanted.

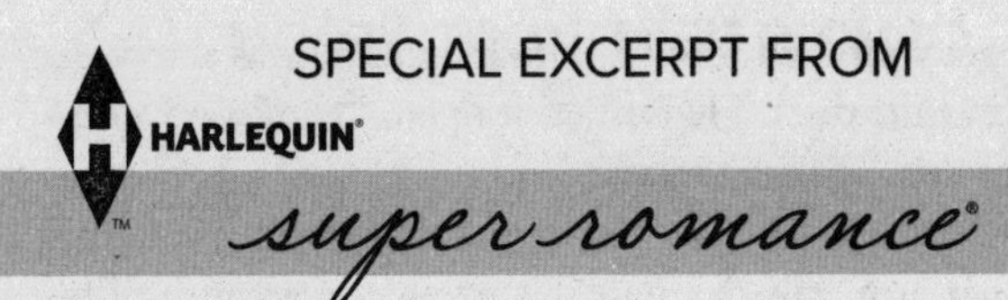

Staying at Joe's

By Kathy Altman

On sale August 6

Allison Kincaid must convince Joe Gallahan to return to the advertising agency he quit a year ago—and to do so, she must overlook their history. But when she tracks him down at the motel he's renovating, he has a few demands of his own.... Read on for an exciting excerpt of STAYING AT JOE'S by Kathy Altman.

Allison tapped her fingers against her upper arm as she turned over his conditions in her mind. No matter how she looked at it, she had zero negotiating room. "So. We're stuck with each other."

"Looks that way." Joe's expression was stony.

"I didn't come prepared to stay, let alone work," she said.

"I can see that." He looked askance at her outfit. "You'll need work boots. I suggest you make a run to the hardware store. Get something sturdy. No hot-pink rubber rain gear."

"I'm assuming you have a separate room for me. One with clean sheets and a working toilet."

"You'll get your own room." In four steps he was across the lobby and at the door. He pushed it open. "Hardware store's on State Street. You can't miss it."

When she made to walk past him, he stopped her with a hand on her arm. His nearness, his scent, the warmth of his fingers and their movement over the silk of her blouse made her shiver. *Damn it.*

Don't look at his mouth, don't look at his mouth, don't look—

Her gaze lowered. His lips formed a smug curve, and for one desperate, self-hating moment she considered running. But she'd be running from the only solution to her problems.

"If I'm going back to the agency and delaying renovations for a month," he said, "then I get two full weeks of labor from you. No complaints, no backtracking, no games. Agreed?"

She shrugged free of his touch. "Don't worry, I'll do my part. Your part is to keep your hands to yourself."

"You might change your mind about that."

HSREXP0713